One Woman's Compelling Journey to Freedom.

THE PRODIGAL DAUGHTER

By Kathleen Steele Tolleson

The Prodigal Daughter
by Kathleen Steele Tolleson

Printed in the United States of America

ISBN 978-1500365462

www.KingdomLifeNow.com

READ IT – LOVED IT!
Here's What People Have to Say

꙰ ꙰

Have you ever wondered if your hurts were too deep or too long lasting for God to heal? As the author takes us through one broken woman's healing journey you will experience God's merciful and amazing healing process. This powerfully written book will open your eyes to the healing principles of God's Word for each of us, and bring you fresh faith and hope.
~ Chester and Betsy Kylstra
Proclaiming His Word Ministry

I read this book at the lowest time in my life, it was awesome and life changing. It helped me hand over my life to God and to let go of a lifetime of bad experiences and choices. God really works miracles!
~ Laurie

The Prodigal Daughter truly touched the very core of my spirit, soul and body. It filled me with a deeper understanding of how much my heavenly Father really loves me and wants simply nothing more than to do just that, LOVE ME; unconditionally and without all the baggage of my past and present getting in the way. It helped me release things that have been buried and to take back what I've lost. It's not only a beautiful story of a journey to inner freedom, but it gently guides you through the steps on how to do it. Thank you.

~ Kim

There were times of tears, times of healing, times of restoration. While reading *The Prodigal Daughter*, the Lord did a work on me, one that was long over-due. It opened up parts of my soul that had been painfully closed for many, many years.

~ Chryl

The Prodigal Daughter brings freedom to those who are living in bondage and helped me realize how God orchestrates situations that bring happiness and fulfill our desires.

~ Melody

This book contains healing, understanding, insight, and reality. I highly recommend it to all women no matter where they are in life. Life impacting!

~ Linda

I found it captivating and could identify with so much of what the main character was going through.

~ Patsy

The Prodigal Daughter tells a powerful story which presents the life-altering influence of prophetic prayer counseling in a non-threatening manner. It is a "must read" for all those who struggle to break free from the bondage of past hurts. I thoroughly enjoyed every chapter.

~ Pastor of pastors, Jeanni Davis

The Prodigal Daughter reads like a movie and will keep you on the edge of your seat! It is a journey into one woman's soul and yet you will find healing for your heart just by reading it. A must for everyone's bookshelf, counselor and lay person alike!

~ Mary Kendall
Co-Founder/Director, School of Worship in Jerusalem

The Prodigal Daughter is a book for the believer and unbeliever alike, for anyone who has come from or in places of destruction, abuse, helplessness, sin-anything! It's an effectual book weaving a story while ministering to areas of unforgiveness, addiction, generational curses, unbelief, and the greatest of all salvation, restoration and redemption.

Being the daughter of the author of this book, I love seeing chapters that relate to my own story, because I, myself, am... a prodigal daughter. Mom, thank you for preparing the way. I love you.

~ Leanne Kaplan

Acknowledgements

৯ ৯

This book could not have been written without the opportunity of ministering to hundreds of courageous people who have opened up the painful secrets of their lives in pursuit of healing, restoration and freedom. I personally want to thank them and the wonderful support system the Lord has given me in my family, church, staff, and counseling team. You are all wonderful and I, more than anyone, know that without you this book would have never been written.

Because of the nature of *The Prodigal Daughter*, I also want to thank the faithful intercessors who supported and prayed for me through all the warfare that accompanied its writing, with special thanks to Linda Fleury, who organized the team of prayer warriors. She has been an armor bearer, a great cheerleader and a faithful friend.

They say that behind every great man there is a woman who is supporting him. I can also say that behind every woman who accomplishes anything, there is a special man. I have several special men in my life. First of all; my husband, Rodney, who has never clipped my wings; my Bishop, Dr. Bill Hamon, who is a great champion of women in ministry; and my pastor, Dr Jim Davis, who has loved, supported and adjusted me when necessary. Thank you Christian International Apostolic Network.

Kathi Rose was a Godsend as an editor. She is not only an editor, but a counselor, as well, which helped bring a special sensitivity to the editing process. I want to thank her for her insights and for helping polish the book along with Sarah Callahan for proofreading under pressure.

One of the most important acknowledgements I can make is to Chester and Betsy Kylstra of Proclaiming His Word Ministry. They wrote *Restoring the Foundations* and introduced me to the integrated process of ministry found on the pages of *The Prodigal Daughter*. They were especially supportive of having the process shared in novel form. Thank you for your contribution to the Body of Christ.

I'd also like to thank my two daughters, Leanne and Tara, for believing in me. Tara, thank you for all the personal things you do to take care of me. Leanne, thank you for your honest and enthusiastic feedback as you read the beginning chapters of *The Prodigal Daughter*. It helped me to keep writing.

Finally, I would like to thank my mother and grandmother who instilled in me a love for reading and for books which I have carried with me all of my life.

Foreword

❧ ❧

    The Prodigal Daughter is a book of living truth written in the form of a novel. Though the characters are fictional their experiences are true to life realities. As on read this book they will be entertained, enlightened and encouraged while gaining insight and hope. It will cause you to laugh at times and cry at others times but you will not want to cease reading the book until it is finished. You will discover you have experienced some of the same things or know someone who has. Read on through the book and into the continuing series and you will be greatly enriched.

    The characters in this story are not fictional characters like the strange beings shown in science fiction films like *Star Wars*. This novel is written like the parables that the Master Teacher used as recording in the Holy Bible. The Son of God did most of his teachings as true-to-life stories which He used to reveal a particular person or incident, but that type of person does exist and such incidents do take place. *The Prodigal Daughter* could be called a hypothetical illustration based on true life experiences of people living on planet earth.

    Kathy Tolleson has blessed us with reading which brings joy and hope that imparts truth that enlightens and enables the reader to live the victorious life. You will be so blessed by this book that you will want to share it with a friend. Truth has the same power to make people free to live life fully whether presented in factual statements or in a novel.

Thanks Kathy for sharing with us the knowledge and answers to life's problems you learned from you experiences and education.

~ Dr. Bill and "Mom" Evelyn Hamon
Bishop of Christian International Apostolic Network
Author of: *Who Am I and Why Am I Here* and 7 other books.

Disclaimer

༈ ༈

Deborah Noble and all the other characters in *The Prodigal Daughter* are fictional. Many times, when we have issues and problems in our lives, we feel that we're the only ones who've ever had that experience. You may say to yourself, "Was she writing about me?" The answer is a definitive "No!" This is a novel, purely fictional, with no specific individual in mind.

Introduction

❧ ❧

    The Prodigal Daughter was written for several purposes: First, to give hope to individuals whose lives have been set on destructive paths as a result of childhood events; and then, to put life changing, effective ministry tools in their hands. Second, to give others an inside look into a restoration and healing ministry and to train and equip spiritual counselors. And finally, to simply offer a novel with a story I hope you enjoy.

Table of Contents

໔~ ๓

Chapter 1: The Drive..3

Chapter 2: The First Day...11

Chapter 3: The Family...21

Chapter 4: Once upon a Time..27

Chapter 5: The Teenage Years..37

Chapter 6: Time Alone..43

Chapter 7: Facing the Past..63

Chapter 8: Living on the Edge..61

Chapter 9: From Bad to Worse...69

Chapter 10: The Second Day..79

Chapter 11: Repentance..87

Chapter 12: Behind the Scenes...99

Chapter 13: Lydia's Story..107

Chapter 14: The Third Day..119

Chapter 15: Revelation..129

Chapter 16: A True Identity...139

Chapter 17: Back Home...149

Chapter 18: A Divine Appointment.......................................157

Chapter 19: Reflections..163

Chapter 20: The Dream..171

Chapter 21: The Fourth Day..183

Chapter 22: The Secret..195

Chapter 23: The Healing Balm..................................207
Chapter 24: The Fifth Day..221
Chapter 25: Freedom..233
Chapter 26: Saying Good Bye....................................245
Chapter 27: Going Home..255
Chapter 28: The Vision...265
Chapter 29: The Arrival..271
Chapter 30: Forgiven..279

The Prologue

෨ ෬

Deborah sat up in bed, disorientated and drenched in sweat. Realizing where she was, she fought back the scream that had almost escaped. Screaming wouldn't help her now; it would just make matters worse. All she needed was to wake up the cell block and have all the other inmates and the guards upset with her.

She tried to lay still but inside she was still shaking. The fear she had of Tommie Lee's reprisal was very real. Tomorrow was the day she was supposed to testify against him. If she did, she would walk away with probation and a chance to get her life straight. If she didn't, she would probably get the maximum, 7 to 10 years, in state prison. She knew that Frank Goldstein, the District Attorney, and Judge Harris wouldn't go easy on her if she changed her mind now.

Deborah replayed the dream over again in her mind. In the dream, Tommie Lee sat on the edge of her bed sharpening his knife. It had been the same bed she had used as a teenager, the antique bed that had been in the family for years. It was covered with the royal purple comforter that she had loved so much. The four-post bed was so high she had needed a stool to climb up in it.

In the dream, as Tommie sharpened the knife, he kept

saying over and over again, "My little girl talked. My little girl talked." Finally, he moved towards her and just as he lifted up the knife to plunge it in her heart, Tommie Lee's face contorted. Suddenly, she was looking into the face of Satan, himself. She had started screaming. It was a blood curdling scream, one full of terror, and it felt like it would never stop.

Now that she was awake, Deborah shuddered and felt the hair on the back of her neck standing up. There was a tangible fear beyond anything she had ever experienced right there in the jail cell; she had nowhere to run and no one to talk to... Should she testify or not?

Wrestling with her decision, she laid awake the rest of the night. If she did testify, would she have to spend the rest of her life looking over her shoulder? Was the dream a warning or was it just her fear?

As morning approached, Deborah found herself doing something she hadn't done in years, she prayed. A still small voice spoke back and simply said, "Fear not." She didn't know if it was her imagination or what, but a strange peace washed over her. For someone who didn't even believe in God any more, it was strange enough to resort to praying, but even stranger believing that God may have responded.

By the time the guards came to transport her to court, Deborah knew what she had to do. Time would only tell if it was the right decision.

Chapter One

The Drive

ॐ ॐ

As dawn was breaking, Deborah drove past the old bus station on the outskirts of Deerfield. Memories of a similar journey over seventeen years ago began to flood her mind as she headed out of town. "The station looks pretty much the same, just a little dingier and the passengers a little rougher these days," Deborah thought as she saw a group of people waiting to board the next bus out of town in her rear view mirror. Tears began to well up in her eyes. She hated any display of emotions and quickly took a deep breath. "Where did that come from? I've driven past this station dozens of times since I've moved back home and have hardly ever given the day I first left Deerfield a thought. Now is not the time to fall apart. I've got a lot of driving to do, and if I break down now, it'll be too easy to turn this car around and forget Florida."

She gripped the wheel even more tightly as she began to switch the dials on the radio, needing something to distract her from the pain that was wanting to surface. The radio only made it worse. The only station free of static was playing oldies. Suddenly, a song that had been in the Top Ten most of the first summer after her graduation was playing.

Deborah's mind careened back in time to a picture of the Greyhound bus she had left town in that summer. She felt helpless to stop the memory now. She had been so young-just seventeen years old-as she boarded the bus. Taking her seat, she had pressed her head up against the bus window and watched the town of Deerfield grow smaller and smaller as the Greyhound bus headed South. Belching black fumes, the bus picked up speed as it had headed toward the Interstate.

That day, all she had wanted was to get as far away from home as possible. As she lost sight of her hometown, she used her intense anger to suppress every tear that was trying desperately to work its way to the surface. With her head still against the window, she allowed the vibrations of the bus to put her to sleep.

Now, as she remembered that day, she wasn't quite as successful in holding back her emotions. Tears slowly streamed down her face as she headed down the very same highway towards I-75.

As she continued the drive south, her memories from the past seemed overwhelming. She tried to squelch the desire to stop and call her friend, Anne. As she wrestled with the urge, Deborah thought, "I know she'll be busy getting the kids off to school and I just can't be more of a bother than I've already been." Besides what's Anne going to do? It's too late. The demons from the past have been unchained, and now I'll just have to deal with them.

The memories continued to flood her mind. She remembered plotting her escape from Deerfield with a vengeance during her entire senior year. As the realization of just how young she had been when she had left home washed over her, she winced at the thought. "I thought I was all grown up, but I was so young, just a baby, really." At the time, the experiences she had been running away from had forced her into a false kind of maturity. She had felt all grown up.

"I can't believe I had the nerve to leave with no family, no friends, no job, and no one waiting to pick me up when I arrived. I was so young, but so determined!" She shivered at the

4

thought of the events that had created such determination.

Seeing an exit sign brought Deborah back to the present, she decided to pull over, fill up the car and get a nice warm cup of coffee. Any distraction was welcome at the moment. As she filled her tank, she was still unable to calm the ebb of emotion she was feeling. The cashier took her money and immediately noticed Deborah's tear streaked face. "Ma'am, are you alright?"

Deborah nodded, unable to speak. She knew that if she opened her mouth there was no telling what she might blurt out because the feelings inside were so intense. In her silence, her mind was screaming, "No, I'm not alright! My life's a mess! I'm a mess and I don't know how to fix any of it!"

As Deborah walked back to her car, she passed the pay phone hanging on the wall outside the convenience store and was unable to pass up the urge to call Anne. She dialed her friend's number, but as the phone rang, she panicked and almost hung up the receiver. However, Anne answered the phone in record time. It was as if she had been sitting right beside it just waiting for it to ring. "Deborah, is that you? Are you okay? You've been on my heart all morning."

Deborah didn't know what it was about Anne's voice, but whenever she heard it, a sense of calm washed over her. This time was no different. "Anne, I'm so sorry for bothering you. I was just having some flashbacks and they're trying to get the best of me. I feel like there's a dam ready to break inside of me, and I don't know if I can handle it. I'm feeling kind of shaky right now."

This was the one thing Anne had been concerned about; could Deborah make it down to Florida herself? She knew that Deborah desperately needed the ministry that was awaiting her there. Anne would have loved to have driven down with her, but the responsibility of her own family prevented it.

"Deborah, I'm so glad to hear your voice. I actually asked the Lord to encourage you to call me so I could find out how you were doing," Anne said. She was very glad that

Deborah had reached out and called. More than anyone, she appreciated how difficult it was for Deborah to ask for help.

Hearing Anne's reply made Deborah feel a little better. Apparently, she considered her overwhelming urges to call simply the prompting of the Holy Spirit. Maybe she wasn't breaking down after all. She breathed a sigh of relief. "When I'm this emotional, it's just so hard to know the difference between my flesh and my spirit," she said.

Anne replied, "Deborah, I know that this trip is critical for you, and it's because of that there's opposition from the Enemy. But I really believe what's happening this morning is not torment from the Enemy. I think the Lord is bringing up some things from the past to prepare you for next week. He's priming the pump, so to speak. Running from your feelings and memories won't help; you're going to have to trust that He won't bring up more than you can bear."

When Anne was through with her pep talk and had finished praying for her, Deborah thanked her and got back into the car with a new sense of resolve. "I will make it to Palm City and I will go through with this ministry. I have no choice. I can't keep running from my past." Thinking about it, she realized that was why she had climbed on that Greyhound bus in the first place. She had been running from everything. And if she was honest with herself, her running hadn't stopped in the eighteen years since.

As she drove, she wondered to herself, "Can God really bring healing to everything that caused me to leave home, much less everything else that has happened since? It just seems like too much; too much pain, too much heartache, and way too much shame!" The Interstate continued to rise up and meet her as she drove towards Florida, while allowing herself to think about the memory like Anne had encouraged.

That morning on the bus, she had drifted off to sleep as

soon as they had pulled out of town. A couple of hours later, she woke up and stared hypnotically out the bus window. Watching the farm fields pass by, she no longer felt the pain; there was just a deadness inside. It felt like Deborah Lynn Noble had died while she slept. When she awoke there was someone else in her place. This new "someone" had no family, no background, no past, and no real future–she was now Debbie Lynn Webster, the name on her fake ID.

Suddenly, as she continued heading towards Florida, she had a revelation. God wanted to resurrect Deborah Lynn Noble! The thought of facing all that emotional pain was overwhelming. Deborah found herself screaming at the clouds as she drove, "God, I can't do this! Isn't there any easier way? I can't believe You are going to make me do this!" As she continued to rail, heaven seemed totally deaf and unresponsive.

Finally the frustration turned to pleading, "God, please help me. I can't do this alone. I surrender it all to You. Please just give me the grace to be able to face it and to do what's right. I simply can't live like this anymore, I really can't!"

For thirty minutes, Deborah had been driving in a light rain; up ahead she saw the clouds clearing and the sun shining. Suddenly, she could make out a faint rainbow over the horizon. Could heaven be responding to her after all? Whether it was simply a sign the weather was clearing or a sign from God that everything was going to be all right, Deborah decided to take it as an answer to her prayers. She began to hum *Somewhere over the Rainbow,* and in just a matter of minutes, the intense desperation began to dissipate.

As the rainbow faded, she decided to listen to some teaching tapes Anne had lent her for the trip. Maybe they would help keep her mind in a more positive place. "The tapes might just be a temporary fix, but if they help, that's all that matters right now," Deborah thought. She continued to play them one after another as she drove.

It had been a very long day, and it was after midnight

when she crossed the Florida State line. As she headed toward her final destination, she wondered what the next five days would have in store for her.

Tommie Lee sat on his prison bed plotting his revenge. He cursed the day he met Deborah. If she hadn't sold him out, he wouldn't be locked up in one of Louisiana's worst prisons. Not only was it old and outdated, the new warden had reinitiated chain gang labor. It was one of the worst prisons in the South. Even though it was only April, the humidity and heat just got worse by the day. The summer would be unbearable.

Tommie Lee continued to talk out loud to the prisoner on the top bunk. "When I get out of here, I'm going to track her down and make her pay. Miss Deborah Lynn Webster is going to be sorry she ever took the stand against me. I may just cut my own deal with the D.A. so I can get out of here and find her." Tommie Lee let loose with a string of obscenities.

Johnson, the young black man on the top bunk said, "Man, I'm tired of hearing what you're going to do to your old lady when you get out of here. They're going to be rattling our cages before we know it and I need to get some sleep." Johnson rolled over and pulled the rough and tattered prison blanket over his head while Tommie Lee continued to mutter to himself on the lower bunk.

Tommie Lee hoped the Renegades were having some luck tracking Deborah down. They were as angry as Tommie Lee because several of their members had ended up in prison based on her testimony. "If I could just remember the name of the town where she grew up, I'm sure I could persuade some family to talk," Tommie Lee continued to whisper to himself in the dark.

During their time together, Deborah had rarely shared anything about her past. She had always been extremely closed mouthed about anything related to her family. But a couple of times, when she had been drinking, she had let some information slip. All Tommie Lee could remember was that she was from somewhere in Ohio. "If I have to, I'll search every town in the state to find her. No matter what it takes, she's going to pay." Tommie Lee finally drifted off to sleep only to dream once again of what he would do to her when he finally found her.

Chapter Two

The First Day

આ ⚬ ⚬

In the morning, Deborah walked next door and up the sidewalk. Now, she was able to see the little sign hanging from the porch roof. It read: His House. Last night when she arrived, it had been so late and too dark to see much of anything. But in the light of day, she could see the unique architecture of the two older renovated homes. The one she had slept in the previous night served as the place where people stayed during their ministry time. It was kind of like a private Bed and Breakfast.

The house she was about to enter was where the ministry was supposed to take place. Deborah hesitated on the porch wondering if she should knock or just open up the door. Her instructions had been to be there at nine o'clock in the morning. It was about five minutes 'til, by her watch. Suddenly, the oversized door opened up. "Hi, I'm Joyce, one of your ministers this week. Lydia's in the office finishing a phone call. I'll get you settled and we'll be with you in a minute," she said. Joyce appeared to be in her late forties and was dressed casually in a khaki skirt and tropical looking top. Deborah found herself just nodding and following her down the hall.

The next thing she knew, Deborah was sitting alone on a couch. Her mind swirled as she took in the room and her new surroundings. The house had a familiar smell. What was it?

Suddenly, memories of her grandmother's house came flooding back to her.

Grandma's house had always been a safe place for her. There was always plenty of love, plenty of food, and everyone was always welcome at Grandma Ellen's house. "Maybe this place won't be so bad after all," she thought.

That thought was followed by a wave of grief, Grandma was gone and she hadn't even had a chance to see her before she died. On the heels of her grief, came that gnawing sense of guilt and shame. Deborah had never forgiven herself for not honoring her by attending the funeral. Grandma had always meant so much to her, but she hadn't been able to force herself to go back home.

Now, she quickly pushed down the unwanted feelings of guilt and shame and continued to check out her new surroundings. The room had a comfortably-used sort of feel. Nothing was brand new, but it wasn't run down either; just comfortable. The room was painted a soft yellow that was warm and inviting, and trimmed in off-white. The floors were a honey-colored wood, worn by time and use, and partially covered by an oriental rug.

The sofa she was sitting on was a neutral color with pillows that picked up the green and blue accents in the room along with the yellow from the walls. The room somehow reminded her of a gentle summer day.

She noticed a basket, of what appeared to be toys, in the corner of the room and thought it a bit strange. She looked closer and saw that it was full of teddy bears and dolls of different types. Then she heard footsteps down the hallway and quickly turned her attention to the door.

The two women entered the room and sat opposite her. Introducing themselves, they seemed friendly enough, but she still felt very guarded.

There definitely was a fight going on inside of her. Part of her wanted to run out of the room and never look back, but another part was relieved that she was finally there. It reminded her of the sense of relief she felt after waking up from a terrible nightmare and realizing that it had all been a dream. Maybe now the running would finally end.

The women began to talk; she had to focus on what they were saying. The older one with the graying hair spoke first. "What was her name again? It was an unusual one." She searched her memory. "Lydia, that's it. Another biblical name," she thought to herself.

She had always hated her own name. Most of her life, everyone had just called her Debbie. Deborah seemed so formal. Now, she felt somewhere in between the two names. She wasn't "messed up little Debbie" any more, but she sure didn't feel like she was a "Deborah" yet. She continued to examine the two women who sat in front of her as they began to talk about what was going to transpire over the next five days of her life.

Lydia seemed to be the leader of the two. She had dark brown eyes that seemed to look right through you. The other woman, Joyce, appeared a bit quieter, but when she did say something, it was direct and confident. Deborah found herself relaxing just a bit as she sank back into the soft, slightly-worn couch.

Now, they were talking about confidentiality. The very thought of what she might have to tell them set her on edge again. "What will these women think of me if I really share everything? What was I thinking to even attempt this? How did I get here anyway?" she wondered trying to keep her face from showing the fear she was feeling inside.

The only thing that made the fear subside was the thought that she could go next door, pack her suitcase and leave after this morning's session. She also knew that decision would cause another decision. She wouldn't be able to return home to Deerfield, either. There was no way she could face Anne if she didn't go through with this.

"Strange," she thought, "the only thing that makes me

feel better is the thought of running away. The revelation she had on the drive down came back to her-that was how she had survived her junior and senior years of high school. Thoughts and plans of running away had been her only comfort. She realized, at 36 years old, they still were.

After explaining that they were not licensed counselors but ministers of the gospel, Lydia and Joyce outlined the steps of what they called "integrated ministry." Deborah was reminded of the circumstances which had begun the journey that had brought her to this room. In her mind, she saw the lights of the police car flashing. What got her here had actually started that night. It sure seemed longer than just two years ago.

She would never forget the feeling of being cuffed and pushed roughly into the police car. She was angry that night at herself, angry at the circumstances that had gotten her there, angry at Tommie Lee, angry at the world.

Deborah was startled as Lydia spoke her name. "Deborah, do you have any questions?"

She shook her head, "no." Everything was so foreign to her that she didn't have a clue what to ask. Then she thought of one question. She blurted out, "Can I use the bathroom?"

Joyce said, "Sure," and began to rise out of her chair. She opened the door and pointed to end of the hallway. "It's the door on the right." Deborah felt clumsy as she got up and headed in that direction.

Lydia also got up from her chair and headed to the kitchen for a cup of coffee. The Florida morning sun was pouring through the windows which made the room bright and cheery. Lydia prayed within herself as she reached for a cup, "Father, You're going to have to send a lot of help with this one."

She had spent last night going over Deborah Noble's detailed application. The same one everyone was required to fill

14

out before coming for ministry. The thirty-six year old woman had been through a lot by the looks of her completed form.

The counselors had nicknamed the application "The Eliminator." Only people who were serious need apply for this ministry. The questionnaire itself discouraged many people who weren't ready to really face the issues of their lives and pasts. Many times after the form was requested, they never heard from them again.

As she went to the bathroom, Deborah checked out her surroundings. The bathroom was clean, sort of homey and casual, like the rest of the house. Washing her hands, Deborah's thoughts returned to the night Tommy Lee had convinced her to go along with him to pick up some crack he planned to sell the next day. Though she had used alcohol and drugs since she was fourteen, she had always avoided the dirty, frightening crack houses where dealers and users found each other.

As she walked out of the bathroom and back to the room, shame suddenly overwhelmed her again. Tears filled her eyes. "How can I face these women and tell them the sordid details of my past? Both of them looked like they had probably spent their entire lives in church. How can they ever understand what I've been through?" She reminded herself that there was one thing she would never tell anyone. She had kept this vow for nearly twenty-four years. Even though the counselors had reminded her earlier that God was only able to minister to what she was able to face and share about openly; there were some things better left unsaid. "There's plenty of work for them and God to work on without going there," she mused.

During Deborah's absence, Joyce and Lydia had met in the hallway as Lydia left the kitchen. They looked at each other knowingly. Lydia reminded Joyce in a whisper, "She'll be okay, we've just got to get her to relax."

It was obvious that the young woman carried a lot of

shame about her past. It wouldn't be an easy task to get her to open up, but they had seen a lot of miracles happen in what they called "The Restoration Room." They chatted for a minute in the hallway about Lydia's daughter, who was pregnant again. They had just found out on Friday that she was having a little girl, and Lydia couldn't contain her excitement.

As Deborah returned to the room and the three women found their respective places, they resumed the conversation of what today would bring. Lydia said, "Today, we'll be interviewing all day. First we'll do the generational interview and then your personal interview."

Joyce added, "The interviews are the foundation we work from all week. They're very important. The depth of the interview will release the heights of ministry."

Sensing that Deborah was apprehensive about what was going to happen next, Lydia shared "We've counseled and ministered to a lot of people and nothing is going to surprise or shock us. We're not here to judge you or preach to you. Our job is to pray for you and to help facilitate what the Lord wants to do in your life this week."

Joyce encouraged Deborah, "Journal any important thoughts that you have outside of your sessions." It reminded her of Anne. Because of her encouragement, she had already started journaling. And just like she had said, it helped her sort out her thoughts and feelings. She could even look back on it now and see how much she had grown. She silently thanked the Lord for the woman who had come to mean so much to her. She hoped Anne was praying for her right now.

Both counselors had clipboards in their laps and appeared to be writing down everything that came out of Deborah's mouth. Although they had shared earlier that all personal notes would be destroyed at the end of the week, she still knew it would be quite a challenge to allow those things she had tried so hard to forget, to live again on Lydia's and Joyce's notepads. One thing was sure, she couldn't do this alone. "God is going to have to help me," she thought.

"It's nine o'clock our time, which means it's ten o'clock Florida time," Anne thought as she unstacked the breakfast dishes from the dishwasher. She wondered how Deborah was doing. She sure hoped that she had not recommended the *Restore Your Soul Ministry* too prematurely to her. There was a time for everything and she hoped this was the right time for Deborah. "Well, it's too late to second-guess myself now," she thought. "The only thing I can do at this point is to pray."

Suddenly she heard a knock at the back door. "That must be Daniel, dropping off Aimee." She had come down with a cold yesterday and had been sent home from school early. Today she would be spending the day at her aunt's while her father went to work.

Anne hoped Daniel would be able to take a couple of minutes and pray with her for Deborah. She knew he was running late, but this was important.

Actually these days, Daniel felt like he was running late all the time. He didn't understand how his wife, Susan, had juggled the home, the children and all of her other responsibilities so well. She had always made it look effortless.

This morning he'd had to run into the corner drug store on the way to his sister's house to pick up some cold medication for Aimee. Hopefully, his daughter wouldn't have to be out of school for too many days.

Daniel knew that Anne already had her hands full with her own three children. At least he didn't have to worry about Anne's children getting sick. They had been the culprits who had passed the virus on to Aimee.

His heart ached as he looked at his daughter buckled in the seat next to him. It was times like this that really hurt, times when a child really needed their mother. He couldn't thank his sister enough for all she had done for him and the kids, but he knew it wasn't enough. Aimee and David still needed a mother. Daniel thought about his promise to Susan, but now wasn't the time to go there.

As Daniel walked into the kitchen, Anne looked up from the dishwasher. It still caught her off guard to see how the trauma and toil of the last several years had aged her brother.

Daniel got Aimee settled in the living room with a box of tissues, several of her favorite videos, and her arts and crafts box. When he returned to the kitchen, Anne was pouring him a cup of coffee.

He immediately said, "I better take that to go, Sis, I'm running late."

Anne laughed and said, "Daniel, you work for yourself. Take a minute and catch your breath."

Daniel reached for the extended cup and slid onto the stool at the kitchen counter. "Okay, okay, but just for a minute," he responded.

Anne reminded him, "Today is the day Deborah Noble is starting the ministry process in Florida that I've been telling you about."

Daniel had to be honest, "I've been so busy with the kids and an important deadline at work I haven't really given it much thought or prayer." He caught the look on Anne's face. Obviously, it was important to her.

The two women had grown close over the past year. Daniel had run into Deborah several times at his sister's house. She hadn't shared anything with him about what Deborah had been through before returning to Deerfield. But by the haunted look in Deborah's eyes, he knew there had been a lot.

Anne was saying, "Just agree with me in prayer that Deborah will open up and really allow the Lord to touch her."

"Lord, continue to minister healing and freedom to Deborah. We bind up all the works of the enemy." Anne prayed, "Fear and shame, you are bound and no longer have authority over Deborah," she continued. Then Daniel found himself praying, "Please give Deborah's ministers wisdom and compassion and give her the strength to face the real issues."

"In Jesus Name, Amen!" they said in unison.

"Deborah Noble." Well, that was a whole other topic in itself; one he didn't have time for now. He kissed his sister on the cheek and headed out the door. It was time to get to the office. His secretary would be wondering where he was.

PRODIGAL DAUGHTER

Chapter Three

The Family

ॐ ॐ

They had completed the generational section of the interview, which hadn't been easy for Deborah. Lydia and Joyce knew she was probably dreading the next couple of hours of her personal interview.

The gathering of family history had yielded some clues as to what they were facing this next week; but like many people, Deborah had been careful not to paint her family in a poor light.

Her answers were especially short and terse when it came to talking about her father and their relationship. He sounded like the typical religious, but emotionally distant parent, that Lydia and Joyce had encountered in interviews throughout the years.

Her father's side, the Noble's, were of English and Scottish ancestry, except for the great grandfather's marriage to a Cherokee Indian which had scandalized the family. The paternal side also included landowners and respected citizens of the community. Deborah's grandfather had been a local judge. He was a stern, unyielding man, and as a result, Deborah's father hadn't received much from him in terms of emotional support and nurturing.

His wife, Regina Remington, came from high society, and her parents had a great deal of money. Though she married an attorney from a respectable family, her own parents had very little to do with their daughter or her children. They had always felt Regina had married down.

After the marriage, she too became disillusioned and made no bones about how unsatisfied she was with her husband and the money the Judge made. However, being full of pride, she was determined not to give her parents the satisfaction of being right by divorcing her husband. So they lived divorced lives under the same roof.

After Regina's father died and she received her inheritance, Deborah's grandmother created a life for herself that basically excluded her children and her husband. She traveled a great deal, especially abroad, served on various committees and spent a good part of her life supporting the "arts."

She, like her husband, had been too busy, aloof, and emotionally distant to connect to her children. As a result, Deborah's father had never been taught by his parents how to give or receive love. This ungodly generational pattern had flowed down and repeated itself in his relationship with Deborah.

As she continued to share her family history, more important information about Judge Noble came forth. Although he had been well respected in the community, it appeared the Judge was involved in a relationship with his secretary for a good part of his life. From the information Deborah shared, it was obvious to the two counselors that, not only had an illicit relationship transpired between the Judge and his secretary for a number of years, but he didn't made much of an effort to hide it.

Deborah was glad the counselor's had given her a twenty minute break. The room had begun to feel like it was closing in on her and it felt good to swallow some fresh air. She decided to take a quick walk around the block. It felt good to stretch after sitting for nearly two hours. Talking about her family members had caused more memories to begin to surface, and tension had seeped into her body. She wondered how she was ever going to get through the next section of the interview.

This morning Lydia and Joyce had told her that they were going to want her to share her life story from birth to the present. "Did they have any idea what they were asking for?" Deborah wondered.

———————————————

Lydia and Joyce also walked out onto the front porch of the quaint house. The first part of the interview had gone fairly well, but both of them knew they had just touched the tip of the iceberg.

They compared notes on the generational information Deborah had shared this morning. "The week has only just begun. Let's not get discouraged." Lydia spoke reassuringly. Both of them had realized in that short time that Deborah was very guarded and it wasn't going to be easy reaching her because of the emotional walls.

"Deborah sure doesn't have a lot of respect for her mother, does she?" Joyce said.

"Not surprising, really. It sounds like Theodore Noble just used his wife as a maid and nanny for their children! Not the atmosphere that breeds respect for a mother." Lydia replied. "But that's all he knew from growing up with Regina and the Judge as his parents."

The one thing they both had learned over the years of hearing personal stories was not to judge anyone. It was so easy to assume things until you heard someone's generational and personal histories. Then even the worst cases became understandable and treatable. It didn't make the sin right, but it helped to discover how people had got there.

They had learned that individuals didn't just wake up one morning and choose to be a mess. They always had plenty of assistance. The sad part was that most of it usually came from their own family members. The two counselors had heard more than their share of heartbreaking stories over the years.

They considered it a sacred trust from the Lord. It was an honor to assist as He performed surgery on those that came to the *Restore Your Soul Ministry*. They knew it was only by His Grace that they were able to continually hear stories that represented some of the worst of humanity's evils without becoming hard and calloused.

Lydia and Joyce now began to discuss Deborah's maternal side of the family, the Millstones. They had found the generational sins of poverty, passivity and addiction in this side of the family line. The pride, control, rebellion and sexual sin issues Deborah had marked on her application apparently came from her father's side. But the sins of fear, unworthiness, shame and co-dependency came predominantly from her mother's side. Both sides of Deborah's family had had their share of premature deaths, which could often be evidence of generational curses.

The one bright light on both sides of the family had been Deborah's grandmother, Ellen Millstone. She had come to know the Lord as a young woman and did her best to instill love and true Christian values into Deborah.

The two counselors compared notes on how Deborah's face lit up when she had discussed her grandmother and the time they had spent together. How sad it was that her father was so possessive of his children that he had hardly ever allowed Deborah to spend the night with her grandmother. It was one thing when Ellen's husband, Eugene, was alive and still drinking. But after he died, it didn't make much sense.

Lydia said, "It's too bad that Deborah didn't get to spend more time with her grandmother. It could have really made a difference in her life.

"I don't think she would even be here if it wasn't for the prayers of her grandmother!" Joyce strongly replied.

From Deborah's sharing about the Millstone family, it was clear that her mother, Elizabeth Millstone thought Theodore Noble was going to be a ticket to a better life. Unfortunately, it hadn't turned out that way. It sounded like Theodore had slowly squeezed the life out of his wife. And then, ironically, spent the rest of his years being angry at who she had become.

The counselors had asked Deborah if she thought her father had fallen in his father's footsteps and had an affair. Deborah had shaken her head negatively and reminded the two counselors that her father had been an elder in their local church. No, Theodore Noble would have never taken the chance of having his reputation sullied with an extramarital affair.

Deborah walked slowly up the front stairs of His House dreading what was about to come. It was time for her to answer questions about herself. It had been hard enough talking about her family!

As she entered the house and walked down the hallway, she heard voices. Without being able to hear what was actually being said, her face flushed with embarrassment as she opened the door. "I wonder what they're saying about me–probably wondering how I ever got here. I bet I'm the worst case they've ever had," she thought.

Lydia and Joyce were already perched like two eager birds on their chairs. They were ready for what Deborah would feed them next. Her stomach began to churn just a bit and her knees felt a bit weak as she headed for the couch.

Lydia and Joyce each had a couple more questions about her family when they resumed. Deborah was glad for the respite. It was still easier to talk about her family rather than herself.

PRODIGAL DAUGHTER

Chapter Four

Once Upon a Time

ও ও

Deborah was surprised at some of the patterns that she had seen emerge while sharing her generational history that morning. In the past she had always seemed so different from her family and simply "messed up" beyond repair.

This morning, as she listened to herself talk, Deborah realized that her life was really a mixture of the sin from each family line. Not that she could blame them for her own choices, but it did make some of the things that had happened in her life a little more understandable.

She had always known that she had battled the Noble pride and anger, but had never really seen how she had been affected by the passivity, codependency, and the addictive behavior of the Millstone family line. Today had been an eye opener. She suddenly saw how those traits had kept her going back to Tommie Lee. They had also rendered her helpless to say "no" to drugs, men or anyone else, for that matter.

Lydia and Joyce had caught the glimmer of revelation in Deborah's eyes as she began to see how there might be something to this generational curse thing they had talked about in the very beginning. They were very encouraging after she had shared the pattern she was seeing. "I've been so strong on one hand and yet so passive on the other hand," she had stated.

The women sitting opposite her now didn't seem quite as intimidating as they had this morning; it already felt like she had known them much longer than just a couple of hours. However, Deborah still felt apprehensive about the things she was going to have to talk about next. It was helpful that they kept asking questions and then gave her enough time to think and to talk things out.

"Thank God, this doesn't feel like an interrogation," she thought. Her mind flashed back to the night at the police station. No, the two detectives hadn't been nearly as friendly or as sensitive as these women.

Deborah took a deep breath and began to answer the first question related to her birth. "My mother's pregnancy was without complication, but I was a little late in arriving. The doctor actually had to use forceps during the delivery. I was born nearly three years after my brother, Paul. Mom had a miscarriage in between the two of us. I think she had a lot of fear while she was carrying me."

Deborah had only recently discovered the existence of the miscarriage as she was asking her mother some questions while filling out her application for the counseling. It had surprised her and caused her to wonder what else her family had kept from her. There had always been an air of secrecy about everything; the adults would often talk in a code that somehow the children could never fully break.

Joyce had led the questioning in the generational part of the interview, but now Lydia was clearly in the lead. Next, she asked about Deborah's infancy.

"They weren't kidding when they had said the personal interview was going to encompass my entire life!" she thought. She tried to remember what she had heard about herself as a baby and infant. "My mother always said that even though I was late coming into the world, once I got here, I was early at everything else. Basically, I was a good baby who crawled, walked and talked early. Being the first girl in the family I think I got my own share of attention."

Lydia then asked, "Deborah, what's your earliest memory?" Deborah had to stop and think for a minute. At first, she wasn't sure if she remembered it from a picture or if it really was a memory. The memory was of her and her father swinging on the big porch swing that had always graced the Noble family home.

One of the first things that caught her attention this morning, as she approached *His House*, was that there was an old-fashioned wooden swing hanging by its chains on the front porch. It was smaller and white rather than dark green like the one she loved as a child, but seeing the swing this morning had stirred something deep in the pit of her stomach. Deborah had simply pushed the feeling down as she walked onto the porch and up to the front door.

"I was only about three and I see myself sitting on the front porch swing with my father. It's a warm summer evening and I'm laying my head against his chest. In the memory, there's a sense of security and freedom at the same time." Lydia silently noted that Deborah never called her father, Dad.

Now tears filled Deborah eyes. Only she knew what made the memory of the swing so painfully bittersweet. It was the other memories that had followed. Memories, she reminded herself, she would not-and could not-talk about, not even with the gentle and gracious women who sat opposite her.

She quickly wiped her eyes, but again she had seen the look between the two counselors, as if to say, "Did you catch that, too?"

———————————

As Daniel drove into the parking lot of the Worthington Advertising and Marketing, Inc. office, he thought about the call he had received from Andrea Kline last night. The woman gave him the creeps.

He remembered awhile ago when Pastor Harrison had taken him aside after a Wednesday evening service and warned him gently that Andrea had set her sights on him. Being an eligible, single man in a small town was like calling an open hunting season; all the women came out, and they were armed and dangerous!

Last night, Andrea had the nerve to call and ask if he needed help with Aimee. Earlier that evening, she had called Anne for a recipe. His sister had innocently mentioned that she was going to be busy the next day taking care of Aimee, who still wasn't feeling well. Afterward, Andrea hadn't wasted any time calling Daniel and offering her assistance.

"No! Thank you, very much!" Daniel had thought to himself as he hung up the phone. He couldn't stand it when women tried to use his children to get to him. Maybe he was reading too much into it. Maybe she was just trying to help. Daniel hoped he wasn't judging the woman too harshly, but he still wasn't taking any chances. If you gave that woman an inch, she would take a mile!

Daniel walked through the front door and greeted his combination receptionist-secretary-bookkeeper and the woman who helped keep his office, and life, from getting totally out of control. Irene McPherson had been with him since the first day he had opened his own business. He couldn't imagine functioning without her. The 53 year old woman was like the Rock of Gibraltar. Nothing seemed to faze her: deadlines, computer crashes, angry customers, and even his own propensity to lose things.

"Good morning, Irene. Sorry I'm late-had to drop Aimee off at Anne's," he said as he dropped some mail on her desk.

"Good morning, boss. Remember, you don't have to answer to me, you own this place," she smilingly reminded him.

That was the second time that morning he had heard the same thing. Daniel wasn't sure whether it was good or bad that he still worked and acted as if he was an employee in his own business. He made a mental note to keep an eye on it. As the owner of the company, he had to make sure he ran it like a business man but yet kept himself humble and served his business, employees and clients. He had seen too many business owners who forgot where they had come from and started acting like kings.

As Daniel began to get ready for his day, he was glad of one thing: he had two safe women in his life, Irene and Anne. They had already appointed themselves to help him inspect and select a future wife for himself, but he hadn't kept them very busy. He just didn't have the heart or desire to date. But he knew he was safe with one thing, Andrea would never get past that committee!

"No if I'm ever going to remarry, the woman will have to be hand selected by God. And even then, a little skywriting would be appreciated!" he thought to himself.

Daniel began to quickly thumb through the e-mails Irene had left on his desk. She returned to his office with the *Sergio* file he had requested. It was a major account he had landed this month. The business had started out as a family-owned pizzeria and then graduated to regional franchise owners and operators. Daniel's father had known the Sergios', who had originally opened the restaurant, for years.

His father had actually been their accountant in the early days. The Sergios' had now taken over the family business and had contacted Daniel at their parents' recommendation. They were about to take the restaurant franchise nationally and were depending on him to create the ad campaign that would guarantee their success.

"What a time for Aimee to get sick!" Daniel knew that this meeting was going to require his full attention. Even though he had been highly recommended and had impressed Tony and Steve with his presentation, Daniel knew that he would have to perform to keep the account. The two brothers had too much invested in "Sergio's, *Pizza You Can Trust!*" Tony and Steve had liked his idea for the ad campaign right from the beginning. Daniel had shared the concept of them sitting around the family kitchen table while their parents lectured them on how to make sure their pizza sauce stayed homemade quality, with fresh ingredients and lots of love. People had always trusted the parent's pizza. Now they had to be able to trust the brothers to carry on the family tradition and business, and that would be his job.

That meeting had gone even better than he had hoped. Now they were actually scheduled to shoot the commercial in the Sergio family home. He checked his schedule for the rest of the afternoon's events.

The morning had flown by. He rang Irene and asked her to run out and pick up some soup and a sandwich for lunch. She ran out and was back in no time.

As he was eating and reviewing another client file, Daniel was surprised when a picture of Deborah flashed through his mind. He remembered the scene like it was yesterday. He had just moved to town, and was in the fourth grade. The family had moved from Chicago because his Dad was tired of commuting and both of his parents wanted their children to have the benefit of growing up in a small community. After the move, they had enrolled him in the private school run by the Deerfield First Assembly Church.

He remembered hating leaving all his friends and how uncomfortable he was that first day at the new school. As he walked into the new classroom, not even a quarter of the size of the one he had attended in Chicago, Deborah was the first person who smiled at him and introduced herself.

He remembered that smile! It would start slowly and then spread across her face. He thought about how hard he had worked after that to try to get her attention and to make her laugh. Her smile was one of those that could light up a room and make a little boy feel like a million bucks. Daniel smiled to himself just thinking about it now. Then he felt the nudging of the Holy Spirit to pray for Deborah. In obedience, he prayed.

As Deborah continued to answer the counselor's questions, it appeared her early infancy and childhood were quite normal. There were the usual childhood sicknesses, bumps, scrapes, and sibling rivalry.

Having her older brother, Paul, to always compete with had been a challenge for Deborah. Because he was older, he was always ahead of her, which had not set well with her competitive nature. Their relationship had helped contribute to the tough exterior she worked so hard at maintaining.

Her younger sister, Mary Rachel, had come along two years later. She was very different in temperament than Deborah. Although they had played together as children, a distance grew between them once Deborah hit puberty.

There was nearly a seven year age difference between her and Tim, her younger brother. She had helped some with his care. Tim had been a sick, colicky baby who demanded a lot of attention from the whole family. Deborah had felt sorry for him and had always tried to protect him from the unmerciful teasing of their older brother.

The counselors then progressed to asking questions about elementary school. Deborah realized that it had been years since she had thought about many of these things. "I attended the private Christian academy run by the First Assembly of Deerfield. It's the church where my father was a deacon."

As she talked, Deborah realized it was the only church she had ever attended, with the exception of two separate occasions in New Orleans when she visited the little Methodist church near her apartment. Deborah suddenly had a strange thought. "Maybe I didn't really have enough information from just attending one church to decide never to be a part of a church again." Before today she had never realized how much she had judged every church by the one she had attended as a child in Deerfield.

When she had visited the Methodist church around the corner, she had only made it through one entire Sunday morning service. Afterward, she was overwhelmed by how dirty and unclean she felt for the rest of the day. She had felt so different from the rest of the people and had even caught a couple of the women looking her over. After that, she had gone back only one other time out of desperation. She had been reminded of the prayers of protection her mother had always prayed over them as children and she was in need of protection.

She had made her way back to the church and had found the door open. There was no one in the sanctuary and she was relieved not to have to face anyone. She made her way to the altar and asked God for protection from Tommie Lee. It was one of those times when he was high on everything he could get his hands on and was threatening to kill her again. Going to the police hadn't been an option. He would have killed her for sure if she had sought their help. Today, as a believer, she wondered just how much that prayer had helped her to get where she was.

As Deborah continued to share her past experiences with Joyce and Lydia, it appeared to her counselors that she had been a pretty well-adjusted student. For the most part, her teachers seemed to like her and she always had a small circle of friends around her. Her father did not allow anything from his children but the best, so Deborah had always made good grades.

As Deborah continued to share about her elementary school years, Lydia caught herself thinking, "Lord, what really happened to destroy the heart of this young woman?" She knew they hadn't uncovered it yet. Performance and perfection were understandable fruit in her life given the pressure of her father's expectations, but it didn't add up to the self-destruction and trail of bad relationships that her application form indicated. And, it didn't appear that anything sexually abusive had happened to her in elementary school, at least not from her responses to the questions the counselors had asked. But, it did sound like things had begun to get more intense at home during those years.

Lydia and Joyce had finally been able to get out of Deborah that her father had been more than just a strict disciplinarian. Her brother had been beaten so badly on several occasions that he carried the marks for days. Lydia cringed inside when she heard how Theodore Noble justified his abuse with scripture. He would remind his son of the 39 stripes Jesus had received upon His back as he lashed him with a razor strap. The mental picture of him quoting scripture with a loud voice as he beat his son turned her stomach. It was the most animated the counselors had seen Deborah as she recounted stories of her brother's abuse and her own reactions. "I've always felt guilty that I never received quite the same treatment. None of us got what Paul did. It was like living with a sacrificial lamb.

"Mary Rachel and I were too afraid to do anything to incur my father's displeasure and Tim was just too weak and sickly as a child. Mom just learned how to avoid her own abuse by getting better at hiding things from my father. Paul received the brunt of his anger physically. I remember getting sick to my stomach and wanting to throw up every time I heard my brother's screams. Sometimes it would happen late at night just when everyone had drifted off to sleep. Something would make my father angry, and suddenly the whole house would be awakened by my brother's screams. Can you imagine the shock and pain of being fast asleep and then out of nowhere have the covers pulled back and being beaten for no reason?" Deborah's eyes were looking past the counselors now as if focused on a distant screen. The memories of her childhood were coming back, and they still hurt.

As the interview continued, Deborah began to open up a little more and share what life was actually like inside the Noble family home. It was clear that her mother had received the onslaught of verbal and emotional abuse from her husband, while the eldest son had received the physical abuse. No matter how many different versions they heard, the counselors still found it strange that sometimes just one child could be the focus of abuse in a home. Other times, it was just the mother who was abused and the children were all treated wonderfully. There were so many combinations of abuse; the combinations themselves carried their own sicknesses and symptoms. Just like Deborah had shared, the ones who weren't abused lived with the guilt and the shame of not being able to stop it. Often, they found that those who listened and watched someone else suffer, often had as much trauma as the one who actually experienced the abuse.

Chapter Five

The Teenage Years

৵ ৵

Lydia and Joyce noticed that Deborah had been more relaxed when discussing her early childhood, than when she approached the topic of her teenage years. Apparently, that was when her rebellion kicked into full force. Even though her fear of her father caused most of her rebellious nature to be hidden, her anger and rejection of authority was obvious as she shared her story. She had also rejected God and church during this time and continued attending church only because Theodore Noble gave her no other choice.

Deborah also shared how difficult a transition it had been from Deerfield Christian Academy to the public high school. She had attended the private school for seven years of her life, including kindergarten. Transitioning to public school made her feel like an outsider; the transition had made seventh grade a difficult year.

"The summer between sixth and seventh grade I had a growth spurt and developed rapidly." She looked down somewhat ashamed even now. That, along with her natural beauty, had caused a lot of unwanted attention from boys and even some of the men in town. As a result, she had subconsciously started to protect herself by dressing in baggy clothes and doing little to take care of herself. She began to avoid any appearance of femininity. This so angered her father that often Deborah would leave the house in one outfit and then change into another on the way to school in order to avoid his wrath.

Her mother had done little to educate Deborah on her sexuality. When she had begun menstruating at the end of the seventh grade, her mother had handed her a booklet on the topic. No, sex was never discussed in the Noble household. Besides a sex education class in school, Deborah's information regarding the subject had come primarily from her friends and classmates. Lydia and Joyce weren't surprised by this. It was amazing how many people they counseled never received adequate information from their parents in the area of their sexuality.

By the age of sixteen, things had changed and Deborah Lynn had begun to see her sexuality as a weapon to use against men. Her clothing had changed with her new perspective; and, rather than dressing in a way that hid her sexuality, she began to dress provocatively. She began to take pleasure in attracting guys, using them and then dumping them.

Lydia asked, "Did you ever love or care about any of the boys in school that you dated?" Deborah responded with a cold look in her eye and a shake of her head. Lydia and Joyce noticed that the only male she had spoken about with any warmth in her voice was an old childhood friend by the name of Daniel. When they asked her if there had ever been more to the relationship, Deborah simply responded, "He was too good for me."

Deborah's life contained some of the typical symptoms which accompany rebellion associated with having parents who exercise control, rather than Godly authority. Her father controlled with anger, abuse and religiosity; her mother, on the other hand, controlled in her own way through withdrawal, appeasement, worry, and enabling. She lived in between her children and her husband's disapproval. Rather than standing up to Theodore Noble, Elizabeth's passivity taught her children how to avoid the wrath of their father.

Deborah's rebellion continued to escalate and she started hanging around the wrong crowd. This led to smoking, drinking and occasional shoplifting. This started when she was about fourteen. Her drug use began by experimenting with pot. It became her drug of choice until she was introduced to cocaine. By sixteen, Deborah was clearly out of control.

Lydia and Joyce both noticed that when asked about eating disorders, Deborah avoided their eyes as she answered. The shame was intense. "I began using laxatives at thirteen," she said almost under her breath. Joyce gently explained that part of it could have been due to the fact that she was trying to stop the development of her body by trying to keep her weight down. Deborah agreed, but also knew there was more to the story. From laxatives she progressed to binging and purging, and by sixteen, bulimia had inevitably taken over her life. Deborah had justified using cocaine because it reduced her appetite, unlike the pot, which had only caused her to binge more. In some ways, she confessed, she felt more in control of the bulimia when using coke. Deborah remembered, "There was only one counselor during senior high that tried to reach out to me. Her name was Mrs. Reynolds. But just as I was beginning to reach out, her husband was transferred and she had to move."

Joyce shook her head as she thought, "It was so sad; over and over again any hope of help had failed Deborah."

It was obvious her parents had used the drug of Denial so they didn't have to face or deal with the true condition of their daughter. And as long as she was in a pew Sunday morning, no one in the church leadership bothered to find out what was troubling the young girl. After all, she was a Noble and everyone in town knew what a fine family that was. She was just going through a "stage" and would outgrow it. Actually, most of the townspeople, and even her own family, were unaware of a great deal of Deborah's rebellion. She had learned to hide it so well that she was on the way to becoming a master of deception. Deborah thought bitterly, "My father taught me well."

While Deborah was going through her interview, Anne had spent the day watching after Aimee and taking care of household chores. With three little ones and a husband to care for, the housework never ended. While Aimee took an early afternoon nap, Anne used the time as an opportunity to prepare for her Tuesday night women's Bible study. She had decided the topic would be *Hearing the Voice of God.* Many of the women were still having a hard time making decisions and were dealing with a lot of confusion in their lives. She felt that it was important to help them understand the different ways God could speak to them. How sometimes the Holy Spirit would highlight certain scriptures, how He could speak to them through dreams and visions, and also how He would speak to them within their own minds and spirits.

The only reservation Anne had about the topic was that she didn't want to give Andrea Kline the opportunity to tell everyone how God had spoken to her that Daniel was going to be her husband. Andrea had never said it directly to Anne, but like everyone else in Deerfield, she had heard the rumor.

"Maybe this would be a good opportunity for me to adjust Andrea. I can explain, through the lesson, how confirmation is needed for major decisions and how our own soul can be deceitful at times when it wants something badly enough."

It was certainly obvious that Andrea wanted a husband. That's all she ever talked about ever since her own husband had suddenly announced that he was gay and came out of the closet. After nine years of marriage, he had packed his bags and headed off to Key West with his male lover. "That was sad and a shock to everyone," she thought, trying to drum up more compassion for Andrea.

It had devastated Andrea when her husband left but she had immediately set her mind on remarriage. She finally understood why her husband had never wanted children all those years. Now, she only had a few more childbearing years left, and she wasn't about to waste any more precious time.

Andrea apparently had decided that with Daniel's two children, and the one she wanted to have, God could redeem her wasted time, and she could still end up with the perfect family. She had their lives together all planned out: they would be in ministry together and end up with one of those Christian television shows. They would look great on TV together.

Anne shook her head and tried to dismiss the things she had been told about Andrea's plans for her brother's life. They were just the thoughts of a grieving, desperate woman. "God, please give me more compassion for her," she prayed softly.

When Daniel stopped by after work to pick up Aimee, he told Anne what had happened at the office. "It was strange, I just started thinking about Deborah back when we were in elementary school together and then felt impressed by the Holy Spirit to pray. Have you heard anything else from her?"

Anne shook her head, "No, I guess whatever was happening today just needed some more prayer. Thanks for being obedient, Daniel.

"I prayed that everything hidden would be exposed. I'm not sure what that really means but I know even as a little girl, Deborah always carried a caution sign next to her heart." Daniel realized that Anne was already in the living room getting Aimee's things together, she hadn't even heard his last statement. He shrugged it off, gathered up his daughter and headed home.

Lydia and Joyce knew exactly what Daniel meant. They had run into the same caution sign and had proceeded slowly as the day went by.

That afternoon as they filled out the paperwork for the next counseling session, Lydia discussed their observations of Deborah Noble and the life story she had told them. Both of them had a nagging feeling that there was something more to it, but neither Deborah, nor the Lord, had revealed it to them yet.

They both knew it was still very early in the process, but committed to some extra time in prayer. Joyce said, "I'll call some of the intercessors for some extra prayer coverage.

"That sounds like a good idea, make sure they pray that everything comes out. I just know she's holding back. But it's still just the first day. We better not get impatient," Lydia responded. "Deborah's given us plenty of other things to work on right now but I also don't want to settle for anything less than God's best."

Chapter Six

Time Alone

ॐ ॐ

After the generational and personal interviews were over, Deborah was alone in her room contemplating what she had just experienced. She was surprised at how much she had been able and willing to open herself up and tell the counselor; but, she was also glad it was over. They had told her that she would probably feel drained and most likely would want to rest. That sounded like a good idea. Deborah fell into the bed and pulled the comforter over herself. She felt chilled inside even though the day was warm and the room was comfortable. Actually, it was more like a feeling of being exposed and a desire to cover herself. It was an old familiar feeling she knew all too well.

When she awoke two hours later, Deborah stayed in bed and allowed her thoughts to return to the events of the morning. Before today, she had never told anyone about the abortion she had at seventeen and couldn't believe that she finally had done so. She didn't know what she had thought would happen when she finally said it out loud to someone. Maybe she had been expecting lightning bolts from heaven. She had never cried about it before. It had actually always seemed like a movie that she had watched. She had starred in it, but it wasn't actually her. Deborah Noble had gone through the motions of the abortion, but she had never been connected to the experience. Lydia had said that this was called dissociation.

As Deborah lay in bed pondering these things, she realized that in most of her life experiences she had felt dissociated. She had always thought that a lot of her feelings of being disconnected had been the result of drug use; but, Lydia and Joyce explained that even though drug use helped the dissociated state, dissociation actually was a defense mechanism developed by children when life became too traumatic for them to handle. Deborah now reflected on the earlier conversation.

Joyce had begun by explaining, "Dissociation is something we all use at times. Have you ever been driving down the Interstate and suddenly realize that you passed your exit without being aware of it?" Deborah nodded in response. "That's a level of dissociation we can all understand," Joyce continued. "It's the same thing that happens when a wife is trying to talk to her husband while he's watching a football game and gets upset because he doesn't respond. He's in a state of dissociation. His mind is in another place and it's not focused on the reality surrounding him."

Lydia interjected, "At the other end of the spectrum, we have dissociation from memories which we call repressed memories and also Dissociative Identity Disorder or DID. This used to be called MPD, or Multiple Personality Disorder. The brain simply compartmentalizes experiences, emotions, and behaviors necessary for survival into different identities. Sometimes these identities actually have different names, or they may simply have identity through their functions or feelings, like the Protector or the Angry One. One compartment or personality may not even have any awareness of other personalities. This condition represents a very high level of dissociation.

"I want to emphasize that this has nothing to do with sanity. People who suffer from DID are not crazy. In fact, they're usually highly intelligent and very creative individuals who develop a very complex way of dealing with trauma at a very young age." Seeing the look on Deborah's face, Lydia instinctively realized what she was thinking. "Don't look so worried Deborah, we don't think that you're suffering from DID, I just wanted to explain the continuum to you." Deborah breathed a sigh of relief as Lydia continued to share.

"The problem with dissociation is that it seemingly works for children because it helps them get away from the pain or trauma on a temporary basis and allows the child to continue moving on through life. But it's still a dysfunctional way of approaching life and can cause many difficulties when the child reaches adulthood."

Lydia then gently helped Deborah see that dissociation was the defense mechanism that helped her survive the tension and abuse that she experienced at home as a child. As an adult, her methods of dissociation through drugs, alcohol and isolation were destructive, and they were now hindering her from mature ways of dealing with issues and relationships. "Deborah, in order to survive you had to create your own little world as a child and then, as you got older, you had to continue to use dissociative mechanisms to help you survive. Now, however, that same dissociation keeps you from being truly connected to your own real feelings and prevents you from experiencing true intimacy with yourself, and the Lord, much less anyone else."

Lydia had shared how even the bulimia helped contribute to the dissociated state because it always consumed so much of her thoughts and kept her so busy that she didn't have the time or energy to focus on the other issues of her life. Plus, it was a way of dealing with the self-loathing she felt inside. Yes, binging and purging had been an escape, too.

The counselors had tried to help her understand that the coping mechanisms she had developed as a child were substitutes, and destructive ones at that, for true healing and the grace to deal with the issues of life. Joyce shared, "Even though you overcame the bulimia with Anne's help and prayers, sometimes when old wounds are re-opened up, the temptation to deal with the pain by throwing up might return. We're not saying this is going to happen, but if the bulimia is triggered at all this week, please be honest and let us know."

The conversation had scared her a little and she sure hoped the bulimia wouldn't try to resurface. It was like a monster-if she let it out of its cage, it would consume her again-and she knew it.

Deborah couldn't believe, looking back on the interview time, that she had even been able to tell Joyce and Lydia so much. Things she had never told anyone before. Besides sharing about the abortion, she had even shared how she had lost her virginity to Justin on her prom night. That night had also been her first experience with cocaine. Although it felt good to talk about it, it also made her nervous because there still was information that she was determined not to share with anyone, and something just happened when she got in that room. Answers to their questions just poured out of her before she had a chance to filter them.

As she thought more about that prom night, she remembered being dropped off at her home in the early morning hours, disheveled and broken. Even in the midst of all her rebellion, her virginity had been the one thing that she had still valued. Now, it was gone too.

Because of the alcohol and drugs in her system, Deborah had not been able to fight Justin off when he had forced himself on her, demanding payment for the drugs he had given her. What she hadn't been able to tell the counselors was what had happened related to Daniel that night. Hurting him had been worse than the loss she had suffered.

She had never used the word "rape" in conjunction with that night or any other night with many other men. But she realized this morning, as she shared her life, with Lydia and Joyce, that she had never given herself willingly to a man. Either she was so "messed up" on alcohol and drugs that they just took advantage of her, or she forced herself to return sex as payment for something they had done for her.

Lydia had pointed out that her following sexual experiences mirrored her first experience with Justin. She had heard the new term "date rape" that was on all the talk shows, but somehow she had never applied it to herself. As badly as she felt about what had happened that prom night, she had been helpless to stop herself. She kept going back to Justin, trading sex for drugs. Prior to losing her virginity, Deborah had only acted seductively around men for the attention and the power it gave her. She had never allowed them to do anything but touch her.

After Justin, her sexual boundaries were completely broken and there were many men. Justin was the only one her age. All of the rest were much older; some of them, she ashamedly admitted today, had been married. She couldn't believe how much she had opened up and talked about this afternoon.

She had shared how Justin had gotten her a fake ID. She already looked twenty and with the fake ID, she had a ticket into another world, one that went far beyond her sixteen years. Things kept escalating. She created elaborate stories to satisfy her parents and then drove to larger towns nearby where no one knew her. There she would find a club and pick up someone for the evening. Never for more than an evening; she wanted no attachments. She always gave the men fake information. Hotel lounges and clubs became her specialty. The men there were usually all from out of town, so she didn't incur the risk of running into them again. Her new identity, created during that time of twenty-one year old Debbie Lynn Webster, was the one that she would carry for the next eighteen years.

Then, at the end of her high school year, she became pregnant. She felt certain that Justin was the father, but there was no way of knowing for sure. In her way of thinking, it made no difference anyway. There was no way she was marrying

Justin or having his baby.

She graduated high school three months pregnant, but no one knew. She had always been in good shape and hid it well. She found an abortion clinic in one of the nearby towns. They wanted $500 for the abortion. To get the money, she prostituted herself for the first time. Deborah remembered shaking as she dressed that night to go out. If her parents only knew some of the outfits she wore under her long dark coat. She realized today that they had never asked to see what she was wearing. They had to have known she was hiding something.

She kept a special box in the back of her closet filled with some of her skimpier outfits. That night, Deborah had put on a short, tight, black leather skirt, high black leather boots and a tight bright red sweater that showed her midriff. Her silver earrings and choker were in the coat pocket as she walked out of the house. She was sick over what she was about to do, but she knew of no other way to get the money.

"After all, it isn't anything different than what I've already been doing," she tried to convince herself. Rather than just receiving the reimbursement of drinks, some drugs and maybe dinner, this time she was going to make the guy pay.

Deborah drove to the southern side of Columbus. She already knew the area where most of the hookers worked. She had driven through with Justin several times on the way to pick up drugs. It felt like a movie that she was watching from a distance. Once she had stepped out of the house that night, she hadn't really felt connected to what she was doing. Now she knew the word; she had been dissociated.

That night, Deborah just knew she had to have that money before the pregnancy went any longer. She parked her car several blocks from Broad Street. She was a little nervous about how she would be received by some of the other women strolling up and down the street-she had heard that the prostitutes were pretty territorial and had a reputation of getting rough with each other.

She already had her strategy and planned on working fast. She parked close to where some of the more upscale strip clubs in the area were located; clubs where limos pulled up, clubs with valet parking. That's where the money was, and that's where she was heading. She only wanted to have to do this once tonight, twice if that's what it took. She needed to find a man with money.

Deborah had decided to catch a man before he entered the club. It didn't make sense to get them coming out of the club after they had already spent most of their money. She was going to find one going in, one who looked lonesome and wealthy. Until then, she would keep her coat on and try not to draw any attention to herself.

Deborah didn't have to wait long. Before she knew it, a silver BMW convertible pulled into the parking lot. A decent-looking man in his forties was at the wheel and he was alone. Looking for the lot attendants, Deborah immediately slipped off her coat and walked boldly to the driver's side of the car. Before the driver had time to swing his car door open, she was leaning on the car, bending just right, so that he could sample the merchandise with his eyes. The man seemed startled at first, and then looked up into Deborah's face. He had taken a deep breath, and then said, "Can I help you?"

Deborah knew it was a good sign. He was polite and didn't look aggressive. She responded by saying, "Absolutely! I need a ride to my car. Would you mind? By the way, what's your name?"

He replied, "Ben." And before he could say anything else, Deborah was already opening the passenger door. She slid in very slowly to give Ben a good long look at her legs. Then she turned and smiled at him.

Ben didn't know what hit him. Three hours later, Deborah walked out of the Paradise Hotel with five one-hundred-dollar bills crumpled in her coat pocket. She had the money and that felt good, but once again in the pit of her stomach, she was sick. Intuitively, she knew that she had sunk to a new low. Strangely, at the same time, it gave her an exhilarating sense of freedom and power. Now she knew there was a way that she could get her needs met if push came to shove.

She remembered glancing nervously at Lydia and Joyce's face as she retold the story. But they hadn't even blinked. It was as if she was telling them she had gone to the grocery store and did some shopping. In some ways, it was comforting that they hadn't looked shocked or disgusted with her. There was still a look of compassion on their faces. Were those tears she had seen in Lydia's eyes?

The sun was going down as Daniel drove Aimee and David home from his sister's. Aimee seemed to be feeling much better. Daniel prayed that David wouldn't get sick, too. One sick child was plenty for him to handle.

There were still some meals in the freezer, thanks to Anne. By the time he fed the kids, helped with homework, and gave them their baths, there would be just enough time for one short video and then the bedtime rituals of bathroom, water, prayers and some individual conversation with each child. Aimee, being younger, always went to bed first. David got an extra thirty minutes. The routine seldom varied from night to night.

Daniel hoped he could get David to open up a little bit tonight. He was concerned with how withdrawn he had become lately.

David was setting the table, supper was in the microwave, and Aimee was looking over her homework assignments that Daniel had picked up from her teacher. Hopefully, she would not fall too far behind in her class work. He had already decided to call Anne and ask her to watch Aimee one more day. She felt a little warm and her cough was still persistent.

Suddenly the phone rang. As Daniel answered it, he was dismayed to hear it was none other than Andrea. Once again, she was asking about Aimee and how she was feeling. He was in no mood to make small talk with her. He quickly escaped the conversation by letting her know that he was right in the middle of making supper for the kids. Hanging up the phone, Daniel hoped he hadn't been too abrupt. She had actually been in the middle of saying something when he said "good bye" and hung up. He hoped it hadn't been anything important.

Chapter Seven

Facing the Past

‰ ‰

It was late in the evening and Deborah still didn't have the energy to get out of bed. She reached for her bottle of water by the bedside and took a long deep drink. She remembered the day she walked into the abortion clinic. It was June 17th. She had forgotten a lot of dates in her life, but that one would never go away.

The clinic was the same place where she had received the news-her pregnancy test was positive. That day the waiting room had several other people in it. Besides Deborah, there were two other girls, both wringing the hands of their boyfriends, and another woman who looked to be in her late thirties. Deborah thought, "Obviously age isn't a factor."

The receptionist handed her a clipboard and a pen. She quickly went over the form and filled it out, putting down totally false information. The receptionist had said, "You're not alone are you? You need to have someone with you to drive you home.

"They had to run some errands and will be back in time to pick me up," she had lied. Back then, there was no way she would trust anyone to help her. Deerfield was just too small of a town. No, she would have to face this herself. No matter how she was feeling afterward, she had been determined to drive herself home.

As she shared the memory with Lydia and Joyce, she found herself smelling the smells and hearing the sounds of the clinic. The sucking sound that had always haunted her echoed in her head. The doctor had been so matter of fact-it had felt like she was part of some assembly line. She waited for him to say, "Next, please," after he was finished. Instead he simply walked out of the room as he stripped off his rubber gloves. The nurse came in to check on her and they moved her to a recovery room and gave her something to drink. They had recommended Tylenol for the discomfort and then released her. She had just killed her baby, and everyone was acting as if she had nothing more than a common cold.

Deborah had been able to drive herself home that day, weak and shaken, but determined that no one in the world would ever find out what she had done. She would go home and act as if she had the caught the flu and her mother would let her rest. She had dealt with work by getting two days off in advance. That should give her plenty of time to recover and get back to work at the café downtown without anyone getting suspicious.

Today, tears streamed down her face as she retold the story. But now, in the privacy of her room, a deep cry erupted from the depths of her belly. It sounded like a mortally wounded animal. The grief and horrible realization of what she had done that day had finally touched her soul. Deborah was no longer dissociated from the trauma and grief of it all. All she could do was let out her pain and cry, "Forgive me God, forgive me." Deborah found herself rocking on the bed, her arms holding a baby that wasn't there. For the first time ever, she wondered if the baby had been a boy or a girl.

After what seemed like forever, the painful memory of the abortion began to subside, and Deborah was able to stop crying. She got up slowly from the bed and made her way into the bathroom. It was as if a huge weight had been removed from her.

Today in the counseling room, as she had been relating the story of the abortion, she had glanced up and seen a picture on the wall of a person coming into the arms of Jesus. As she looked deeper into that picture, there was the shape of the Father with arms encompassing the whole scene. Then above the whole scene was the Holy Spirit, descending like a dove. It was beautiful she thought, but she couldn't imagine herself being received and embraced so lovingly. But this evening, as she had finished crying and repenting, she had suddenly seen herself as that person in the picture, safe in the arms of Jesus. The Father and the Holy Spirit were with her, as Jesus comforted her and eased her pain. She felt a deep peace come into her soul. For the first time, Deborah felt forgiven for the abortion.

She washed her face and looked in the mirror. It was a new experience. For years, all she had been able to do was give a quick glance. This time, she really looked hard at herself. Now she realized that she hadn't been able to even meet her own eyes in a mirror for years. Just like avoiding the eyes of others had become a habit. She stood there for a moment examining herself carefully. Her green eyes, flecked with gray and gold, looked back at her; they were swollen from crying. Her face was a little red and blotchy, but she was still able to look and face herself in the mirror.

Then she realized that her stomach was growling. She was hungry. She made her way into the common kitchen hoping that she wouldn't run into anyone else. There she fixed herself a salad with some tuna on top and a glass of iced tea with lemon. The food actually tasted good and the desire to vomit afterwards was not there. Deborah was relieved. She did not want the bulimia to return. It had frightened her today when the counselors had even suggested that it might try to come back as she got in touch with traumatized areas of her soul. As she ate, she continued to replay pieces of the morning's interview in her head.

———

That spring, Deborah's father had been pressuring her to enroll in the local community college. She had already missed her chance at Ohio State, not because of grades, but because she just hadn't bothered applying. But Deborah had other plans and she wasn't telling anyone.

Ben, the man who had unknowingly funded her abortion, would be back in town on business in two weeks. He had given her his cell phone number and wanted to see her again. Another five-hundred-dollar night and she would have enough money to get out of Deerfield for good. She already knew where she was headed: New Orleans. She wanted to be somewhere warm, somewhere exciting, and somewhere where she wouldn't stand out.

She had told Lydia and Joyce how she had left home a few weeks after the abortion. She had met up with Ben one more time and had earned another five-hundred-dollars. It was only when she got to New Orleans that she appreciated the amount of money he had given her for one night with him. Well, not even a whole night, just several hours.

The morning Deborah had left Deerfield for good, her family received a note that she was leaving but with absolutely no information of where she was going. The note informed them that she wasn't ready to go to college and didn't want them to waste their money on her. When she was ready, she would let them know where she was.

It was all downhill from there. From the age of seventeen and a half until she had arrived back in Deerfield at thirty-four years old, Deborah's life had played out like a bad movie.

She had told the counselors, "I left the car that was mine to use while living at home in Deerfield and caught a bus to New Orleans. I wasn't about to take the chance of my father accusing me of car theft. I didn't want to owe him anything."

"I actually lived a pretty quiet life for the first eighteen months after arriving in New Orleans. Everyone there calls it "The Big Easy" but what I didn't know was that there would be nothing easy about it for me. I found a "Help-Wanted" sign in the window of a restaurant my first day in town. They were looking for a dishwasher but the manager liked me and told me to come back the next day for training. It was called Bayou Bill's and specialized in Cajun cooking and Southern cuisine. The restaurant and other servers became home and family to me for the first year and a half I was in the Big Easy," she said.

After finding a job, Deborah went on to explain how she had found a place to live. "I picked up a paper and found an ad that caught my eye. It was only a one-room efficiency but at a price I thought I could afford. I went to a pay phone and called the number. An older woman, who sounded pretty safe, answered the phone and gave me directions.

"When I found the place, it wasn't in the best of neighborhoods, but it also wasn't in the worst. The efficiency was a little run down and threadbare, but it was livable. It was a little room that Miss Paula, as she introduced herself, had added on when her mother had come to live with her. Her mother had died of old age six months before and she was finally ready to rent out the place. I guess Miss Paula was probably around seventy.

"She made me feel safe so I agreed to the $35 a week which included all the utilities. I think Miss Paula took a liking to me. I did lie to her and told her that I was nineteen; I've always felt bad about that. Anyway, Miss Paula was satisfied, I didn't even sign a lease-we just shook hands. I went straight back to my motel room, got my things and made my way back to Miss Paula's place. I was glad that the city bus ran two blocks from her house. I had just brought a few clothes and toiletries with me, so moving in only took a few minutes. Looking back, I realize that I probably hadn't done as great a job at fooling her as I thought I had. It must have been pretty obvious that I was under age and needed some help. Miss Paula was a real Godsend."

As Deborah reflected back, those first eighteen months

hadn't been so bad. She had made a couple of friends at work and went out occasionally, but over-all, life had been pretty quiet and uneventful. It was when she first met Tommie Lee that everything began to change. Deborah remembered the night. Donna, one of the other waitresses, had asked her if she wanted to go out, shoot pool and have a couple of beers. It was a Friday night, and Deborah decided it would feel good to get out, relax, and have a little fun.

She had gone home after her shift, showered and changed into a pair of tight blue jeans, boots, and a t-shirt. Then she met Donna outside of the Thunder Bolt Lounge. It was a place they had both been before. This time, however, Deborah noticed a number of motorcycles out front.

The tables were all full, so Deborah and Donna slid onto two bar stools and Deborah ordered a Michelob Light. They hadn't been there more than five minutes before the stool next to her was suddenly occupied. Out of the blue, the man sitting next to her reached out, took her face by the chin, and turned it towards him. As Deborah looked into the darkest eyes she had ever seen, Tommie Lee said, "I just wanted to look into the eyes of an angel." Then he let go of her face.

It had startled her, but admittedly, he had also captured her attention. Tommie Lee had dark, long, shaggy hair, a black leather jacket, intense eyes and a handsome face. Before long, they were deep in conversation. The next thing she knew, Deborah was saying good bye to Donna as Tommie Lee James led her out of the bar and unto the back of his chopper. Deborah had never ridden on a motorcycle before, and she wasn't sure if she had fallen in love with Tommie Lee or the thrill of the ride.

The night air was cool, but it still felt like the closest thing to freedom that she had ever found. They rode for a number of miles, and then Tommie Lee had pulled onto a small dirt road. Deborah had felt a moment of fear, but it passed as Tommie Lee got off the bike and said, "I just need to use the bathroom."

He disappeared into the woods and was back in a minute. As he came back to the bike, he took Deborah in his arms and kissed her deeply. She had had enough to drink earlier and her body responded to his kisses and the pressure of his body against hers. Despite all of her sexual activity before she had left Deerfield, Deborah had actually been celibate since moving to New Orleans. Soon Tommie Lee was pulling a bedroll out of the bag on his bike. He was quite a lover. And for the first time in her life, Deborah experienced an orgasm. As the waves of pleasure washed over her body, Deborah finally understood what she had only read about. She didn't even know this man, yet she felt strangely in love.

That night he had dropped her off at Miss Paula's and promised he would return the next afternoon. Sure enough, Tommie Lee showed up like he said he would, and they had gone out for another ride.

She was impressed. He hadn't pushed her for sex that afternoon and he seemed to genuinely enjoy her company. When she had returned home, Miss Paula had been on the porch but slipped inside as they pulled in the driveway. After Tommie Lee had left, the screen door opened and Miss Paula came back outside before Deborah had time to get to her room. Before she knew it, Miss Paula was lecturing her. "That boy is nothing but trouble. I can smell it," she said. "You need to stay away from him." It was the first time that Miss Paula had ever gotten in her business.

But Deborah was already hooked, and it was too late. In less than a month, she moved away from the safety of Miss Paula's home into a one bedroom apartment with Tommie Lee.

How often Miss Paula's words had haunted her in the months and years to come! If only she had listened to that warning. One day she would get in touch with the older woman if she was still alive and tell her how right she had been!

Chapter Eight

Living on the Edge

჻ ჻

As soon as Deborah became Tommie Lee's official "old lady," life changed. He became jealous, possessive, and more controlling than her father. She discovered all too soon that Tommie Lee had a violent temper when crossed.

One night she had to work a little over-time and hadn't thought to call home. By the time she got home, he was furious and had punched a hole in the wall, calling her a whore and a slut. Deborah had finally gotten him calmed down and kept apologizing for not calling him from work. From then on, she walked on egg shells, never knowing what might unleash Tommie Lee's temper. Only six months later, he made Deborah quit her job. He said it was because he just wanted to take care of her, but Deborah knew better. Tommie Lee wanted to know where she was and who she was with at all times. But there wasn't a whole lot to do in the one-bedroom apartment, and without any other outlet, Deborah found herself getting high more and more.

Tommie Lee had told her that he was a bike mechanic, but Deborah had discovered after moving in with him that he actually made most of his money dealing drugs. The mechanic work was just a real, good cover. He was seven years older than Deborah and had been raised by his mother in the Bayou country of Louisiana. Tommie Lee's mother had just turned fifteen when she got pregnant with him. Her parents had thrown her out, and she had survived by moving in with a series of men. Because of his upbringing, Deborah intuitively knew that, deep in his heart, Tommie Lee really hated women. She remembered thinking at the time, "After all, if you can't trust your own mother, how can you trust any other woman?"

Now, she instinctively put her hand to her face remembering the first time Tommie Lee had knocked her across the yard. Before that incident he would only scream or break something. But that day, he took his anger out on her.

She had gone out for a walk that afternoon and had found herself at the park; the day was pleasant and it felt good to get some fresh air. She had stayed a little bit longer than she normally would dare. Tommie Lee had called home several times while she was out. He had finally left work and driven home to see why she hadn't answered the phone. He was standing in the front yard of the apartments, seething, as she had walked up the sidewalk. As she approached him, he backhanded her with an intensity that had shocked and stunned her. Afterward, he simply started up his bike and went back to work. She lay weeping in the yard. That night she found herself making him a special dinner, hoping to appease his anger. He had come home and acted as if nothing had happened. He had never said he was sorry for that or anything else he had ever done to her.

Looking back, Deborah saw how sick and crazy it all was. But at the time, she had nowhere to go and her definition of love was all messed up. Sadly, she had believed the lie that if she loved him hard enough and good enough, Tommie Lee would change. In reality, what changed was Deborah. She became harder and more addicted as she found herself caught in the cycle of abuse and Tommie Lee's possessive jealousy. Every time she even thought of leaving, Tommie Lee would let her know that she would be sorry. Over time, he started threatening to kill her if she ever left him.

Tommie Lee had been prospecting with the Renegades motorcycle club when she had met him. He finally became a patched member when Deborah turned twenty one. Life really went down hill after that. He eventually left his job as a mechanic and began working full time for the club. Whether it was drug running, robbery or threatening someone's life, Tommie Lee lived for the Renegades. They were the family he never had and the fathers and brothers he had longed for all of his life. Any semblance of a normal life from that point on was gone.

Deborah had moved from one prison to another. Now her life in New Orleans was no better than the one she had left in Deerfield. There was just a new warden, and his name was Tommie Lee James.

Fifteen years of her life became consumed with either running from him or running back to him. She remembered how Tommie Lee loved to show her off and made sure she dressed in as little as possible when she was on the back of his bike. But heaven help the man who ever dared talk to her. Most of the time she just felt like bait as Tommie Lee took out his anger in another fist fight over her. She remembered one time when a man simply asked for some directions. Before she knew it, Tommie Lee had punched him in the mouth.

Actually, it was Tommie Lee's temper that finally gave her a reprieve. He was finally arrested for assault and battery and ended up spending three years in prison. The judge hadn't been lenient because of Tommie Lee's extensive juvenile record. Deborah remembered the wonderful sense of freedom she felt when Tommie Lee was led out of the courtroom that day. She had gone back to their apartment, packed her bags, and left the rest of the stuff for the Renegades to take care of. She knew if she didn't get out fast, they would watch her every move and report everything back to Tommie Lee.

The previous year, she and Tommie Lee had gone to Daytona Beach for Bike Week and Deborah had decided that she would go back if she ever had the chance. Here was her chance and Deborah caught the first bus out of town. She landed in Daytona Beach in the middle of August. It was hot, humid, and dead.

During Bike Week, the city had been teeming with bikers, parties and life. Now it seemed like a sleepy small town. All the snowbirds had gone back up North. There were no special events and nothing much was happening.

It took Deborah a couple weeks to find a job; she survived by visiting the homeless shelter for meals. How she hated the women who handed her plates of hot food as they smiled and said, "Remember, Jesus loves you." Finally, one day, Deborah got sick of it and decided to get a job at one of the local strip clubs. It was another first for her, but it beat standing in line with the smell of homeless people all around her. The club owner took an immediate liking to her and before long, she became his mistress.

Roy Teems put her up in a condo on the beach and she found herself dancing less and less. She would, however, go to the club with Roy nearly every night. Deborah found herself enjoying this different lifestyle. There was no passion or real relationship with Roy, but there was also none of the abuse she had experienced with Tommie Lee. Deborah would get back to the condo at about four in the morning; she would sleep until noon and then hit the beach. Tanned to a golden brown and fed properly, Deborah began to feel more and more like her old self. However, all of that changed the next Bike Week.

The nightmare began when one of the Renegade members had come into the club and recognized her. She could have kicked herself for offering to help out because the place had been so busy. What had she been thinking? She was actually dancing when they walked into the club. She quickly ended her number and slipped out hoping that they weren't club members who would recognize her. She kept her mouth shut and didn't say anything to Roy, something she would later regret. She should have warned him and gotten out of town. But by the next night, it was too late. As they came out of the club to head home, Roy was jumped and beaten to a pulp by four of the gang members right in his own parking lot. Hootch, one of the gang members, forced her onto the back of his bike. Roaring out of the parking lot, she knew that life as she had known it was over. They had taken her outside of town past the campgrounds where they were staying. There in a secluded spot, the four bikers in a drunken stupor gang raped her. Each of them took his turn with her until they were sure she had gotten the message. She belonged to the Renegades. She was their property.

It had taken all she had to retell the event to Lydia and Joyce today. She remembered the coldness which existed in the hatred and anger that had penetrated her soul that night. She had refused to cry out, refused to move. No, she wouldn't give them the satisfaction of knowing how scared and devastated she really was. The night had been silent, except for the disgusting grunting of the man on top of her, and the occasional cheers of those watching.

The scream within her had never been released until today as she shared the story with Lydia and Joyce. After she finished the story, Lydia had asked her if it was okay if she put her hand on her. She said, "I believe there's a scream inside of you that you were unable to get out that night. It's still there waiting to be released. Will you trust me as I pray for you?" Deborah didn't know why she had nodded, "Yes," but she had. The next thing she knew Lydia was praying for the scream and pain to come up and out of her. Suddenly a blood curdling scream of, "NOOOO!" came rushing out of her. And then it came again and again. She screamed until she finally fell weeping into Lydia's lap.

She had been shaking all over as Lydia and Joyce prayed against trauma. Lydia comforted her and rocked her, just as one would rock a small, frightened child until peace came. Finally, she was able to continue with the story. She never saw Roy Teems or Daytona Beach again. The next morning the Renegades headed out of town with Deborah on the back of Wolf Man's bike. Everything hurt, and she remembered the long, painful ride back to New Orleans.

Once she arrived back in New Orleans, she immediately went to the Louisiana State Penitentiary to see Tommie Lee, prompted by the threats of the Renegade gang members. Although he was initially angry when she first got there, he eventually softened. Being sober and clean from the alcohol and drugs had, to some degree, changed him. He even talked about getting a job when he was released, and about leaving the Renegades. Deborah actually left the prison that day wondering if she dared to hope that things could be different.

She went back to work as a waitress. The club members kept a close watch on her until Tommie finally got out of prison. He actually only served a little over two years because of gain time. Until that day, Deborah made occasional visits, and Tommie Lee continued to make promises of a better future.

One of the mandates of Tommie Lee's probation was that he get a job upon his release. He soon found one at a garage as a motorcycle mechanic. Because of the terms of his probation, he was not allowed to have anything to do with any of the gang members. Thankfully, the next eighteen months of probation were some of the better times Deborah and Tommie Lee experienced together. However, it didn't last. Soon after his probation was over he was back with the Renegades. Not long after that he lost his job. Alas, nothing had really changed.

Deborah began planning another way of escape. She started saving money and had finally built up enough courage. One afternoon, when Tommie Lee was out doing a job for the Renegades, she walked out of the place where they were living.

She left with only the clothes on her back and the couple hundred dollars she had pilfered from Tommie Lee's drug money over the last couple of months. She was now nearly twenty-nine years old, and she decided life had to change before she turned thirty.

Chapter Nine

From Bad to Worse

ॐ ॐ

This time, Deborah headed in the opposite direction and went to Houston, Texas. Because it was the only life she had ever known, she found herself another job as a cocktail waitress in one of the downtown clubs. While it was true that life had been very hard on her so far, she could still "clean up" pretty well so getting a job wasn't hard. Once again she found a one-room efficiency and moved in. She led a fairly quiet life during that time, working and keeping to herself.

Unexpectedly one night she met Moses. He was a good looking, very charming and very persuasive black man. Reflecting back, Deborah could see that he had the same demonic spirit that had controlled her all of her life.

Moses complimented Deborah. He began buying her nice things and taking her to nice places. He was the perfect gentleman and never pressured her for sex. He also started sharing drugs with her. Except for occasional use of alcohol and pot, Deborah had been clean since she had made it to Houston. This time, the drug was bigger than her ability to control it; this time the drug was heroin. The first night Moses shot her up, Deborah couldn't believe what she was doing. She had always made a vow to herself that she would never use needles, but it didn't take long for the drug to take control and every vow she had ever made was swept away with the warmth of the first rush. It was a high like no other she had ever experienced.

As time went on, Deborah discovered that Moses actually supported himself by pimping off a stable of women. He had all his girls working the streets for their share of heroin. Moses always called her his "special girl," but he had done that with every girl he had under his spell. She also found out that Moses was into witchcraft and considered himself a warlock. Cold chills went up and down her spine just thinking about it.

Moses started grooming her for prostitution by just dressing her up and strolling her up and down the street. He loved the attention the long-legged beauty received as the men drove by. He had told her not to be afraid, he was just using her as advertisement for his other girls working the street. It wasn't long, however, before one of the men pulled up beside them and negotiated a deal with Moses, a deal he couldn't resist. Deborah remembered the words, "Just this one time, for Daddy, Sugar, and if you don't like it, you'll never have to do it again." But Moses was hooked on the money she could bring in, and Deborah was hooked on the heroin he supplied.

In a short time, she was consumed by the cycle of drugs, prostitution and then more drugs. Finally, Deborah ended up in the hospital. She had passed out with one of the johns she was with and he dumped her outside the emergency room door of the hospital. She was sick from malnutrition and had a bad strain of flu that was going around. Deborah was thankful that it wasn't hepatitis or, even worse, AIDS. After a couple of days of hospital food, rest, and a chance to clear her head, Deborah knew she had to get out.

Deborah had seen some of the girls who had worked for several years for Moses and what that life had done to them. One of them, Connie, had come to see her and warned her to get out while she still could. She had jumped from the frying pan in to the fire. She actually found herself missing Tommie Lee. He had been a part of her life for ten years and now Deborah hardly knew how to live any other way than at the mercy of a man like him.

Moses had tracked her down in the hospital and was scheduled to pick her up the next afternoon. That evening, she found herself placing a long-distance call to Tommie Lee from the hospital. Out of desperation, she asked him to come and get her. Once again swearing his undying love and willingness to change, Tommie Lee was back in her life. This time, she had no one to blame but herself. He rode all night and was at the hospital the next morning to pick her up. She had convinced the nurses that she had to get out early before Moses came back to get her.

Tommie Lee and Deborah spent a couple of days in Houston at a cheap motel while she got her strength back. Within a few days, she found herself on the back of his bike and heading back to New Orleans.

What Deborah didn't know was that since she had been gone, Tommie Lee had started free-basing cocaine; smoking crack was a whole new level of drug use for him. And as soon as she was back, Tommie Lee introduced her to the new love of his life. Once she started doing crack, Deborah was hooked like she had never been hooked before. For her, it was even worse than the heroin. Tommie Lee continued to smoke up his drug profits, and the Renegades were beginning to lose their patience with him.

Finally, late one night, several gang members took Tommie Lee out of town and beat him up badly. He had come home bruised and bloody. It was their way of sending him a serious message about the money he owed the gang. The next thing Deborah knew, they were both leaving town. This time they were headed to Missouri. Tommie Lee had some family there. His aunt and uncle took them in, and there Deborah nursed Tommie Lee back to health. She actually enjoyed the couple of weeks spent at their farmhouse. Life almost felt normal. But Tommie Lee couldn't sit still for long, and soon they were on the move again.

From Missouri, they headed out to Jackson, Mississippi. After a few months there, Tommie Lee had contacted some of the Renegades back in Louisiana, swearing that he had gotten his drug use under control. Before Deborah knew it, they were back in New Orleans, back to the Big Easy.

No sooner had they arrived when Deborah had finally caved in and agreed to go with Tommie Lee to the crack house. Normally, she avoided those places, but in a moment of weakness, she gave in to his pleas to go along. Neither she nor Tommie Lee knew that the house they had just entered had been under surveillance for some time. That night, they had barely walked out of the house with the drugs when they were surrounded by police. She was eventually faced with the choice of either turning State's evidence against Tommie Lee and the Renegades and getting probation, or facing time herself.

Tommie Lee was facing another ten years, probably seven with gain time for good behavior. She knew one thing for certain. Her life with him was over. She thought about how much time had been lost. She felt like her life was nearly over and she was only thirty-four years old. Those years of her life had been a haze of drugs, alcohol and abuse; years that were lost forever. The pain of regret felt like it could over take her at any moment. "How could I have been so stupid?"

Throughout the course of all those years, she had never once spoken to her father. She had never gone back to Deerfield, not even for his funeral. In truth, she had not even known that he was dead until three months after the family had buried him. Occasionally, she would call her mother on Christmas or Mother's Day. A few times she had dropped a card to her sister, Mary Rachel. For the most part, however, she had no relationship with her family during those years.

Deborah realized that talking about the past this morning had stirred up a plethora of memories and emotions. She walked into the library to watch her video assignment. It was on something the counselors had called bitter-root judgments. Deborah curled up on the couch, covered herself with an afghan, and picked up her notebook.

In a quiet living room in Deerfield, Daniel had also settled down to watch a football game after the kids were tucked into bed. Suddenly the door bell rang. "Who could that be at this time of night?" he thought to himself. As he opened the door, Daniel found Andrea Kline standing on his steps. He was totally unprepared and uncomfortable with her presence.

She held out a casserole dish and said, "I tried to tell you on the phone that I was going to run this by later, but I think we got disconnected."

Daniel realized he had hung up before he heard exactly what Andrea had been saying. Not knowing what else to do, he reached for the casserole dish and said, "Thanks. That was nice of you."

But Andrea wouldn't let go of the dish and rather than fighting for it, Daniel let go. Before he knew it, Andrea was slipping into the house and walking toward the kitchen. She acted like she owned the place, opening the refrigerator door and placing the casserole dish inside. Then she went to the little message board near the telephone and began to write the directions for heating up the dish on the board.

Daniel felt paralyzed. He couldn't just throw her out, but this was not how he planned on spending his evening. "I'm sorry, Andrea. I was just right in the middle of the Monday night game," he said, thinking she might take the hint.

Andrea, however, seemed oblivious to Daniel's discomfort and replied, "I would just love to watch the rest of the game with you." Before Daniel could say anything, she walked straight to the living room sofa and made herself comfortable. Daniel deliberately walked over to his favorite recliner and sat in it. There was no way he was going to give her the satisfaction of his sitting next to her on that sofa.

So there he was, in his own family room, with a woman he didn't really know and didn't really care to know, watching a football game. "So much for a relaxing night at home," he thought. "I can't let my guard down for a minute." He couldn't believe the pushiness of this woman and was angry with himself for his own inability to tell her what he really thought. Then, wouldn't you know it, the game went into overtime. "What on earth will the neighbors think with a strange car in my driveway at this time of night?" Daniel prayed that no one would notice or recognize Andrea's car.

Andrea kept trying to make small talk during the commercials. Daniel's response was always as minimal as possible and bordered on rudeness. He couldn't believe that she didn't get the message. He just wasn't interested in any conversation with her!

As soon as the game was over, Daniel stood up and walked to the front door. Andrea followed, looking a little disappointed. Daniel opened the door and said, "Good night, Andrea. Thank you for the casserole."

Not knowing what else to do, Andrea walked out the door and down the front steps. She then turned and said, "I can't tell you how much fun this was Daniel, I would love to do it again sometime."

Daniel wanted to slam the door after her, but he simply closed it with a half-hearted, "Bye now." Part of tonight's debacle was his own fault, but he was going to be careful not to let it happen again. It wasn't that Andrea was unattractive; actually, she really was a good looking woman, blonde hair, blue eyes and a pretty nice body. Her personality, on the other hand, turned him off totally. There was something about her that made the hair on the back of his neck stand up. Daniel was going to need some of his sister's advice on how to deal with this woman.

Anne and her family were all in bed early. It had been an uneventful night. As she crawled into bed next to her husband, her thoughts once again turned to Deborah. She wondered how she had made it through the first day of ministry.

She prayed within her mind so as not to disturb her husband, who was almost asleep; "Father, please make Yourself real to Deborah this week. Let those whom You have appointed to minister to her use grace and wisdom. Give her hope for the future and heal the wounds and even the scar tissue surrounding her heart. Lord, I pray that You would give Deborah rest this evening." She continued, "I bind every tormenting spirit that would harass her. Let her see You as the God who is able to redeem all things." With that, Anne was quickly off to sleep, curled up comfortably beside her husband.

Deborah had just finished the video on bitter-root judgments. What an eye opener! Lydia and Joyce had asked her to make a list of some of the judgments she saw while she was watching the video. The list had gotten longer and longer. Most of them were related to her father and mother. The meaning of "judge not, lest you be judged," began to take on a whole new meaning for her.

The teachers on the video had shared that in the book of Hebrew, Chapter 12, verse 15 explains that we are to be careful not to let the root of bitterness spring up because many can be defiled by it. For the first time in her life, Deborah saw how her bitter-root judgment of her father had ended up causing her to be drawn to the type of men who would use and abuse her. Some of them could have even treated her worse as they were defiled by the bitterness that lived inside of her.

She also saw that she had judged her mother harshly when it came to her passive reaction to Theodore Noble's anger and abusive behavior. Yet, she herself had acted no differently with Tommie Lee or any of the other men in her life. She became exactly what she had judged and hated in her mother, a woman that took abuse from a man, helpless to do anything about it.

Could life really change by repenting to God for her judgment of others, especially her parents? It almost sounded too good to be true. Deborah was glad that the video had pointed out that it didn't mean that everything they had done was right or okay, but that it just released the right of judgment back into the Lord's hands. "It couldn't hurt," she thought as she took the list of judgments she had compiled while watching the video and repented to the Lord for each and every one of them.

Deborah had almost completed her list when Maureen, the lady who oversaw the facility, came down from her upstairs apartment. It was the first time that she had seen her since she had arrived last night. Even though there were several other rooms in the big old house, Deborah was the only other person staying there this week. She had been relieved to hear that. God knew she could only take so much. She was having a hard enough time facing herself this week, much less having to face other guests in the house.

Maureen was very sensitive to the needs required by the special guests of the ministry. Deborah felt the anointing and presence of God as Maureen walked by the study. Rather than entering the room, she simply poked her head in the door and asked Deborah if she would like a cup of hot, chamomile tea before bed. Deborah just shook her head yes. Maureen disappeared for several minutes and came back with a cup of steaming tea in a lovely china cup. By that time, she had finished with her list and prayer.

While she and Maureen exchanged a few words, Deborah discovered that Maureen had lived in the house for nearly three years; she looked after the guests and made sure they all felt welcome. Maureen had a ministry of hospitality and it was obvious that she loved the old house as if it were her own.

The women said, "Good night," to each other and made their way back to their own rooms. The tea had felt good, warm, and comforting, "Just what I needed," she thought as she got into her pajamas. As she climbed into bed, Deborah reflected, "It's only been one day. I already feel like I've been here a week. No telling what tomorrow will bring." But she was tired and the thought barely surfaced before she drifted off to sleep.

Chapter Ten

The Second Day

ॐ ॐ

Lydia rolled over in bed as the alarm went off and snuggled up next to her husband. "Seven thirty already! It feels like I just fell asleep." The sun was already streaming into the bedroom window. She could tell it was going to be another one of those beautiful, inviting spring days. April had always been one of her favorite months in Florida. The weather wasn't hot and humid yet, and the summer rains were still several months away. It was a perfect day, and she was going to have to spend most of it in the counseling room.

As quickly as the thought crossed her mind, she caught her attitude and prayed, "Forgive me, Lord. You know that I have laid down my life and I know only You could have brought Deborah here. I trust You to redeem the time I give today."

She knew that once she got to His House and began ministering, there was no place she would rather be. It was so exciting and such a privilege to see God work on a life so up-close and personal. She felt like a head nurse assisting a gifted surgeon, able to see his miraculous work first hand. "No, there's no way I would trade one day of the last seven years of ministry for a day at the beach," she thought to herself.

Lydia reached for her Bible on the night stand and began to read out of the book of Isaiah. Chapter 52 caught her attention. It sounded just like it was written for Deborah.

Awake, awake! Put on your strength, O Zion; Put on your beautiful garments, O Jerusalem, the holy city! For the uncircumcised and the unclean shall not longer come to you. Shake yourself from the dust, arise; sit down O Jerusalem! Loose yourself from the bonds of your neck, O captive daughter of Zion! For thus says the Lord; you have sold yourselves for nothing. And you shall be redeemed without money.

The words read like the story of Deborah Noble's life. She began to pray for Deborah's redemption as she got ready to get out of bed. She nudged Stephen who began to stir, "Good morning, honey, time to get up." Stephen placed a light kiss on her neck and rolled out of bed.

As he got up to take his shower, Lydia made her way into the kitchen. "I hope Joyce got a good night's sleep," she thought. "We're both going to need all the energy we can get for today's session."

Back in Deerfield, Daniel and Anne went through the morning rituals of getting their children up and off to school. Tuesday morning looked no different than Monday morning. Daniel got Aimee to his sister's house ten minutes early. He wanted to make sure he had time to talk because he definitely wanted to let Anne know about his uninvited visitor last night.

Aimee seemed to be feeling much better. This was the first morning she had an appetite since she had gotten sick. In spite of her improvement, he thought that it would still be good for her to have one more day of rest before she went back to school.

Anne yelled, "Come on in," as Daniel and Aimee approached the back door. As Aimee came in and hugged her aunt, Anne could tell that she was feeling a whole lot better. "Good morning, Aimee. You're looking like you're feeling better. Tomorrow it will be back to school for you."

Daniel, on the other hand, looked troubled, and Anne wondered what was wrong. He went to the cupboard, found a mug and poured himself a cup of coffee while Anne got Aimee settled into the living room. When she returned, he wasted no time telling her about his late-night visitor. As Daniel relayed the story, Anne was more than a bit shocked. She knew Andrea was desperate, but she couldn't believe the woman's forward behavior. She suggested, "Daniel, you need to talk to Pastor Harrison. I think it's time you received some advice from him. He might even be willing to have a talk with Andrea."

Daniel breathed a sigh of relief, "That sounds like a good idea. I'll have Irene call and set up an appointment this week." He knew he could count on Anne to have some good advice. She always did.

It felt good just talking about what had happened the night before. These were the times he missed Susan so much. Having someone as a sounding board was so important. After he finished sharing with Anne, he felt relieved. They spent a few more minutes chatting about the Sergio account that he had just landed, and then Daniel left his sister's house ready to face his day.

Deborah slept in until 8:00 a.m. She couldn't believe it when she looked at the clock. It was a rare occasion for her to sleep a whole night through; she hadn't even bothered to set an alarm the night before. Now, she only had an hour to get ready for her session. She quickly jumped in the shower, got dressed and applied a minimal amount of make-up. "It appeared that Lydia and Joyce's goal is to get me to cry it off anyway!" she thought.

After such an emotionally draining day yesterday, she was amazed at how good she felt this morning. She had actually caught herself humming under her breath. She hadn't done that in a very long time-in fact-not since she was a little girl.

As she made her way into the kitchen, Deborah ran into Maureen who was doing laundry in the utility room. Maureen greeted Deborah with a cheery, "Good Morning! How did you sleep last night?"

Deborah responded, "Great! Thank you!" and made her way to the refrigerator and pulled out some juice. She popped a bagel into the toaster and reached for a banana out of the fruit basket. She ate the banana standing up, while the bagel toasted.

Grabbing her bagel and juice, she walked out the back door unto the attached deck. "What a beautiful morning!" The azaleas were blooming all around the back of the house.

Deborah suddenly realized that she had never really appreciated Florida during her short stay in Daytona Beach. Now she was taking it all in, the beauty of the palm trees, the clear blue sky, and the spring flowers in bloom. Sitting on the deck furniture, Deborah drank her juice and ate her bagel. "Don't want to be late for my morning session," she thought.

After eating, she made her way back to her room, brushed her teeth and then headed out to the house next door. She was a few minutes early, and the door was still locked. Deborah sat on the porch swing and began to swing back and forth. It was as comforting now as it had been when she was a child.

Lydia and Joyce pulled up separately but within minutes of each other. One look at Deborah and they were immediately put at ease. She looked more peaceful and less guarded today than she had the day before. She actually greeted them with a "Good morning" and a smile, and the women all made small talk on the porch before going inside.

Back in the counseling room they all found their places, as if actors finding their marks. Lydia and Joyce opened the session with prayer. The words were so personal and caring-so unlike the religious prayers her father used to pray over the family-that brought tears to Deborah's eyes.

Joyce opened the session with a discussion of scriptures related to generational sins. She got up from her chair to give Deborah a physical illustration. Joyce had Deborah hold her own arm up, bent at the elbow. "Now, Deborah, if this area to the left is sin, you can move your hand in that direction by your own free will. Just move your hand downward and to the left."

Deborah did so and then looked at Joyce as if to say, "So, what's your point?"

Now, Joyce said, "I'm going to take my hand and push your hand into the sin area, and I want you to resist."

Deborah did and Joyce said, "Do you feel that weight and force that your arm is fighting against? Let's call that generational sin." All of a sudden, Lydia saw the light of recognition in Deborah's eyes. She had received the understanding.

Deborah inquired, "So in other words, even when I decide not to sin, I have to fight against generational curses, and if I get weak at all, they'll overcome me."

Joyce explained, "Exactly! Generational curses give the Enemy the right to put greater pressure on you. It's a weight that actually pushes you into areas of sin. Without the weight of the generational curses, it's much easier for a person to withstand the temptation and pressure of sin. With the pressure, it's very easy for a person to quit resisting and simply succumb to the sin."

Lydia interjected, "Now, that doesn't take away your accountability for your sin. It just helps people to understand why certain sins in their life are so much harder to overcome. Why do some people have such a hard time with alcohol, or anger, or depression, or poverty, and others have no problem at all? Many times it's because of the generational curses that are affecting them."

Joyce noted, "The Word says, 'My people are destroyed for lack of knowledge.'"

It made sense now. The physical illustration helped

Deborah "get" the picture. Yes, everyone has free will but there were times when she had felt helpless to exercise hers. She thought of the mornings she could hardly get out of bed because life had felt like a huge weight that was ready to crush her at any moment. She realized that she had never really heard anything about generational curses before yesterday, and she hadn't fully understood even then what they had to do with her.

Joyce was sharing Galatians 3:13: *"Christ has redeemed us from the curse of the law, having becoming a curse for us for it is written, 'Cursed is everyone who hangs on a tree.'"*

Lydia added, "Jesus made a way for all of us to be redeemed from the generational curses of the law by dying on the Cross, but each of us has to appropriate it personally by faith. And we must also do what the Word of God says in order to receive anything from the Cross. To *appropriate* means to take something for one's own exclusive use. We all have a responsibility to receive the sacrifice Jesus made on the Cross as our own. People often say that Jesus would have died for us even if we were the only person on the earth, and that's true. What He did was very personal for each of us and must be appropriated by us in a very personal way." Lydia continued, "Jesus died that everyone might be saved, but many are not - not until they personally appropriate salvation by faith. Healing, deliverance and redemption are all available through the cross. It's our job to claim our inheritance by faith and application of the Word of God."

Joyce shared several other scriptural examples, from the books of Nehemiah and Daniel, of how people confessed their own sins and the inequity of their fathers whenever there were seasons of revival and restoration. She also shared that there is only one way to deal with sin and that is through repentance.

Lydia explained, "Deborah, many times generational sins magnify and multiply as they come down the family line. Today, you have the opportunity to stand as righteous seed and ask for forgiveness. What you are doing today is not just for you, but for any children you might have and all the generations that will follow. Curses empower us to fail while blessings empower us to succeed. The Word says, 'choose this day blessings or curses.' It's up to us, we have a choice."

Deborah's breath caught. She had really given up all hope of ever having children. Now, as Lydia spoke, it actually sounded like a genuine possibility.

Lydia continued on by using examples of the kings in the Bible who would do evil, followed by their sons who would do more evil, and then by the next generation would do even more evil. "It took a righteous king, who would repent for the evil of all the kings before him, to make changes for the entire nation. Today, you have the opportunity to come before the Lord as that righteous king or priest ready to make atonement."

Deborah took all the information in intently and jotted down some of the scriptures they shared. She wanted to be able to remember everything so she could share it all with Anne: Leviticus 26:39-42, Exodus 20:4-5, Nehemiah 9:2 and Deuteronomy 23:2.

Joyce gave some specific examples of generational sin. "The sin of idolatry carries consequences for four to five generations and the sin of illegitimacy causes the offspring for ten generations to be cut off from the assembly of the Lord." She said, "People operating under the curse of illegitimacy always have a sense of not belonging. They have a difficult time entering into worship and into the presence of the Lord. They often feel as if they're on the outside looking in."

The seriousness of sin and its consequences had never impacted Deborah like it did after hearing what Lydia and Joyce shared. Deborah thought, "Thank God, Tommie Lee was unable to have children." As a young man, mumps had rendered him sterile. Deborah shuddered visibly at the thought of bringing a child into the insane life she had lived with that man. "No, God spared me when He left me childless after the abortion," she concluded. For years, she had always secretly felt that her barrenness was punishment for killing her unborn baby. Now, she fully understood why they had wanted so much family background information when she had filled out her forms. At the time, it had seemed a little over the top.

The revelation of the need to repent for generational sin created a new sense of hope. Even though she had been doing much better in life since she had become Born Again, each day still seemed like such a battle, especially in certain areas. Finally, she understood why. Rather than feeling nervous about this next session, Deborah actually felt a sense of anticipation.

Chapter Eleven

Repentance

ॐ ॐ

Joyce handed Deborah the prayer that she was going to be using during this session. "Deborah, let's take a look at the steps of this prayer. In the first step, you're going to repent for a certain category of sin committed by yourself and members of your family line. Repentance is the act of taking responsibility for your sin, but you're also letting God know that you're choosing, from this point on, to walk in the opposite direction of the sin.

"When you repent of the sin of pride, then you are choosing to walk in humility. When you repent of the sin of lust, you're choosing to walk in holiness. It's not just simply saying, 'I'm sorry for what I've done,' like a lot of people think. Repentance is much more than that. It's asking for forgiveness while also committing to God that you are going to make a one-hundred-eighty degree turn. So you need to be sure that you just don't read the prayer. Your heart has to come into agreement with it. Repentance is not something to take lightly."

Deborah looked down at the prayer, trying to follow along, sobered by what she had just heard.

Joyce continued, "In the second step, we want you to get in touch with how the sins of your parents and ancestors affected your life and then forgive them. In order to have true forgiveness, it's important to assess the damages so you really know what you're forgiving. Many people just minimize, deny, or shrug things off, and that's not true forgiveness."

Lydia interrupted gently, "This is not about blaming your family for all of your problems. By identifying the sin areas in your family line, it helps you to get in touch with your predisposition to sin in certain areas. For example, the generational sexual sin of your grandfather, and possibly of your father, opened the door in the spirit realm for the enemy to visit that curse upon your life."

Deborah thought to herself, "If Lydia only knew how true that statement was!

"Step three of the prayer is where you ask for forgiveness for your own participation in the sin." Joyce went on, "Step four is where you forgive yourself." Deborah thought about yesterday when Joyce had drawn the forgiveness cross on the white board. She had explained that throughout the week Deborah would be asking for and receiving forgiveness from God as she drew a vertical line on the board. It represented forgiveness between her and the Lord. Next, Joyce explained, "You'll also have to forgive others," as she drew a horizontal line over the vertical and formed a cross. "And then you'll have to forgive yourself," and she drew a circle around the area where the two lines intersected. It made so much sense, but Deborah had never really thought about forgiving herself before. She was thankful for the opportunity to do that today.

Joyce was continuing, "Step five is where you will renounce the sin, break all agreement with the enemy, and receive, by faith, a blessing to replace the curse. *Renounce* means to make a formal, public statement, to give up all rights, claims, and allegiances. You will be declaring before heaven and earth your position regarding the generational sins that have encumbered you and your ancestors."

Deborah was glad for the piece of paper to hold onto and follow. "I'll never be able to remember all the steps with everything running through my mind right now," she thought.

Lydia began to speak again, "We've seen so many testimonies of what God has done in families after someone has stood in the gap and repented of generational sin. In my own life, my oldest daughter was illegitimate. We couldn't get that girl to attend church. Remember the scripture says that the curse of illegitimacy is that they and their offspring, up to ten generations, can not enter into the Assembly of God. Once Marie became a teenager, she just refused to go to church, and then she ended up in total rebellion and on drugs." Lydia paused as tears filled her eyes. "Six months after my husband and I went through this same process my daughter was home and back in church. It made a believer out of me! I know now that after the generational curse was lifted from her life through my repentance, her own free will was finally strong enough to make some right decisions for herself. And now, there's no one who is more serious about attending regular services than Marie. She also loves to worship and easily enters into the presence of God."

Deborah was shocked for two reasons and thought to herself, "I can't believe Lydia is so open with details of her own life." Plus, it surprised her that Lydia had anything but a perfect life and family. "Maybe these women could understand me more than I've realized."

Then Joyce began to share that her grandparents on both her mother's and father's sides had divorced. Her parents subsequently had also divorced and remarried. Her mother had been married twice before and her father once. In her own life, Joyce had been divorced twice. Joyce shared how understanding that she had the curse of divorce made it easier to forgive herself.

Again, Deborah had to guard against looking shocked. She would never have believed it. Joyce looked so happy and content. Deborah could only imagine the pain of two failed marriages. Now, it was she who was having compassion on the two women sitting across from her. "I guess you never know what other people have been through," she thought. Most of the time, she believed everyone else's life was perfect and hers was the only one that was "a mess." "Maybe I'm not the Lone Ranger after all," she thought.

Joyce continued to explain, "We have compiled a list of categories of generational sins from the questionnaire you filled out before arriving and from your interview yesterday. The rest we have to trust the Holy Spirit to show us."

Lydia interjected, "The prayer may feel a bit awkward at first, but you'll get into a flow after the first couple of times through. The most important thing is for you to get in touch with what the Lord is showing you.

"If you have any questions about anything as we move through the list, please stop and ask us," Joyce also added. "Are you ready to get started?"

Deborah nodded in agreement and picked up the prayer lying on the couch beside her. Joyce read the first category to her: abandonment, rejection, and favoritism. Deborah confessed the sin and repented to the Lord for both herself and her ancestors.

The next step of the prayer took some coaching from Joyce. She wasn't exactly sure how her family's sins in this area had affected her life. It made her stop and think. As she talked it out, she realized that her parents had suffered from their own share of abandonment, rejection, and favoritism. Her father had been totally rejected by his maternal grandparents, and his mother, Regina. Plus, he had been emotionally abandoned by his father, the Judge. Judge Noble's only concern in life had been his own work, accomplishments and his illicit relationship with his secretary. The Judge had avoided home because of the pain his wife's rejection caused him. His sister, Liberty Noble, had always been the family favorite, which probably always caused the Judge to strive for recognition and approval.

For the first time, Deborah saw her family in a different

light. She was actually beginning to feel a bit of compassion for her father. That was definitely a first! She also saw how her maternal grandfather, Eugene Millstone's, drinking and passivity had created abandonment and rejection in her mother's life. The premature death of her maternal great grandmother had also caused Grandma Ellen to experience her own share of abandonment. She had had to raise herself, her brothers, and sister from the time she was thirteen years old.

Deborah felt like a ray of light began to shine through the darkness of her past as she worked through the prayer.

On step number three, when she was confessing how she had participated in the sins, Joyce had gently pointed out that Deborah had abandoned and rejected her entire family. She had never seen it as sin before, simply self-preservation for them and for her. Now, as she forgave herself, she realized that she had rejected the whole world.

By the time she got to the last step, it was easy to renounce and break agreement with all the sins, curses and demonic influence related to abandonment, rejection and favoritism. And at the end, she prayed to receive the blessing of acceptance and unconditional love from the Lord.

Deborah took a deep breath as she finished. "That wasn't so hard," she thought. "It really felt good once I made it to the bottom of the page." She was ready for more!

Throughout the morning, the women patiently worked Deborah through the list of generational sins. As the list went on and on, she told them, "I know I probably have had the longest list of anyone." When she commented on the fact, they both immediately replied, "Just about everyone who goes through the ministry has that same thought. The Word isn't kidding when it says that 'all have sinned.' When you compile the sins of generations, most people have quite a list."

The category of sexual sins was one of the hardest for her

to face. It carried so much shame. Confessing the prostitution, harlotry, pornography, perversion, fornication and adultery was very painful, but even more painful was what she couldn't bring herself to confess. She did it in her heart, but she couldn't get past the vow she had made years ago to never speak it aloud.

The areas of addiction were also an eye opener. She had never seen her father's work or religiosity as a form of addiction before. She didn't even know there was such a thing as religious addiction. Then as Joyce and Lydia explained, Deborah's eyes were opened and she saw that the activities her father found in church and work caused him to avoid his pain, just as much as the drugs and alcohol had helped relieve her pain. She also had never realized that a workaholic needs an enabler in the same way an alcoholic does. Her mother had enabled her father. She had always made excuses, tried to appease him, and taught her children how to do the same thing. Now, she could see it clearly.

Suddenly, Deborah felt rage stirring within her. She had lived her whole life with a deep-seated anger related to the abuse of her brother. Her anger had always been aimed solely at her father. Today, however, she realized that she was also angry at her mother for never stopping the abuse, for pretending it wasn't happening, and for encouraging her brother not to upset Theodore Noble. The counselors gave her time to work through her anger.

Lydia and Joyce decided to help her by doing some role-playing. Lydia prayed and asked for the Lord's protection and stood in the gap for Deborah's mother. She moved her chair directly in front of Deborah and asked her to be honest and tell her mother how she really felt. The untapped anger and rage she began to express amazed and frightened Deborah as the words came bubbling up from some unknown place.

"I hate you. You're weak, pathetic and miserable. You never protected any of us, especially Paul. You didn't deserve to have children. Why didn't you leave him? Why did you put up with the abuse? You just became his doormat. You let him and everyone else walk all over you.

"I have no respect for you. You made me hate being a woman because I never wanted to be like you!" At this point she broke down in tears. She was shocked at what had just come out of her, and realized that she had never been in touch with how she really felt. Suddenly she understood why she had never had any close female friends. She not only hated men; she hated women too!

She heard Joyce's voice faintly in the background, "Now that you've gotten your anger out, tell the Lord about the pain it caused you."

Obediently, she began to share, "I lived in fear, fear of my father and fear that there was no one to protect us. I had no role model, no one to look up to, no one to try to be like. It hurt that I didn't like my own mother." At this point she broke down again; a wail of deep pain flowing out of her.

As she quieted, Lydia spoke softly, "Deborah, will you forgive me for not being strong enough to stand up to your father, for allowing him to abuse all of us, and for not being someone you could look up to?"

Now, she found herself at a crossroads, taking a deep breath, she said, "Yes, Mom, I choose to forgive you." Suddenly a dam of feelings broke inside and she found herself in Lydia's arms, "Yes, Mama, I forgive you. I really do love you." She felt like a wall had been broken down within her heart. Part of her could hardly wait to get home and really hug her mother, to forgive her for the past and to begin a whole new relationship with her.

At the end of the session, Lydia helped lead Deborah in a prayer that broke the word curses which she had spoken over herself and those that others had spoken over her. She had a difficult time repeating some of the curse words Tommie Lee had called her.

"In the name of Jesus, I break the power of the words that I will never amount to anything, that I'm a wild child, that I'm nothing but a whore, a bitch, and a slut and those words I just can't say out loud but You know, God. I rebuke every demon assigned to them, and I forgive myself, my father, Tommie Lee, and any other man for speaking them over my life." After she finished the first group of word curses some others came to her mind, some from her brothers and sister, and other people in her life, so she repeated the prayer several times, not wanting to miss anything.

Next, Lydia showed her how vows had affected her life. As she drew a big circle on the white board, she said, "Now, Deborah, let's say that this whole circle represents your life. Whenever you make a vow, you take a slice of your life into your own hands." With that Lydia carved out a piece of the circle that looked like a slice of pie. "When you make a vow out loud or in your heart that says 'I will' or 'I will never,' you're basically telling God, 'Hands off of that area of my life.' Plus, most of the time, when we make vows, we make them in judgment of others."

Joyce said, "And then the scripture that says 'by whatever measure we judge, we will be judged' comes into play."

Lydia said, "It's like a double whammy. First, we remove God's power from that area of our life, and then when we judge others, we set ourselves up to be judged. When I finally understood this, I could understand how people who had been abused ended up becoming abusers. Even though all of them, at some point, had probably said out loud or in their hearts, 'I will never abuse my children like I was abused.' Then eventually, they are judged by others for committing the very sin they hated so much."

She felt a little overwhelmed with this concept because she knew that she had made a lot of vows out of her own strong will. She had tied the Lord's hands in so many areas of her life by exercising her will out of hurt, anger, judgment and self-protection. She hadn't done such a hot job of running her life up to this point and now she was more than willing to put every area back into the Lord's hands.

Lydia handed her the prayer to read and she began to pray without hesitation, "I release my life from the vow that I would never be like my father. I give that portion of my life back to Your grace, power, and authority. I repent for judging my father and rebuke every demon assigned to this vow," Deborah prayed. She had vowed that she would never be like her mother, that she would never let anyone hurt her again, that she would never need anybody, that she would never be weak like her mother, that she would never be stupid like other women, that she would never let anyone see her cry, that she would never trust anyone again, that she would never bring children into such a "messed up" world. And the list went on and on...

As she continued to work through the list, Joyce reminded her gently, "Remember, if you think of any others at any time, you can pray this prayer yourself. This is also an equipping process. We want to deal with as many things as possible while you're here, but the Holy Spirit will continue to be faithful even after you leave. He will help to complete anything we may not have time for this week."

At that, Deborah said, "I really can't think of anything else, but if I do, I'll write it down and share it with you. Thanks for reminding me that I can continue to identify and pray over other things that come up later. I start feeling a little desperate, wanting to make sure we don't miss anything."

Lydia said, "We totally understand, and we want the Lord to do as much as possible over the next few days. But over time, we have had to become realistic knowing there are just so many hours in the day. We're often amazed at how much the Lord can accomplish in a week. But we also know that the He is jealous over you and some things are going to be just between you and Him."

As the session ended, they ministered over her in prayer. They laid hands on her, and Lydia said, "As ministers of the gospel and by the power of the Holy Spirit, we release forgiveness for all the sins and iniquities that have been confessed today. I command every curse to be broken and every demonic influence to be bound." Then Joyce prayed, "We open up the spiritual gates that have been shut up by sin and release generational blessings to flow to Deborah and her descendants. Lord, protect her and prepare her for the next session. Lydia concluded, "Lord, we thank You for Your shed Blood and Your grace that made today possible."

As the session closed and she rose from the couch, Deborah felt like a huge weight had been removed. For the first time, she felt like she had a chance in life. Before she had always felt defeated, but now she realized that had been due to the effect of the curses. She had been set up to fail. "Christ has redeemed *me* from the curse," Deborah said out loud as she personalized the Scripture. That word 'redeemed' had a whole new meaning now. It's not just a religious word anymore. It's actually an experience, an experience that carries with it hope, freedom, and forgiveness. How can I thank you enough for the time you've taken with me today?"

After exchanging hugs with Lydia and Joyce, she walked out of the house. "I've been redeemed" Deborah said to herself again as she stepped out onto the porch. She had an urge to run and tell someone else about redemption. It felt so good! Now she understood why people had the desire to share the Gospel. It wasn't just a gospel of do's and don'ts, it was the Good News of redemption. Redemption! What a wonderful word!

Deborah decided to get in her car and have lunch somewhere. It was still a beautiful day. She found a terrace restaurant on the beach where she ordered a fish sandwich and fries. Today, she had an appetite.

As she ate, Deborah reflected back on the morning session. It had lasted three and a half hours. When she had first started on the list of generational sins, Deborah had figured that it would probably take all day-given her past.

After lunch, Deborah found a pay phone and used a calling card to call Anne. She just had to let her know how she was doing; she knew Anne was praying for her. The phone rang several times and then she heard her voice. "Hello, you've reached the Erickson residence, please leave a message." Deborah was disappointed to get the answering machine, but as she began to leave her message, Anne picked up the phone. "Deborah, is that you? Hold on a second while I shut this machine off. How's everything going?"

At that moment, she realized that it was going to be pretty hard to put into words what she had already experienced. "Anne, it's better than I could've ever imagined. Yesterday was pretty tough, but today was great. Thank you so much for recommending this ministry to me. My counselors' names are Lydia and Joyce. They're just wonderful. They've been really patient with me and have great insight."

Deborah realized that she hadn't given Anne a chance to respond, so she paused for a moment. Anne replied, "That's wonderful, Deborah, I'm so proud of you for taking this step. I'll sleep better tonight knowing that you're in good hands."

Deborah replied, "Let all the girls at the Bible study know that I appreciate their prayers and I'll tell them all about it when I get back to Deerfield. I only have a couple more minutes on this card." Anne said her goodbyes and Deborah hung up. It felt good to call someone she knew really cared about her.

She went inside the restaurant and used the bathroom. Her hands smelled a bit fishy and as she was washing up someone knocked on the door. Previously, something as simple as that would have made her angry; today she responded, "I'll be done in a minute," and actually smiled at the lady as she headed out the door. She decided to take a short walk along the boardwalk before heading back to the house. She actually found herself humming as she walked.

After returning to her room, Deborah started her homework assignment. She tried listening to the two tapes on anger and addiction, but dozed off halfway through the first tape. She had to re-listen to it when she woke up. This time, she took notes as she listened. After she had completed the tapes, Deborah got out her journal and began to write down some of the insights and thoughts she had about the morning's session.

Chapter Twelve

Behind the Scenes

ଛ ଈ

After finishing up the paperwork for the next day's session, Lydia and Joyce parted. They were both pleased at the progress that had been made that morning, but they both still had that underlying feeling that there was more to the story. Deborah just wasn't ready to go there yet-it was pretty typical.

Shame often worked in layers. People would peel off enough to satisfy the counselors and themselves, while hiding a core area. Only the Holy Spirit could prepare hearts to face those difficult areas. From past experience, Lydia and Joyce had both learned not to go there prematurely. To do so would usually cause a greater wall of defense to rise. No, they had learned to just pray and trust God to do the rest.

As she drove home that day, Lydia thought about what a great team she and Joyce made. "Thank God, we found each other." They complemented each other well. Each had different gifts and personalities, but when blended as a team, the combination just worked. Lydia was a little more direct and tended to operate with discernment and revelation, whereas Joyce was very compassionate and gentle and had a lot of wisdom.

Lydia found herself thinking of how they first met. She had been attending Grace Fellowship for a number of years with her family and had already been participating in their counseling ministry when she met Joyce. She thought about how different Joyce looked now compared to the first time she had seen her. She had been a broken woman. Her eyes were full of grief and pain and her hair had been dyed a platinum blonde in a former attempt to please her husband. Now, she had gone back to her natural auburn hair and on most days her eyes were peaceful. At times, they even expressed joy.

Joyce had moved from up North after a painful divorce. Her realtor had actually been the one to recommend the church to Joyce. Lydia had found herself counseling and ministering to Joyce as she recovered from her second divorce.

Joyce had first married at the tender age of seventeen. The marriage hadn't even lasted two years. They were both too immature, too selfish, and both were unsaved. They simply broke up, as if they had just been going steady. The second marriage break-up was much more painful. Joyce and her second husband, Bill, had been married eighteen years. Their only daughter had just left home for college. The breakup was the result of the exposure of a sexual addiction that Bill had kept covered for years. Even though they had been faithful church goers, he had led a double life.

Joyce was not only devastated by the divorce, but her faith in God and her own discernment were shaken to the core. Once the addiction was uncovered, Bill refused to get help. His shame was so great that he was unable to face his wife, the church, people at work, or anyone else who could have helped him. He packed up and moved out to California and divorce papers followed a few months later.

Joyce had difficulty finding closure because Bill had never been willing to talk to her after the day she finally confronted him. During the confrontation he had broken down and confessed it all but after his shame became a wall. He had grown up in a family where pornography was easily accessible, and even encouraged by his father to use it. After getting hooked as a teenager, Bill had never been able to give it up. He had always been afraid to tell Joyce, assuming she would never understand. His problem had escalated with the advent of the Internet. Joyce discovered that his late nights at the office were not spent working, as he had claimed, but on chat lines and web sites.

Everything had unraveled when he had eventually agreed to meet one of the women he encountered on the Internet. She drove in from out of town for the occasion. This was a whole different experience for Bill. Pornography had been safe, in a sense. Over the years, he had gotten very skilled at not getting caught. He had always told himself that the women he was viewing were not real women, and so it could not be adultery. Bill had even justified what he was doing by believing it enhanced his sex life with his wife.

"Trixie" was the chat room name used by the woman he was meeting. Bill knew in his heart that things had gotten badly out of control, but the spirit of lust in him was no longer satisfied by pornography-he wanted more. Once again Bill lied to himself; he told himself if he could just do it this one time, he would get this desire out of his system.

Despite all of the pornography he had viewed, Joyce was actually the only woman Bill had ever had intercourse with. Because of this, he had been able to deceive himself into thinking that he was being a faithful husband.

"Trixie" was a whole lot more than Bill could handle and the next thing he knew, she had him talked into going to a local sex house. Bill hadn't even known that such a thing existed in their town. But Trixie informed him of a whole other area on the Internet, which included houses and clubs where people actually met. These were places people could go for a simple cover charge. They were even listed and described on various web sites. Suddenly, Bill, the man who attended church every

Sunday with his wife and their daughter, was walking into a place that he would have never gone to on his own. He had no clue what was really waiting for him there. The enemy had set the perfect trap to destroy as many lives as he could.

Unknown to Bill or Trixie, the local police department had been watching the sex house for several months and finally had collected enough evidence to bust them. Drugs were also being sold in the house. Minutes after he and Trixie walked into the house, the place was suddenly swarming with police.

In the spirit realm, the Enemy was rejoicing. He had destroyed another so-called Christian family. This scandal could tear up the whole church. After all, Bill was an elder, and Joyce was always trying to counsel and help other families. This was a Grand Slam. The family would be destroyed and the church would be discredited and weakened. "Those stupid Christians," the Enemy thought as Bill was led out of the house in handcuffs. "Gotcha! And that stupid church of yours!"

The demon that had finally led to Bill's demise had been assigned to him by the territorial spirit over the city. The spirit of lust already in Bill had opened the spiritual door for the spirit of destruction, which reigned over the area, to enter and have authority over the unsanctified areas of Bill's heart and mind. The demonic presence-assigned to keep the people in Greenville, Indiana-oppressed was delighted to capture Bill. He was a valuable POW. The Christian Community Church had begun to affect both the people in the community and the spiritual atmosphere over Greenville. Taking one of its visible members hostage was a major triumph. "Take that, Christian Community!" Tomorrow the bust would be on the front page of the local paper.

That night the clock read 1:00 a.m., when Joyce began to get frantic. She had no idea where Bill was. She had called all the hospitals and then the police stations. That was how she learned that her husband was in jail, though the police would not give her any more information. Bill had not been able to face Joyce and hadn't called her from jail. He didn't come home until late the next morning.

a friend had bailed Bill out and dropped him off at home. When he had arrived at the house, Bill, not knowing that Joyce had discovered where he had spent the night, tried lying toher. Joyce simply said, "I know you're lying. Tell me the truth." Not having slept all night, and with his defenses down, Bill spilled it all. The truth came tumbling out.

Afterward, Joyce realized why she had been having so many troubled dreams about Bill cheating on her and why many times, when he worked late, there would be that uneasy feeling in the pit of her stomach. The Holy Spirit had tried to get her attention, but she had pushed the feelings down and ascribed them to her own insecurities. Now, as the whole story unfolded, she was overcome by nausea and pain. Her world had crashed to pieces in what seemed like moments.

After Bill had walked out of her life with no intention to deal with what had happened, Joyce had to make plans of her own. With her daughter in college and her marriage destroyed, Joyce had made the decision to start over. She had prayed and felt a leading to go to Florida. One of the things that had led her to Grace Fellowship in Palm City was a brochure someone had given her about the *Restore Your Soul Ministry,* which was connected to the church. Someone had actually put it in her hand a month before the situation with Bill was exposed.

Initially, the brochure had caught her interest because they also offered more training for lay counselors and ministers. It had even more value now that she desperately in need of ministry herself. After a visit to Palm City, Grace Fellowship and much prayer, she made the decision to relocate.

Pastor Mike at Christian Community Church gave his

blessing for her departure because he felt it might be the best thing for everyone. He definitely wanted the blemish Joyce and her family had caused the church to be removed and he didn't know what to do with her or her husband. Outwardly, he went through the motions of being sad to see them go, but secretly he was relieved that both Bill and Joyce had decided to relocate. Now Christian Community Church could go on with business as usual. Hopefully, in a short time, the whole scandal would be forgotten. "What a mess!" He remembered opening up the newspaper that Thursday morning and seeing one of his elders being led out of a house by police. The article that went with the picture was an expose on the local sex house and the drug bust.

The church phone had rung off the hook that day. Pastor Mike had been secretly glad that Bill and Joyce had not called for his help; in fact, he had not seen or talked to Bill since. That day, he retreated to his study in preparation for Sunday's message which he could have easily entitled, *Damage Control*.

"Yes," Lydia thought, "Joyce was a mess when I first met her. But God lovingly restored her and matured her through the process and today she's one of my favorite people to counsel with at the center. Out of her broken situation God has done a deep work in Joyce's heart." In the midst of it, despite all of Bill's deception and the pain he had caused Joyce, the Lord had also given Lydia compassion for him. She was all too aware of how the Body of Christ had created a facade of holy perfection and the pressure it put on many people. It left no room for real people with real problems to receive ministry.

Recently, things had begun to shift, but the Church still had a long way to go in meeting the needs of so many broken people and broken families. She continued to pray for Bill regularly, hoping that one day he would reach out and find some real help for his sexual addiction. She had never shared with Joyce the fact that God had given her the faith to believe that one day the marriage might be restored. It wasn't the timing of God to say anything yet, and Lydia was also praying for confirmation. In the meantime, it certainly wasn't going to hurt to keep Bill in prayer. Realizing that it was still a very touchy subject with Joyce, she was very careful about what she said. Right now, the woman was still recovering from a broken heart and thoughts of marriage of any sort were not what she needed. In fact, when Joyce had gone through her own ministry time, one of the vows that had to be broken was that she would never remarry. Lydia remembered the difficulty Joyce had that day when she had to release that portion of her life into God's hands. It hadn't been easy, but Joyce had seen enough of how vows bound people and hindered the plans of God. She finally prayed and gave the vow to the Lord.

Most vows came from people just trying to protect themselves, but they still caused havoc in peoples' lives. More times than not, when Lydia ministered to people, in areas where they had repeated difficulties, there was often an underlying vow. When people genuinely desired freedom, God was always faithful about uncovering them. She knew that if restoring Joyce and Bill's marriage was the Lord's plan, He would also prepare Joyce's heart. It was only God who could bring the healing and forgiveness she would need to receive her husband back. Of course, it would take some real repentance on Bill's part, and they both had work to do on other issues that had also led to the divorce. Lydia smiled to herself, "You just never knew what God might do!"

PRODIGAL DAUGHTER

Chapter Thirteen

Lydia's Story

❧ ❧

Off in her own world, Lydia suddenly realized that she had arrived at the grocery store parking lot. She quickly ran in to pick up food for supper. She actually had the evening off and was looking forward to fixing a nice meal for her husband, Stephen. He was always patient with her busy schedule and she took every opportunity to bless him. As she was making her way through the produce department, she ran into Betty. She had ministered to her over two years ago. They embraced each other and Betty immediately began to recount how much her life had changed since she had received ministry.

Betty had been free from panic attacks ever since her deliverance. Recently, she had also been reconciled with her oldest son. Betty delightedly acknowledged that, since going through the *Restore Your Soul Ministry,* she had also been able to join the praise team at her church. It always had been a desire of her heart, but she had been bound by so much fear she could never step out and try.

Lydia was happy to see Betty so full of life and joy. She was quite different from the woman who had initially graced the couch in the counseling room. Back then, Betty could barely hold her head up or look Lydia in the eye. Her whole countenance had been downcast. Once Betty had told her story in the first session, Lydia could understand why. Everyone always had a "story."

After they parted and she continued with her shopping, Lydia's heart filled with gratitude. The Lord was so faithful and always brought testimonies to encourage her. How wonderful to know Betty's family was blessed and changed by the time she had sacrificed.

People who came for ministry gave what they could. Sometimes it wasn't very much. The counselors had to be dedicated and willing to do the work of the Lord. However, at times, there were individuals who had the ability to sow bountifully, and they did. Thank God for them! They were the ones who helped the ministry stay alive. In the meantime, the ministers had to trust that the Lord would provide and bless their lives. As she pushed the cart down the aisle, adding groceries as she went, Lydia continued to reflect on the faithfulness of God. The rewards were great, not just the promised ones to be received one day in heaven, but here on earth.

Once the groceries were successfully checked out and loaded into the car, Lydia headed toward home. She dialed her cell phone to check on her youngest daughter, Diana, who was pregnant. She had been having some challenges with morning sickness and Lydia wanted to know how her day had gone. With a two and one-half year old at home to care for, Diana had her hands full already. The phone was busy. She would try again later.

Meanwhile, there was another woman walking out of a grocery store in Deerfield. It was Elizabeth Nobel, Deborah's mother. She had felt peculiar all morning. It was as if she could break down crying at any moment for no apparent reason. But it was strange; it felt more like tears of relief rather than pain. As she got back into her car, Deborah's face suddenly flashed before her eyes. Could it be connected to what she was feeling? She offered up a simple prayer for her daughter. No sooner had she finished praying, when another strange picture came to her mind.

Elizabeth saw a vision of the Lord handing her a baby and placing it tenderly in her arms. As she felt the baby come into her arms, she suddenly broke down in the SaveMore parking lot. The depth of her broken mother's heart came rising to the surface as she cried out, "My baby, my baby, thank you for giving me back my baby."

When she was finally able to pull herself together and start driving home, there was real hope in Elizabeth's heart for the first time in years. The baby in the vision had looked exactly like Deborah when she was first born. "God is going to restore my relationship with my daughter, I just know it," she thought.

She didn't know what was happening to Deborah down in Florida, but she felt in her heart that it had to be connected to what she had just experienced. Years of grief were suddenly replaced by peace and assurance that everything was going to be all right. As Elizabeth entered the townhouse, she and her daughter were sharing, she felt an urgency to pray for Deborah every day while she was away. Change was in the air, and she wanted to be a part of it.

Back in Florida, Lydia was pulling into the driveway of their three bedroom townhouse. Although they had purchased the home two years ago, it still took a little adjusting to whenever she drove up. Sometimes it felt like she was visiting someone else's life.

She and Stephen had been married for twenty-five years. They were actually planning an anniversary cruise at the end of the month. Lydia was ready for it. The past winter had been full of ministry and family events, and the schedule hadn't afforded much time off. Unloading the groceries, her mind went to some of the things she needed to pick up before the cruise. "Better write them down or I'll forget," she thought. Her cell phone started ringing as she was juggling too many groceries at once. The number was her oldest daughter, Marie's. Lydia found herself talking to the cell phone unable to answer it in time, "I'll call you back as soon as I get the groceries put away." Her arms full of bags, Lydia made her way through the front door and into her kitchen. As she was putting the food away, a sense of contentment filled her heart. She was truly happy in their new home, despite how different it was from the four bedroom home they had sold.

Lydia loved the light and airy kitchen that overlooked the golf course. It was far enough away from the green so as not to hear too much noise, but close enough to still enjoy the green velvet beauty of the course. There was a man-made lake with a beautiful fountain that continually purified the water as it faithfully spouted upward every day. They could see it from their screened in porch out back. It was their favorite place to just sit and relax, surrounded by the plants and flowers that Stephen loved to tend. All in all, this was the perfect place for this stage of their lives. The yard work was taken care of by the development. There was a community pool and whirlpool they could use without having the concerns of upkeep and maintenance. They used one of the bedrooms as a home office and the other remained a guest room.

It felt incredibly good to have a late afternoon and evening off and she hoped Stephen would be able to get home on time. They both worked with hurt people all day long and sometimes you just couldn't control some of the emergency situations that arose. His chiropractic practice often demanded long hours, as well.

Supper was in the oven slowly cooking itself, the kitchen was in order and there were even cut flowers on the dining table. She decided to relax and went into the large master bath and began to run a tub. She still had another hour before her husband came home for dinner. As the tub was running, she gave her oldest daughter a call back. Marie answered the phone a little breathlessly. "Hi Mom, thanks for calling me back, I just needed to ask what you're doing tomorrow evening. I need someone to watch the kids for a couple of hours." Lydia agreed that between her and Stephen, they would be able to handle the kids so Marie could attend a business banquet with her husband.

As Lydia climbed into her bath, she was glad they weren't babysitting tonight. As much as she loved spending time with her grandchildren, tonight she needed her own battery recharged. Three children under the age of ten was a handful. Their combined energy overflowed the confines of the three bedroom townhouse so that, upon their departure, even the walls seemed to breathe a sigh of relief. They weren't bad kids; just creative, inquisitive and full of life.

As Lydia relaxed in her garden tub, a deep sense of gratitude arose in her heart again. How incredibly grateful she was to the Lord for restoring her relationship with Marie. It had been a long painful battle, but God was faithful.

———————

Lydia's own story was quite different from Deborah's in many ways, but she did know what it was like to be pregnant, unmarried, and forced with the difficult decision of abortion or keeping the baby. In her case, she had been nineteen. "Old enough to know better!" she thought to herself. Lydia had been in her second year of college when she became pregnant, and she remembered the pain surrounding the family scandal. After the decision to keep the baby, she had dropped out of school.

The baby's father, Bob, had wanted her to have an abortion, but Lydia could not bring herself to do it. She hadn't known Jesus then as she did now, but she had been raised in a family with a traditional Catholic background. She knew that abortion was wrong and had made the choice to keep the baby. Every action in life, however, has a consequence, and the illegitimacy had created pain for both herself and Marie.

Once Bob learned of the pregnancy, he had dropped her

like a hot potato. He actually had the unmitigated gall to question whether or not the baby was his. It was so painful to face the truth that he had never intended to marry her. She was no more than a college fling. Unbelievably, Bob, who had been a college senior at the time, wasted no time in going on with his life. He went home after graduation and married his high school sweetheart. She had been the girl his family had originally decided was the one for him-she was from a prestigious family. Lydia never knew if Bob had ever told his parents that she was pregnant.

Life and times were different then; Bob just waltzed out of her life and the baby's without taking any responsibility. There was no DNA testing, no court-ordered child support. Her unwillingness to force him to do the "right thing" let Bob completely off the hook. He went on with his life like their relationship and the subsequent pregnancy had never happened.

Lydia, on the other hand, had to drop out of school and find employment to support both her and the baby. She shivered in the bath tub even though the water was still warm and relaxing. She reflected, "How did I do it working, going to night school, and raising a daughter all at the same time?" No wonder Marie had felt abandoned, unimportant and angry! At the time, Lydia had also felt angry at the sacrifice she had to make. It had been difficult raising a daughter on her own. Then when Marie was seven, Stephen had showed up.

At the time, Lydia just knew things were going to get better. Stephen genuinely loved Marie, as well as Lydia, and he was a Godly, Christian man. Lydia had gotten Born Again two years earlier and started to attend church regularly. Marie, however, saw her mother's new found Christianity as yet another thing that would rob time and attention from her. Consequently, Marie not only hated church, but acted out every Sunday morning. There was always a fight over something. It was as if she purposely plotted to make them late for church.

Rather than seeing Stephen as a man who was willing to be a loving father and someone who would ease the financial pressures they lived under constantly, Marie saw him as the enemy. He was just one more target for her anger. Despite Marie's reactions, Stephen and Lydia feeling certain the Lord was putting them together and decided to marry the next year. In the meantime, Stephen had made a commitment to try and win Marie's heart.

Marie was eight years old when Lydia married Stephen. The wedding pictures served as an all-too-familiar reminder of how her daughter felt at the time. Not one picture captured her smiling. While everyone else was smiling and happy, Marie looked as if she was attending the funeral of her best friend. Two years later Diana was born, and that was the final straw for Marie. There was no way she would or could compete with this baby who had captured everyone's hearts. The day Diana came home from the hospital was the same day Marie left home, in a sense. She still lived there, but she wanted no part of anyone or anything that had to do with the family.

Stephen and Lydia tried to be patient. They understood that her behavior was a result of the deep wounds she carried within, but it was still challenging to live with day after day. They also struggled with the guilt they felt every time Marie saw them expressing love to Diana. Even though Marie was very bright, there were constant trips to school to deal with the behavior issues that arose as a result of the inner turmoil Marie was experiencing.

Marie's pain and rebellion began to spill over into every area of her life. By the time she moved into her teenage years, her behavior was causing constant turmoil in the home. It was sad to say, but the only moments of peace the family experienced, were during the times when Marie ran away. No one dared to say it out loud, and they all felt guilty about their feelings, but it was almost a relief when she was gone. They had tried it all: counselors, drug treatment programs, special family vacations. They read all the books and listened to all the tapes they could find. Nothing and no one seemed able to penetrate the wall that Marie had put up around her heart.

It had been devastating the day Marie had finally moved out. She had finally quit school and left home at seventeen. One day she climbed into a van, loaded with her things, and pulled out of the driveway and out of their lives. Though she lived less than two hours away, they only saw her once or twice a year. She stayed with friends and went from one job to another, always seeming to get by some way, somehow.

All Lydia could do was pray, and pray she did. Nothing had tested her faith like God's seeming inability to reach her daughter. But finally one day, with one phone call, it all changed. It came six months after Stephen and Lydia were offered an opportunity to go through *Restore Your Soul* ministry. Lydia had chosen to go through the process for training purposes, and Stephen had agreed to support her. What neither one of them expected was how deep and profoundly the ministry would impact their personal lives and family.

Through the process, Lydia really received revelation regarding the generational sin of illegitimacy. It had been in her paternal family line for several generations. She had repented for the sin and also received more healing for the pain and resentment she carried because of her own unwanted pregnancy. In the course of the ministry, she experienced a deep unconditional love towards Marie-it just dropped into her heart. She had always loved her daughter, but this was different. Now Lydia knew she not only had her own love for her Marie, but she was experiencing God's unfailing love for her. It gave her a new sense of hope and promise for their relationship.

Sure enough, six months later the phone rang and Marie was on the other end. She was twenty-four years old, living with a man, a drug dealer, who had just thrown her out. She had nowhere to go. Marie asked if she could come home for a couple of days until she could find another place to live.

Lydia and Stephen knew the phone call had to be a miracle since she had never asked for their help before. They had some concerns about how Marie's rebellion would affect Diana, who was sixteen now. Diana was fairly well adjusted, but still had areas of hurt from being rejected by Marie.

The family prayed together, concerning the decision, and each came up with the same conclusion, "This is God ordained." So within hours, Lydia had gone and picked up her daughter. Just like Deborah, Marie had ended up addicted to crack. Now, because of her drug use, she no longer had a car or a driver's license for that matter. They had agreed to meet in a Donut Delight parking lot. It had been over eighteen months since Lydia had seen her daughter.

Now as she sat in her tub, tears still slipped from her eyes as she thought about Marie's condition that day. Her beautiful daughter, broken and aged beyond her years, had slept in a homeless shelter for the last couple of nights. Without even a comb or a change of clothes, Marie looked dirty and unkept, but even worse than that her eyes showed a look of total defeat. Lydia was jolted by the stark reality; her own daughter could be one of the street people she drove by every day, living off the streets of Palm City. That day was the first day of Marie's long journey back home, and back to the Lord. She had also been a prodigal daughter like so many Lydia had ministered to over the past years.

The personal heartbreak Lydia had experienced with Marie gave her the understanding and the compassion which made her so effective in the counseling ministry. She had comforted and encouraged many mothers just like herself-mothers who felt like they had failed, mothers who were frustrated, defeated and in despair.

Now, Lydia actually found herself on numerous occasions thanking God for all they had been through as a family. Out of the pain, out of the ashes, God had called their family to be a demonstration of redemption and restoration. Their testimony always ministered faith and hope to others.

She was climbing out of the tub as she heard her husband pull into the driveway. She had been lost in the past and stayed in the tub too long. She quickly hurried to get dressed, and put on a pair of comfortable capris and a T-shirt.

Stephen was putting away his briefcase in their home office. As she came out of the bedroom, the couple embraced and lingered in each other's arms, both of them looking forward to a night off together. Stephen went into the bedroom and took a quick shower while she went to get dinner ready. As she set the table, thoughts of Marie's homecoming were still running through her mind.

One of the most amazing things that happened after Marie came home was the special relationship she developed with Stephen. As her relationship with the Lord was healed, so was her ability to receive a father's love from her step-father. Today, they were extremely close. She realized that she was smiling as she dished up the beef stroganoff Stephen loved so much. Sometimes the goodness of God was so overwhelming she couldn't help but smile.

Stephen kissed her lightly on the cheek as he entered the dining room. They sat down together and bowed their heads to say grace. Over dinner, they downloaded the details of their day to one other. She was so grateful that God had given her a husband who not only believed in what she did, but supported her whole heartedly. What a difference it made in her life!

They finished dinner, cleaned up the dishes and then went for a walk, conversing casually, as they strolled down the street.

The evening air was soft and balmy. Eventually, their conversation turned to the young woman Lydia was counseling this week. Without sharing details, Lydia let Stephen know how much the young woman reminded her of their daughter, Marie. Soon their conversation turned to prayer as they interceded together for Deborah and the ministry still to come. Lydia shared how she and Joyce both felt there was more to the woman's story than what she told them so far. Stephen and Lydia prayed and bound all demonic fear and shame over Deborah, and then asked the Lord to allow the desire for total freedom to overtake her. Lydia knew that it would take a intense desire to help Deborah press through and eventually tell them everything.

That evening, after journaling and completing her homework, Deborah relaxed on the bed. Listening to the peaceful instrumental CD playing and enjoying the sweet presence of God, she suddenly began to feel an uncomfortable struggle inside of her. A still, small voice from within said, "You have to tell, it will open the prison door."

She knew that it wasn't her thought. It had to be the Holy Spirit speaking to her. Could God really be expecting her to tell someone else, to say those things out loud? Fear began to rise up within her. Almost instantly, the women she had begun to grow so close to over the past two days, became strangers again. She didn't really know them. They would never understand. She found herself begging God, "Please God, don't make me tell! Please God!" She waited and didn't hear anything else. Maybe she had just imagined it; maybe it was just her fear talking. She picked up a book and began to read. She tried to put it out of her mind, as she read herself to sleep.

The next morning there was still a nagging feeling deep down inside. "You have to tell," her heart whispered. Well, if that was the voice of God, He was going to have to confirm it and make it very clear that it was time to share everything. Deborah got ready to walk next door, wondering what today's session would bring.

Chapter Fourteen

The Third Day

৵ ৵

Upon arriving at *His House* the next morning, Lydia shared with Joyce about the lovely evening she and Stephen had enjoyed together. She was refreshed and ready to get started with the day. Joyce was glad that her partner was full of life and energy this morning. Her evening had not been quite the same. She wasn't sure if it was just spiritual warfare or what, but last night she had battled some real oppression. It was nothing she could put her finger on, but even during the night she had experienced troubling dreams. One of them was a recurring dream that she had dreamt many times since Bill had left. In it, she would watch helplessly, as her ex-husband fell off a cliff. She could not find her voice to scream and was too paralyzed to move. She would watch him fall and fall but would always wake up before he hit bottom. No matter how many times she had the dream, she would wake up feeling shaken and helpless. All she said to Lydia was, "I had that dream again," as they walked into the counseling room together.

They had already talked over the interpretation of the dream when Joyce was going through her own counseling. Today, Lydia was glad that Joyce was mature enough to press into God and leave her own personal problems in the Lord's hands. She knew that the dream always managed to get to Joyce.

Lydia felt that through the dream the Lord was speaking to Joyce to pray and intercede for her ex-husband. It was still very difficult for Joyce to have compassion on Bill. He had hurt her so badly, but she was diligently working on forgiveness. Joyce so wanted to put the whole mess in the past and get her ex-husband totally out of her mind. Now, here she was dreaming about him and then having to pray for him.

It was one issue she and Lydia disagreed on. Joyce thought the dream was the Enemy tormenting her with a sense of helplessness, while Lydia felt it was a call to prayer. Joyce finally agreed with Lydia that certainly it could never hurt to pray for someone. She had begun to pray and ask the Lord to intervene in Bill's fall before his life was totally destroyed. Most of the time, Joyce was well aware that her prayers were half-hearted; but, it was the best she could do at this point in time.

The women had also agreed to take authority over any night torment the Enemy might be using against Joyce, in case the dream was demonic activity. Sometimes, when emotional issues of the soul were involved, it was hard to get discernment. Joyce had a nagging feeling that Lydia's evaluation was probably correct, but it was still hard for her to imagine that the Lord would require her to pray for a man who had deceived and then abandoned her.

Now, however, it was time to put all that aside and to concentrate on Deborah and her freedom. They left their own lives in the Lord's hands as they prepared for the morning's session.

That same morning, Anne called Daniel's office. She was clearly upset. "Daniel, have you called for a meeting with Pastor Harrison?" Daniel was concerned when he heard his sister on the phone. Anne was normally very calm and pleasant, but today there was am obvious tone of anger in her voice.

"Yes, Sis, I had Irene call yesterday. I have an

appointment Friday morning at ten o'clock." He heard his sister breathe a sigh of relief and then she said, "I'm so glad to hear that because we have to do something about this situation with Andrea. Her infatuation with you is bordering on witchcraft."

Daniel immediately knew something must have happened at the women's Bible study the previous night. "Tell me what happened last night," he inquired.

"It was simply awful. My spirit is so irritated with that woman," Anne responded.

Daniel knew she had to be talking about Andrea, "So what happened last night?" he persisted.

Anne began to explain her topic was *Hearing the Voice of God.* "I really hoped that I might be able to deal with the deception Andrea has fallen into concerning you. I knew there was a risk that she might take the opportunity to emphasize the fact that God told her you were supposed to be her husband, but I felt the truth outweighed the risks. Boy was I wrong! I'm so mad at myself for giving her any opportunity. I couldn't believe her audacity, Daniel. It's been one thing to hear the rumors from some of the women at church, but last night I finally heard it first hand."

Now it was Daniel's turn to be shocked as his sister continued to share. She told him that Andrea not only informed the group that the Lord had spoke to her in a dream and confirmed that Daniel was her husband, but that God had taken his wife from him because Andrea and Daniel were destined to be in ministry together. Anne shared how she had sat back in helpless silence as Andrea had shared the dream. In it, she and Daniel were in a boat together and they were pulling people out of the sea. Andrea had interpreted the dream to mean that that they were in a ministry together saving lost souls.

The thought that Andrea could possibly think that a loving God would take a man's wife and the mother of his two children so another woman could "fulfill a destiny" was beyond Anne's conception. She was infuriated at the mention of her sister-in-law, much less in that context. She had quickly moved on to the next woman in the group knowing that she was too angry to deal with Andrea on her own and in front of the other women.

An unavoidable wave of anger flooded over Daniel as she continued to recount the events of the previous evening. He could not believe Andrea's nerve to even suggest God had taken Susan from him in order to make room for her. Not only was she full of deception but now she was spreading it like a cancer. He was grateful his appointment with Pastor Harrison was already set in motion.

Anne interrupted his thoughts. "Daniel, I believe I am supposed to be at that meeting with you and Pastor. You know I don't like to interfere, but I believe he needs to hear this from me, first hand. It's obvious that he's going to have to get involved. You and I are just too close to this." Daniel immediately agreed. He needed Anne's discernment and wisdom on how to handle this with Andrea, as well as his Pastor's. With everything else on his plate these days, this was the last thing he needed right now. Daniel had heard single ministers joke before about the *wishions* they had to deal with from single women desperately looking for a husband, but this didn't feel very funny right now. He almost felt like he was being stalked by the woman.

When Anne hung up the phone she felt some relief after venting her anger to Daniel. It also helped to know a meeting was already set with Pastor Harrison. Her thoughts turned to Deborah. She certainly had sounded good yesterday afternoon when they had talked. Anne was thankful that Deborah had received her recommendation to go to Florida for ministry. Clearly, God was already working. It was only Wednesday morning so she wasn't even half way through the process yet.

Anne knew she needed to keep praying for Deborah to continue to be receptive to the Holy Spirit's work in her life through the rest of the ministry time. She would also pray that

Satan would not have any opportunity to thwart God's plans for Deborah. As she thought about Deborah, she felt a distinct prodding from the Lord that she was to fast for her on Thursday. Obviously, that was going to be an important day. Anne decided that she would only drink liquids. "Your ways, Lord, are so different from man's ways," she thought. But Anne had learned from experience how fasting could facilitate spiritual breakthrough and answered prayers. "So fasting it is," she said out loud as she added juice to the grocery list hanging on the refrigerator.

Anne also expressed gratitude to the Lord for giving her the self-control not to tear into Andrea in front of the other young women in the Bible study. All she had simply said was that it was always important to have the Word of the Lord confirmed and that God would never tell you something that didn't line up with His Word, His Character and His Nature. She hoped the other women were mature enough to know that God would not take a man's wife through premature death to make room for another woman. She had caught the looks of incredulousness on a couple of their faces as Andrea had shared. Several women looked to Anne immediately to evaluate her reaction. Some of them had even rolled their eyes in disbelief as Andrea shared the dream.

She was glad to be meeting with Pastor Harrison Friday because she knew it was going to have to be somehow addressed before or at the next Tuesday night Bible study. Now it was time to concentrate on other things, like her housework. She had gotten a little bit behind taking care of Aimee the last couple of days.

It was good that Aimee was well enough to be back in school even though Anne had enjoyed spending the time with her. Tears of grief welled up in her eyes as she began to think about those children losing their mother. Suddenly, she felt another wave of anger. She knew that she was going to have to forgive Andrea or the anger would consume her. "Lord, please give me the grace to forgive Andrea," she prayed to herself as she straightened the living room.

"My grace is sufficient for you," she heard the Holy Spirit speak softly. As the words touched her heart, she began to weep. She found herself saying, "Lord, I forgive Andrea for her obsession and deception concerning Daniel. Please open her eyes so she can receive truth." It wasn't easy but God's grace *was* sufficient; and immediately, a new peace washed over Anne. The Lord would have to deal with Andrea now. She was in His hands.

Meanwhile, Lydia and Joyce prayed over the upcoming session. They called it the "Transformation Session." As they finished, a simple prayer rose out of Deborah's heart and out of her mouth, "Lord I receive Your truth today." It startled her as she heard her own voice. Praying in front of people was something that Deborah was still not comfortable with and she was surprised that she had prayed out loud at all.

Today, Joyce was obviously in the lead as she shared some of the opening scriptures. She started with Romans 12:2: "Be ye transformed by the renewing of your mind." Next she read Ephesians 4:22: "Be made new in the spirit of your mind, putting on the new man." Then she shared 2 Corinthians 10:4: "The weapons of our warfare are not carnal but mighty for the pulling down of strongholds and every thing that would exalt itself against the knowledge of God bringing every thought into captivity." Finally, she talked about Exodus 23:32-33 where the Lord warned Israel not to make covenants with false gods or they would become a snare for them. Joyce explained that when there is agreement with the Enemy in our thoughts, it's like being in covenant with him. That agreement gives him legal spiritual access into our lives.

Lydia interjected, "This session is so important, Deborah, not just for what we will accomplish today, but to equip you for continued transformation and spiritual warfare. We've identified fourteen core ungodly beliefs that we're going to deal with this morning. However, we all have numerous ones to deal with. I'm still in the process of discovering areas where my heart thoughts do not agree with God's word."

Joyce went on to explain what Lydia meant by heart thoughts, "These are emotional thoughts which have been formed through our experiences. We might know what the Bible says about something in our natural minds, but do we believe it in our hearts? The Word of God says, 'As a man thinketh in his heart, so is he.' We need revelation from the Lord to help change our emotional thoughts created by our experiences."

Joyce walked to the whiteboard on the wall opposite of Deborah and began to write. "We all start off in life with EXPERIENCES," she noted as she wrote the word on the top of the board. Then she drew an arrow curving down and to the right as she wrote the word "BELIEFS." "Out of those experiences," she explained, "our belief systems are formed. We develop beliefs about ourselves, about life, about God, and about others from our experiences. If we have had ungodly experiences, we'll have ungodly beliefs. These are beliefs that do not line up with God's Word."

Lydia added, "Our experiences are facts. They really happened, but we cannot live according to facts. We have to live according to the truth of God's Word. It might be fact that someone was abused and rejected, but the truth is that God loves and accepts them and He wants to heal them from the abuse."

Joyce was writing another word, "EXPECTATION," on the bottom of the board with an arrow pointing from the word "BELIEFS." "Out of our beliefs, we develop expectations. If we have had the experience of rejection, we begin to expect that we are going to be rejected or misused. Our expectations will affect our behavior," she said as she drew another arrow upward and wrote "BEHAVIOR" on the left-hand side of the board. "Then it becomes a cycle," she stated as she drew the final arrow back to the first word, "EXPERIENCES." "We continue to have reinforcing experiences that cement the ungodly belief into place.

"The negative expectation acts like a demonic faith that continues to draw wrong behavior from yourself and others. Pretty soon we just *know* that the ungodly belief is true, because it's happened to us over and over again. And it will continue to happen until we break agreement with it.

"Our experiences help develop our beliefs which create expectations that affect our behavior and the behaviors of others," Lydia added, "it looks pretty simple spelled out on the board, but sometimes it's hard to see our own ungodly beliefs. That's why we help you get started. From then on, it's between you and the Holy Spirit to continue to renew your mind to the Word of God. Look at it like laser surgery. Today, we're going in and pinpointing very specific ungodly beliefs."

Joyce noticed that Deborah was looking a bit confused, quickly said, "We're going to use a prayer much like we did yesterday in the Redemption Session to help you get started. And we already have a list of ungodly beliefs to work on. The most important thing for you is to focus on what God is showing and speaking to you. First, we want to look at where and how the ungodly belief got planted and how you have lived it out in your own life. Then, we're going to renounce and break agreement with it and allow the Holy Spirit to speak truth to your heart so that you can establish a new Godly belief."

Lydia added, "It's important that the new Godly belief aligns with Scripture, but we also want it to be in your own words. We'll help you develop it. The main thing to get in touch with is this: if Jesus walked through the door today and said to you, 'Deborah, I don't want you to believe this anymore, this is what I want you to believe.' What would He say? That's your job, to hear the truth with your heart."

Joyce continued, "Afterward, your assignment will be to go over your list of new Godly beliefs a couple of times a day for at least 40 days. Some people do theirs for over a year. You can read them or say them into a tape recorder and play the tape. Some people learn more visually and others are more auditory learners. If you're a kinetic learner, we recommend doing something physical while saying or reading your list of Godly beliefs.

"You'll know when it's gotten into your heart. You'll start seeing different fruit in your life as your emotional and mental responses and reactions begin to line up with your new Godly beliefs," Lydia said. She quickly discerned that Deborah didn't understand what she meant by "fruit" and explained further. "I mean by changes in the fruit is that you'll see changes in relationships, your own attitudes, behaviors, reactions and responses. As your belief systems and expectations change, your behavior and even the behavior and reactions of others is guaranteed to change."

Deborah nodded and Lydia could tell she had it now.

"The Lord may add other ungodly beliefs to your list immediately," Joyce disclosed, "I have seven new ones I'm working on in my own life right now."

Lydia added, "We suggest 40 days minimum of meditating and confessing the new godly beliefs because it takes work to change a habit, and because of the spiritual significance of 40 days. In the Bible, one of the names for Satan is Beelzebub which means, lord of the flies. That means we can learn about his attributes by studying flies. The life cycle of a fly is 40 days long. All the major fasts in the Bible where the enemy was defeated were 40 days. So we believe a minimum of 40 days is necessary, but the longer the better, in order to defeat Satan and bring down the demonic stronghold.

"Well, are you ready to get started?" Joyce asked as she returned to her chair. "Let's look over the prayer and make sure you understand the process."

Deborah reached for the piece of paper Joyce was handing her. She felt like she understood what was expected, but she had a little apprehension about the list of ungodly beliefs Joyce had on her clipboard. Her stomach felt just a little queasy again. "Will this ever get easy?" she thought to herself. She scanned the prayer and then Joyce handed her another piece of paper covered by green construction paper. The only thing showing was her first ungodly belief. "We cover them so you can concentrate on one at a time. When we're finished with the first one, you can move the green paper down and expose the second one," Joyce shared.

"Well, here we go," Deborah thought as she looked down at the paper.

Chapter Fifteen

Revelation

ॐ ॐ

As Deborah studied the first ungodly belief, the neatly-typed black and white words virtually jumped off the page. The simple four-word sentence seemed to sum up her whole life: "You can't trust anyone." Anger and fear began to rise up inside. "But that's really true; I haven't been able to trust anyone," Deborah blurted out. "Are you going to tell me that I have to trust everyone? Because I just can't do that!"

Joyce calmly replied, as she had done countless other times with other people, "Deborah, we know that this feels true based on your life experiences. We're not denying the reality of what has happened to you. Let's just go through the prayer and see what Jesus wants to reveal to you."

Lydia was nodding her head in agreement and spoke up, "Deborah, with that belief in place, you'll have to live a guarded life with no real, true relationships. It leaves you totally on your own, and it even prevents you from trusting God." Deborah knew she was right, but didn't they understand that the ungodly belief had been her only protection? Now they were asking her to give it up.

As if reading her mind, Joyce said, "The Lord won't leave you defenseless and without protection, Deborah. Let's just try going through the prayer and see what happens." She took a deep breath and started.

"Lord, I forgive the people who helped me form the ungodly belief that I can't trust anyone." One by one, Deborah began to name the each individual and talk about what they had done to help form, and establish the belief that she couldn't trust anyone. What a list! From her own family, to teachers and kids at school, to the men in her life, the list went on and on. Tears began to flow down her cheeks and Lydia gently reached over and put the tissue box on the sofa next to Deborah.

Then Deborah moved to the next part of the prayer, "Lord, forgive me for how I have participated in this ungodly belief by isolating myself, by not ever asking anyone for help, by never sharing my real thoughts or feelings with anyone else and by not even trusting that You will answer my prayers." At that point, Deborah broke down sobbing. The loneliness that this ungodly belief had created began to surface. She knew where it really came from. Yes, many things had affected it. But it was the one particular event she couldn't bring herself to talk about, that had really cemented the ungodly belief in her heart. She remembered the feeling of just wanting to tell someone, anyone, but there was no one she could trust with that kind of information. Even now, as badly as she wanted to, she still couldn't bring herself to tell Lydia and Joyce. Deborah sobbed louder and buried her face in the tissue, reaching for more with the other hand. Lydia and Joyce looked at each other, "If every ungodly belief brought this kind of emotion, they were in for a long morning."

Deborah finally composed herself and read number three on the prayer, "I forgive myself for believing this ungodly belief." She looked up at Joyce and said, "But what if I don't really feel it inside?"

Joyce replied, "This is not about feelings, it's about faith and confession. As the new Godly beliefs are fully established, your feelings will follow. Forgive yourself by faith and soon you will feel it in your heart."

Her answer satisfied Deborah and she went on to number four, "I renounce and break agreement with the ungodly belief, 'I can't trust anybody.'" It felt a bit strange-like she was giving up an old friend. Even though the "friend" of mistrust hadn't really protected her, it was at least familiar. But she had to admit, there was a genuine sense of relief as she came to the end of the prayer. "Now I choose to believe and receive my new Godly belief..." Deborah drew a blank. She had no idea what to say next. She looked helplessly at Lydia and Joyce.

Joyce smiled encouragingly and said, "Just take a moment and ask the Lord what He wants you to believe." Deborah prayed and immediately words filled her mouth, "I can trust the Lord to give me discernment and wisdom on who I can trust and to what degree. He will never fail me."

Lydia was writing fast and furiously to keep up with the words as they tumbled out of Deborah's mouth. "That's great." she said. "We won't have to add a thing to that one."

What a relief! Deborah had done it! She had heard from God. Now the scripture, "The truth will set you free," suddenly made sense to her. She felt even more freedom as she repeated the new Godly belief. The ungodly belief had been like a heavy yoke she had carried all her life. She said her new Godly belief softly to herself again and smiled. That did feel better! She was ready to tackle the next one.

She slowly slid the green paper down the page and uncovered the second ungodly belief, 'Life would have been better if I had been a boy.' "Wasn't that the truth!" she thought as she silently read it. This was going to be another tough one. It was like Lydia and Joyce had gotten inside her head and heart, she sure hadn't remembered telling them this.

Even though Deborah had seen her older brother bear the brunt of physical abuse from her father, he still had freedom in more ways than she ever had. Because of Deborah's strong personality and adventurous spirit, she always felt she would have been better off as a boy. Then, as she got older and was involved with Justin and Tommie Lee and all the other men, it confirmed to her that men were in control and women got shortchanged. She knew it was one of the things that she still fought concerning the Word of God. "How could He set up a world where women had to submit to men in marriage? It just didn't seem fair!" As she worked through the prayer, she realized that this ungodly belief not only caused her to reject her own womanhood, but it caused her to reject her mother and sister as well. In fact, she had a low opinion of all women in general. "It's a miracle that I respect Anne like I do," she thought to herself.

The steps of the ungodly belief prayer were so simple. Yet, as the Holy Spirit brought truth and revelation, she began to see things from a completely different perspective. By the time she got down to the end of the prayer, she was more than ready to hear what the Lord wanted to speak to her. This time it came without hesitation, "I choose to believe God ordained my womanhood from the foundations of the earth and created me for adventure with Him. And He's given me the strength of a warrior. The Lord loves me and will bring a husband into my life who will be a Godly man, and I will find delight in submitting my life to him." Deborah could hardly believe her ears as the words rolled out of her mouth. It was almost like she was prophesying over her own life. Through her own words, God was revealing her future. The words had to be from the Lord because the last thing she had on her mind was a husband. She had decided that living her own life was hard enough. The thought of having a husband and family was out of the question. Surprised, she looked at Lydia and Joyce and said, "Do you think that was God?" They both nodded simultaneously.

Lydia asked her to repeat the Godly belief again making sure she wrote down every word. "You're a natural at this. Deborah, you have a very keen ability to hear God's voice." Lydia said as she continued writing.

Joyce added, "A lot of times, the Lord has to use us to

help other people prime their prophetic pump, but for you it's just a natural flow."

As she looked at the next ungodly belief, Deborah saw how it had to be confronted and changed or she would never be able to believe what the Lord had just showed her. "I am dirty and defiled, and no good man will ever want me." The words felt like a sharp slap of reality across her face as they leapt off the page. It was true, she thought, no "good" man would ever want me.

Lydia immediately began to bind the spirits of Shame and Condemnation as she saw the look of oppression across Deborah's face. Once again, Deborah knew that she would have to hold back a portion of the truth from her counselors, even though in her mind and heart, she was confessing it privately to the Lord. Lydia could see her struggle and silently prayed that the hidden thing would be exposed.

Nothing really new surfaced as Deborah went through the steps of the prayer. She listed and forgave the men who had defiled her with a matter-of-fact attitude. But when it came to the second step of how she had participated in it, her struggle began. It was hard to confess how she had defiled herself by dressing provocatively, prostituting herself, dancing in clubs, and staying in the relationship with Tommie Lee. It took all she had to forgive herself for how she had participated in this one.

Finally she was at the last step, "Lord I choose to believe I have been cleansed by Your blood so I can walk through life with dignity and self-respect. You are giving me the faith to believe for a Godly husband who will love and cherish me."

Deborah continued to be amazed at the things that were coming out of her mouth. She had to admit that her heart felt good when she said her new Godly beliefs, but there was still a battle going on in her mind. It was as if a sneering, sinister voice was in her mind, saying, "Yeah right, do you think it's that easy? All those years of sin and now everything is going to be okay. I don't think so." She finally shared with her counselors the battle being waged in her mind. They didn't seem alarmed at all. Lydia simply stated, "We'll deal with the Enemy on Friday when we minister deliverance. Right now, he's not happy because his strongholds are being torn down. He is being exposed and defeated, and you are being transformed."

Joyce said, "We all have to war for our freedom. We have to fight to believe the truth because of the lies the Enemy creates through sin. It's God's truth that will set you free from the enemy's plan for your life, a plan of destruction, defeat and unfulfilled destiny."

They continued through the list of ungodly beliefs, each one piercing Deborah's heart as she saw them in black and white:

All men want to do is use you for sex and then discard you. I will always need some form of escape; life is just too painful on its own. I am all alone, there's no one to take care of me. I have wasted the best years of my life. Church is a dangerous place, full of hypocrites.
Women are weak, pathetic creatures who no one respects. If I'm not in control, bad things will happen to me. I will always have to be ashamed of my past.

The list seemed to go on and on.

Deborah went through the prayer and said each of her new Godly beliefs out loud. As she did, she continued to feel better and better. A couple of them required help from Joyce and Lydia, but for most of them the words just flowed naturally. Lydia had shared the scripture from Isaiah 61:7: "For our shame the Lord has come to bring us double honor" when they had come to the ungodly belief about the shame of her past. Deborah had never heard of that scripture before, but she felt a renewed sense of peace and hope when she confessed her new Godly belief, "My life has been redeemed. I've been forgiven, and I receive double honor from the Lord and others as I boldly share my testimony."

In the past, the thought of telling anyone about the things that had happened to her or the things that she had done would have turned her stomach. Now, she had to admit, there was a certain excitement stirring on the inside of her. "Maybe I can actually help someone else because of the things that have happened to me." The thought brought a smile to her face.

Upon completing the list of ungodly beliefs, the women decided that a ten minute stretch break was in order. Deborah stood up from the couch and was overcome with a desire to hug the two women standing opposite of her. She felt awkward as she took a step forward. Before she knew what had happened, Lydia and Joyce had seized the moment and took turns hugging her and telling her what a good job she had done. She was beginning to realize that she felt like a very dry, shriveled sponge inside. She had let Anne in so far; but even though she appreciated their relationship, she still was very guarded. Anne had respected her walls and had been quite careful not to push past her physical and emotional boundaries. For some reason, in this room, the walls weren't there and it felt good to be hugged and touched in such a pure way.

Deborah also found herself receiving the words of praise and encouragement. In the past, words of that nature just bounced off and fell flatly to the floor. In moments of praise she would just tell herself, "If they really knew me or knew what I had done, they wouldn't be saying that." Not only did Lydia and Joyce know, but they probably knew more about her than anyone. And they were still saying good things! Somehow it made it easier to receive. She didn't feel like such a fake and it felt good inside. She thought, "No, those two definitely aren't people pleasers." They had also said some hard things to her as well, but they had been honest, direct and firm, yet understanding at the same time. The combination was irresistible to Deborah and she found herself believing them, whether it was something corrective or positive.

———————————————

Deborah walked next door to get an energy bar while Lydia and Joyce went into the kitchen in search of some fruit to hold them until lunch. They were both excited at how well the first part of the session had gone. Deborah had participated wholeheartedly. They compared notes on the participant from the week before.

Lydia said, "I am so glad we haven't had to battle a religious spirit in Deborah. Last week was tough."

Joyce replied, "This is so refreshing. It's so much easier when they haven't been programmed to believe they're perfect before they've really been perfected." They were talking about Shelly, a young woman they had ministered to that prior week. She had been deeply steeped in a religious church and knew all the right words to say and what to believe in her head, yet it really hadn't penetrated her heart. The fruit of her life was evidence of that. It had taken a lot of work trying to get across to her that her heart was still holding ungodly beliefs. Each ungodly belief had felt like a full twelve-round fight.

Shelly had experienced a lot of trauma early in her life but had never really dealt with it; she was overly sensitive. Fear governed a large portion of her life but she couldn't see how much it was still affecting her. Shelly would continually respond to each ungodly belief presented to her with, "Well, that's not what the Word says so that's not what I believe." She then would follow up that statement with a scripture, which she quoted like a parrot.

When Lydia or Joyce would point out behaviors or attitudes reflecting the ungodly belief, a defensive battle would ensue. It had been a lot of work, and they really weren't sure how much had been accomplished in Shelly's life. She had come primarily because she had wanted more training herself, but the possibility of her being involved in this type of ministry made Lydia and Joyce shudder. They both understood why Jesus always had the hardest time with the religious order of his day. It was hard to find compassion for someone who was always right, always knew better and had everything completely figured out.

How refreshing it was to work with Deborah. She knew she needed help and even though she was guarded at times, it was more out of fear, rather than spiritual pride. This was a lot more fun, they both agreed, as they went back into the ministry room.

Chapter Sixteen

A True Identity

ও্ঠ ওঠ

As Deborah walked across the room and positioned herself comfortably on the couch, Lydia went over to the white board and picked up a marker. "Now, let's talk about the big ungodly belief that you believe about yourself. We want to identify and look at the false identity the enemy tried to create for you." She then drew a black line down the middle of the board. "On this side, we're going to write down everything the enemy has tried to make you believe about yourself. These words may have come from what others have said, from generational sin and from your own sin. We're going to expose the perversion plan of the enemy for your life."

Joyce interjected, "Satan always wanted to be like God, but he could never be our creator because he has no creative powers. All he can do is pervert what God originally intended."

Lydia said, "On this side of the board we are going to put down the words that help create the false identity and then, when we get through, we're going to put down the truth about who you are in Christ on the other side."

Joyce piped up and said, "The first side will probably sting a little, but the other side of the board will be exciting so we don't want to leave anything out."

On the top of the board Lydia wrote "False Identity" on

the left side of the black line and "True Identity" on the right. As she did, Deborah felt herself taking a deep breath and releasing it. It was as if she preparing to face something that she had avoided looking at for years. Lydia added, "We'll help you work through this just like everything else we've done. What is most important is that we want you to allow the Holy Spirit to help you, so listen for His Voice."

The first word that came out of Deborah's mouth, before she knew it, was "broken".

"Good!" Joyce immediately said, as Lydia wrote the word on the board. Tears fill Deborah's eyes after she said the word and she had to gulp back the emotion she felt rising up inside.

Joyce immediately picked up on the reaction and said, "Deborah, please don't hold back any of your pain, its okay to cry."

Tears rolled down her face as the next word came out of her mouth, "bad." It was a simple three-letter-word but Deborah realized that she had felt like a "bad girl" most of her life. The list went on as Lydia and Joyce helped: unloved, afraid, unworthy, ashamed, used, abandoned, different, hard, mistrusting, insecure, cold, proud, afraid, angry, perverted, ugly, dumb, rebellious, addicted, self-mutilating. The list continued until it covered the whole side of the board. While it was true, that the words were hard to look at, the greater truth was that it felt like a splinter was being dug out of her soul. Those words and what they represented had penetrated deep inside her, and they now had to be taken out in order for her to heal.

Finally, Lydia seemed satisfied that they had every word they needed under the "False Identity" side. "Time to move to the other side of the board," she said. Under "True Identity," Deborah began to share the words that aligned with God's Word and who He said she was. Lydia quickly wrote them on the board. Instead of "broken," Deborah was "mended." God had never called her to be a "bad" girl; He had purposed her to be

"Godly."

At times Deborah could hear the Holy Spirit whispering in her mind, "You're loved; you're courageous. You are not used; you are cherished. You're not addicted; you're free. You're not proud and rebellious; you are humble and submissive." Joy and peace began to bubble up inside her as her true identity in God unfolded on the other side of the board. This was a person even she could love. This was a person God could use. "Can I really live up to my True Identity?" she wondered. Once again hope began to fill her heart.

Joyce watched Deborah's countenance change moment to moment. She was actually sitting up straighter and her head wasn't hanging down. The transformation process was already beginning. Joyce just loved this part of the ministry!

Now the board was completely filled on both sides. What a difference from one side to the other. Lydia laughed and said, "Don't feel badly, everyone has a false identity that was formed before they came to Christ. Each person's false identity may be different, but it's just as crippling." She tapped on the side of the board containing the false identity and said, "Believing this about yourself will make you want to stay in bed and pull the covers over your head."

Deborah laughed with her, knowing that most days that was exactly the way she felt.

Next, Lydia explained, "What we'll do is take each of these words and weave it into a paragraph. Your job will be to meditate and confess it several times a day along with your new Godly beliefs. But first, you're going to erase and renounce your false identity, as Joyce and I pray for you."

Joyce said, "Remember, words are powerful. God created the universe with the spoken word. We're going to pray in the Spirit, as you renounce and break agreement with these words."

Lydia added "And as you do, you'll erase the word."

Deborah felt a little shaky as she stood up from the

couch. "Good bye, Debbie Lynn Webster. Hello, Deborah Noble", she said to herself as she walked across the room to the white board and reach for the eraser Lydia was holding out to her. She repeated after Lydia, "I renounce and break agreement with the false identity of broken, bad, afraid, ashamed...." As she said each word, Deborah firmly wiped the word from the board-it felt so good. "Before, the words had power over me. Now, I have power over them," she thought. Deborah felt as if she was passing through the Red Sea and the Enemy's armies were being wiped away. "There is no more turning back, no more going back to Egypt. The only way now is forward into a land where I've never lived before."

As she got to the last word and then wiped the whole side of the board clean, Deborah saw a picture of herself in her mind. An old dirty robe was being taken off of her and a new robe was being placed on her. It was white, yet shining. Brilliant was the best word to describe it. And even though it covered her, it was translucent. The only word to describe it was "heavenly."

Deborah stopped and shared the picture with Lydia and Joyce. Joyce quickly picked up her Bible and read out of Isaiah chapter 61:10: "I will greatly rejoice in the Lord, My soul shall be joyful in my God; for He has clothed me with the garments of salvation, He has covered me with the robe of righteousness." Deborah felt a shiver go up and down her spine. It was a good shiver, and she realized it was the Holy Spirit bearing witness to the truth.

Lydia took the eraser from her. "Now, let's receive, accept and choose to believe the True Identity."

Deborah began, "I receive, accept and believe my true identity, that I am mended. I am Godly. I am loved. I am courageous. I am worthy and I have double honor, I am cherished. I am a part of the family of God. I am special, healed, trusting, secure...." Her voice got stronger as she went down the list. The last word was "victorious" for the false identity "defeated." As Deborah declared, "I am victorious," her hand went up in the air as if a referee had lifted it to declare the winner after a long and hard fight. Lydia and Joyce began to clap and praise God. There was an atmosphere of joyful celebration in the room. Deborah turned to both Joyce and Lydia and mouthed the words "thank you," as tears once again filled her eyes. The difference in Deborah's tears was apparent-these were tears of joy not tears of pain.

Lydia motioned to a chair and said, "Now, let's pray."

Deborah sat down and Lydia and Joyce laid hands on her and began to pray. This time Joyce led, "We curse all the fruit in her life from the ungodly beliefs and the false identity. I pray that every habit and pattern of living and thinking will be changed to align with her new Godly beliefs. I take authority over the strongholds and every demon assigned to them. You have no right to Deborah's mind any more. I bind all demonic activity and communication."

Then Lydia prayed, "Lord let her new Godly beliefs and true identity take root, grow and prosper in her life. I command your heart, mind, will and body to line up with the truth of your Godly beliefs and true identity, in the Name of Jesus. Give her the faith and discipline to establish the mind of Christ within her. We bless you!"

Before they left the room, Lydia reiterated how important it was for Deborah to read or listen to her Godly Beliefs and True Identity several times a day. They both hugged her and told her what a great job she had done that day. As she left the room, Joyce turned to Lydia, "I'll take care of typing out the Godly Beliefs if you'll do her True Identity?"

Lydia replied, "Sure, I'd love to, but before we go, let's spend a little time praying. Tomorrow is going to be very important. I still sense there's something that she hasn't told us and she needs to in order for her to receive everything God has for her. I might be wrong, but normally when I have this feeling there's something that hasn't come out yet. I know that Deborah has shared a lot with us, but I keep sensing there's something more."

Joyce knew from past experience that it was best to trust Lydia's experience and discernment and so they knelt down in front of the couch that Deborah had been occupying for the last few days.

"Lord, please help Deborah to come clean with us. Give her the supernatural ability to trust us. Please speak to her and encourage her not to withhold anything," Lydia prayed.

"I bind every spirit of fear and shame that would try to hold that memory in darkness and secrecy," Joyce found herself praying. It took barely five minutes to genuinely intercede for Deborah, but when they arose from their knees, they both felt a peace and an assurance that the time was well spent.

As the two women gathered their paperwork and rinsed a couple of dishes, Lydia chatted about what a nice evening she and Stephen had had together the night before. The conversation caused a little ache to rise up in Joyce's heart; she missed some of the simple things of married life. A picture of Bill came to her mind, "No, not again," she thought as she struggled to dismiss the thought. Bill had caused her far too much pain-how she wished God would simply erase him, and everything about him, from her memory bank. Lydia caught the distant look in Joyce's eyes. "I'm sorry," she said instinctively knowing that her conversation had caused memories of Joyce's own marriage to surface. She reached out to hug Joyce.

Joyce stated, "It's not your fault, the dream last night didn't help either. I've broken soul ties. I wish I understood why I keep dreaming. He just won't go away!"

Lydia responded, "Remember, we committed to pray for Bill every time you have the dream. If it's the Lord we can't go wrong. If it's the Enemy, he'll have to stop if we keep praying." Lydia launched into a prayer of conviction, repentance, and the return of Bill's life, to God. As much as she loved her friend and fellow worker and knew how much this man had hurt her, she could still feel God's heart for Bill. She knew his sexual sin and cover-up was something the Lord desired to forgive and heal, and she could feel the Lord's desire to reach Bill.

The best Joyce could muster was a soft, "Amen" as Lydia completed the prayer. They hugged again, said their good-byes, closed up the house and walked to their cars.

As Joyce headed home, her thoughts were not on this morning's session. She found herself returning to last night's dream. She certainly trusted Lydia's discernment and judgment, but sometimes Joyce found it more than a little irritating that her friend always had such a heart to pray for Bill. In her better moments, she knew it wasn't true, but sometimes it seemed like Lydia had more compassion for Bill than she did for her. "After all," she thought to herself, "he was the one that sinned; he was the one that left me."

Feelings of bitterness began to rise up from her heart towards Bill, the "other woman," and for that matter, all the other women who allowed their bodies to be exposed and used in pornography. Joyce knew that she was treading on dangerous ground. God had been gently and lovingly healing her, layer by layer. She had made a decision to walk in forgiveness even when sometimes her feelings or her thoughts didn't line up with that choice. Letting her thoughts go in this direction could be dangerous. Lydia was always reinforcing how God would give Joyce the grace to forgive as long as she continued to set her will toward forgiveness. Some days were harder than others. Today was one of those days.

Joyce made a concerted effort to focus on her Godly Belief that had come from her own *Restore Your Soul* ministry time: "As I choose to forgive others, God's grace is sufficient for me and will set me free." Joyce repeated it to herself several times. As she did, she found herself taking several deep breaths.

First, breathing in and then letting the breath out, slowly and deliberately. As she began to relax, her focus turned to another of her Godly Beliefs. "I am a woman healed of the past and focused on the future."

Rather than turning right to head to her apartment, Joyce turned her car left towards the church. She had felt a quiet nudging by the Holy Spirit-maybe there was something useful she could do there. There would be ample time later to complete her paperwork for tomorrow's session.

The church had been such an oasis of healing and restoration for Joyce. She always felt so rewarded to be able to give something in return. She never felt that anything was expected or that there was a spirit of obligation; it just felt like the right thing to do. Today, she simply wanted to obey the prompting from the Holy Spirit.

There was always something happening at Grace Fellowship. The church was so different from her former church, Christian Community. Even though Christian Community was beginning to have more impact in the community right before Bill had been exposed, it still was a far cry from the transparency and depth of intimacy she found at Grace Fellowship. As she drove toward the church, she silently thanked the Lord for her new church and the Body of Christ. Many of those who came to Grace Fellowship were people who had come out of broken situations. Some, like herself, already knew the Lord; and others had found God through Grace Fellowship. "It sure was named right," she thought. She had found more of God's grace and mercy there than anywhere else she had ever been.

She pulled into the church parking lot of Grace Fellowship. It had been expanded to extend into the lot of the recently-purchased shopping center that had been vacated not long ago. The city had grown westward and many businesses had moved in that direction. The old shopping center was only a couple miles from the previous church location. The entire congregation was excited about the expansion. The ministry had grown so significantly that the last building could no longer serve the needs of the growing congregation. Joyce was glad that she had been a part of their move to this location. It helped her to feel even more a part of the fellowship. The congregation had a two-fold vision: to take over the whole shopping center and actually use it as a church, and to become a place to help birth Christian businesses.

The church secretary, Katie Jo, greeted Joyce as she walked in the door. Katie Jo always seemed to have a great attitude despite the chaos and crisis that seemed to be part and parcel in ministering to hurt and broken people. A person could always count on her for a smile and a hug when needed. Katie Jo, who had been at the church for years, always seemed to have a timely answer for everyone, regardless of the subject.

"So what needs to be done around here?" Joyce asked. "I've got a couple of extra hours and felt like the Lord said I needed to stop by."

"Praise God!" Katie Jo quickly exclaimed. "I had a volunteer lined up to help get this mail ready to go out and she called in sick. I was just praying for some extra help. Here grab those brochures and start putting on these mailing labels. I just love it when people listen to the Lord!"

Joyce quickly got into a rhythm of applying labels to the brochures and stacking them in the mailing bins. A quiet contentment settled over her. She began to hum as the repetitive activity soothed and relaxed her. The church always felt like an ark of safety to her. The continual prayer and worship in the building created an atmosphere where the presence of God always seemed so tangible and strong. She once again silently thanked the Lord for leading her to Grace Fellowship. "If only Bill could have experienced the unconditional love I've felt here, maybe he could have received healing for his sexual addiction.

"Now where did that come from?" Joyce thought to herself. Rather than fight the thoughts of Bill, she lifted up a simple prayer. "Lord, please lead him to a safe haven, a place where he can find healing, a place where people will love him unconditionally, and a place where he can really be open and honest. Help him find a place like Grace Fellowship. Well, Lydia will be pleased. I actually prayed a heartfelt prayer for Bill. Perhaps it's because of the strong anointing in this place today!" she thought. Once she prayed, Joyce had to admit to herself that she felt better. The combination of feeling useful and being obedient to the Lord had averted the depression she knew she would have faced had she gone directly home. Thankfully, now she would actually be able to go home and enjoy the evening.

Eating out alone had been very difficult for her after Bill had left home. Since moving to Florida, however, Joyce had been forcing herself to occasionally visit different local restaurants alone. Today, the thought of an early bird special at one of the places on the beach sounded good-inviting actually. She felt prepared to enjoy her own company for a change. She was coming to realize that, as painful as her divorce from Bill had been, God was getting a lot of mileage out of it. She certainly was feeling more confident than she had had in years and her intimacy with the Lord was greater than she ever dreamed it could be. "Maybe God does work out all things to the good," she thought to herself as she finished the last of the brochures.

Chapter Seventeen

Back Home

ॐ ॐ

The Florida sun was warm and inviting as Deborah walked along the beach. She was glad Lydia and Joyce had convinced her to get out of the house and get some fresh air. She reflected back on the morning's session. What had they called it? That's right, her "brain transplant day." Tomorrow would be "open heart surgery." It was the day she was dreading the most. If it turned out to be anything like the last three days, she knew that it most likely would be difficult, but worth it. Deborah was really beginning to develop a trust in Lydia and Joyce. It was obvious that the Lord had sent them to help her deal with what seemed like a lifetime of pain and all the old baggage that comes with it. Her thoughts turned to the events that had led her to Florida.

When she had first arrived back in Deerfield, Deborah had felt so out of place. She was so angry that after all those years she hadn't really made her escape; she was back in Deerfield. Somehow the town always held her captive in ways she simply could not articulate. She had been forced to come home because she was totally out of money and her health was in such poor condition. Her probation officer was the one who had finally convinced her that she wouldn't make it on her own. It was either go back to Deerfield and face the demons of her past or be court-ordered to a year's residential drug treatment program. Because she didn't have the money for a good facility, Deborah opted for the only alternative-to return home. "Home." That was a word she hadn't used in awhile and really didn't describe how she felt about Deerfield.

Deep within, Deborah had intuitively understood that her probation officer was actually giving her a break. Officer Brenda Stanley had personally called her mother and explained the situation and asked if the family could take her in and support her for at least a year as she recovered her health, stayed clean, and got back on her feet. The answer was "yes," subject to a few conditions. Her initial reaction was anger at the conditions placed on her return, but Deborah's emotions quickly turned to resignation because she knew there was no other choice. She was going to be forced to face her family, her past, and the provincial town she had grown up in for the first seventeen-and-a-half years of her life.

As it turned out, Officer Brenda was a Christian. "Why am I always running into these people who want to pray with me and get me to go to God with my problems? God, they make me sick. I can't stand their pat answers and hypocritical lives! Where was God when I needed him? Why hadn't God stopped the abuse? My father acted like he knew Him better than anyone, and it sure hadn't changed him. No thanks! I'll kick this drug problem myself. There hasn't been a higher power that has helped me yet. No reason to think He will now."

Walking and still thinking about the past, Deborah watched the gentle waves dance in the sunlight. The blue-green water met the horizon in front of her; it had a wonderful calming effect. Her return to Deerfield looked quite different to her now then it had at the time. She had felt defeated that day; a failure, who had been unable to conquer her own world. Today, she saw the hand of the Lord guiding her life. He had allowed her to become broken and humble in order that He might heal and restore her. She finally found a place that was a bit more private, away from the other beach goers, and spread out her towel.

Still lost in her own thoughts, Deborah covered herself with sunscreen. Her counselors had warned her that the Florida sun could be deceiving. Even though it was comfortably warm and not hot this time of year, her Northern skin was not used to the strong rays of the sun. Lydia and Joyce had learned from past experiences with others, and now they always warned everyone to use sunscreen. A bad sunburn could be a distraction from what God wanted to accomplish. She was grateful for the advice and applied the sunscreen liberally, and then stretched out on her beach towel. Slowly, the healing warmth of the sun began to draw the tension from her muscles. As the sunlight warmed and relaxed her body, she soon found herself dozing off.

Two children playing on the beach woke Deborah. At first she was disorientated but then she realized where she was. Soon, the thoughts of Deerfield and the return to her childhood hometown began to drift through her mind again. Deborah could still visualize her mother the first day she was back: she was distant, virtually silent, and still very much the martyr, as she showed Deborah to her room for the next year. She now lived in a two bedroom townhouse in a newer section of Deerfield.

After her husband's death, Deborah's mother had quickly settled her husband's affairs and put the Noble family home up for sale. It had sold quickly and shocked the rest of the family-no one believed that Elizabeth would ever part with the place. She had always seemed so attached to it, not only to the old house itself, but to all of the items within it. It encompassed many years of Noble family life. But she sold it all, right down to some baby clothes salvaged from the attic. It had all been sold: old Christmas decorations, toys discarded long ago, boxes of her husband's books, and most of the furniture which had become worn and a little threadbare over the years. Yes, she had sold it all, with the exception of a few family heirlooms.

Deborah had never seen her mother's new home until her arrival that first day. It was comfortable and admittedly, warm and inviting. The room she would occupy was simple, almost bare. It was as if her mother had run out of steam before she had completed the guest room, but it suited Deborah just fine. The sparseness of it would give her an opportunity to make it her own. Her mother made apologies for the condition of the bedroom and Deborah remembered the familiar pattern of her mother's empty chatter whenever she was uncomfortable. It was always a source of such irritation to her father, "Elizabeth, I can't stand that noise anymore," as if her mother was simply a noisy kitchen appliance that could be turned on or off with the flip of a switch. It always worked. Her mother would become silent until, once again, her nervous energy would spill out like a river that over flooded its banks in the spring time. Throughout the years, the times of silence had increased and lengthened, and the chatter had lessened, until it seemed her mother barely talked at all. Deborah had lived with the pattern for years. She caught herself before she spoke what was running through her mind, "The more things change, the more they stay the same!"

That evening as Deborah crawled into bed, she realized what had been missing in this place her mother now called home. There were absolutely no reminders of a husband or a marriage which lasted nearly thirty-five years. Nothing except for pictures of the three children they had raised together. There were absolutely no pictures of him and none of his things dotted shelves or end tables. It was as if her father had been erased from her mother's life.

Deborah was actually very thankful that there weren't any obvious reminders of her father. That first night snuggling under the heavy quilts on her bed, she was reminded of her childhood. The familiarity of the quilts offered her a bit of comfort her first night back home, which was appreciated. Eventually, she drifted off to sleep.

She had settled into her room and back into life in

Deerfield with a cold indifference. She was there, but not by any choice of her own. She mentally noted the conditions of her stay and probation: first, she had to attend an AA meeting at least twice a week; then, she had to get a job. Now that would be "rich," an ex-drug addict with a record, seeking employment in Deerfield, Ohio.

Next, Deborah had to take a driver's education class in order to have her license reinstated. No drinking, no smoking in the house, home by 10 p.m. She felt like she was fourteen again living in a state of perpetual restriction! As a teenager, she used to think "restriction" was her father's favorite word.

Deborah rolled from her back to her stomach. The spring sun felt hotter than when she had first arrived at the beach. Her thoughts played out like a movie in her mind; she could not turn them off no matter how hard she tried. Perhaps the Lord wanted her to see the events of the past few years in a different light. She sat up and reached for her water bottle and took a long refreshing drink. Settling back on her towel, she closed her eyes and allowed her thoughts to drift again.

Her first nine months back in Deerfield were uneventful. She had felt like the walking dead. Although she had finally gotten a job through one of her mother's friends at the church, deep in her heart she knew she had been hired more out of the charity of her new employer's heart, rather than her own employment skills.

Deborah had started out answering phones at the only travel agency in Deerfield. There certainly weren't many people in the sleepy little town that had the desire, or the money, to do any real traveling. The owners, who were getting older and needed some help, didn't actually attend her mother's church but were members of the First Baptist Church. "Oh great! More Christians!" she had thought. Could God have been orchestrating her footsteps all along? She had to admit the office was the most peaceful place she had ever worked. All of the clubs she had worked in had bands that played so loudly, no one could talk above the clamor. It was hardly any wonder then, that the Mitchell's Worldwide Travel office seemed like a refuge.

Staying clean and sober was a daily battle, but this time she was determined to make it. Jail was one option she simply didn't want to face. Her periodic drug tests, which were one of the conditions of her probation, were something she didn't want to fail. Deborah remembered the first time it happened again, that old familiar feeling when she stuck her finger down her throat to induce vomiting. Here was one thing no one could take away from her. The only thing that had ever given her any sense of relief from the bulimia had been the alcohol and drugs that helped numb the pain of the past. She had suffered from it since she was fifteen years old in some form or another. The bulimia seemed to be greeting her from the toilet bowl. "I'm b-a-c-k!" it seemed to call out as if it were a returning, old friend. At least it wouldn't land her in jail and it wasn't a violation of her probation. Her mother had never recognized the symptoms when she was younger and Deborah was sure she wouldn't notice now.

At times Deborah would be overwhelmed with shame and self-loathing after binging on her way home from work, but she felt helpless to control the urge. She was thankful that her room had an adjoining bathroom so she didn't have to worry about facing her mother going in or coming out.

Armed with bulimia, smoking and the anxious chewing on the sides of her fingers, Deborah would somehow make it through each day. When she was at home, the TV was still her constant companion; the incessant chatter drowned out the reality of how alone she really felt in the world. She and her mother seldom talked, and when they did it felt as if they were unattached roommates thrown together by chance. They were polite and respected each other's privacy, but each had their own life.

Elizabeth Noble had begun volunteer work with the local hospice organization after the death of her husband. Everyone around Deerfield had always called him Ted, except for Elizabeth, he had always been Theodore to her. She had always felt intimidated by her husband and his family and years of marriage did nothing to change that.

The Noble family had lived in the area for years; they were well known and well respected. "No," Elizabeth had thought in those days, "a man like Theodore Noble would never look at me twice." She had no family pedigree, and she didn't have the Noble beauty which was so well known throughout Deerfield. Elizabeth had certainly been too simple and plain for Theodore Noble's taste.

One day, though she could not imagine why, all that changed. Theodore had looked in her direction, and then sauntered over to talk with her; she had felt so honored at his attention. In no time at all, his charm had swept her off her feet. Before she could even process it all, they had been married. How quickly the honor turned into a life sentence once the ring was on her finger.

Now that Theodore had passed away, she was free, free at least from the years of emotional abuse from her husband. Now she felt that her personal pain helped her have compassion to reach out to other people in their suffering. She knew what it felt like to be dying inside while everyone around was living. She knew everyone else thought that she had taken the volunteer position at hospice because of her husband's lost battle with cancer. But the real reason was that she identified with her own emotional death even more deeply. Her spirit and soul had died a slow death inflicted upon her by years of marriage to Theodore Noble.

There were signs of life again. After so many years of being dominated by Theodore Noble's likes and dislikes. She was beginning to rediscover what she liked in life. She was finding out what having her own desires felt like. She had actually caught herself laughing out loud while watching an old movie on TV. The sound virtually startled her. She couldn't remember when more than a quiet smile had crossed her face. Having her daughter come home was more than a bit challenging while she was in the midst of her own recovery. She did not want to lose the ground she had gained in her own life and she knew that if she wasn't careful, Deborah's depression and anger at life could easily overwhelm them both.

Elizabeth couldn't begin to count the number of nights over the years, when the Lord would awaken her from sleep to pray for her daughter. Not knowing what kind of danger she might be in, Elizabeth would quietly slip out of bed and kneel at its side. That's the way her mother had first taught her to pray as a little girl and the old habit had never left her. In her heart she still believed that God might hear her just a little bit better from that position. She remembered how angry Theodore would get if she disturbed him even the slightest, while getting back in to bed. "What a pity it was," Elizabeth thought, "all those hours we spent in church and we never once prayed together over our children's lives." A few tears slipped down Elizabeth's face at the sadness of that thought.

All those nights and all those prayers, and now it seemed as if God had chosen Elizabeth to play a part in the answer to her own prayers for her daughter. It was the last thing she had expected in this time of her life. She felt as unequipped and helpless to deal with Deborah now, as she used to with her own husband. All she could do was pray, and she did.

After a couple months it seemed that their lives together had taken on a quiet, but comfortable rhythm. Elizabeth began to relax a little bit. "Maybe God does have a plan," she found herself thinking.

Chapter Eighteen

A Divine Appointment

 презентация⁓ ⁓

One morning after she returned home everything changed for Deborah. That was when Anne Erickson walked back into her life. She had always known Anne as Daniel Worthington's little sister. Actually, Anne had only been a couple of years younger, but as teenagers, just a couple of years seemed to make a huge difference. Deborah didn't recognize her the first time she saw her. She hadn't seen her since Anne was fifteen and she was seventeen-and-a-half. It was the summer Deborah left home and Deerfield for good.

Anne came in to the Worldwide Travel Agency to check on flights for an upcoming conference she and her husband were planning to attend. She recognized Deborah instantly. Who could forget those unusual green eyes and the chiseled Noble features: high cheek bones, a slightly squared jaw and that beautiful olive complexion that tanned so easily? Deborah's great, great-grandfather had not only scandalized the entire region by marrying a woman who was full-blooded Cherokee, but then brought her back to Deerfield to live. The Indian features had added yet another dimension of beauty to the already handsome Noble family line.

Anne had already known Deborah was back in town; everyone in Deerfield seemed to know everything about everyone. What she hadn't heard was that Deborah was employed by the Mitchell's. As Deborah finished her phone call, Anne had time to take a quick survey. Yes, Deborah was still beautiful, but the wear and tear of the past seventeen years had aged her considerably. Her eyes, still unusual, had no life in them. Her hair was still long and straight, brown; almost black-it had hardly changed since high school. Yes, that was Deborah Noble alright."

Anne remembered that Daniel, as a young boy, had an intense crush on the woman sitting in front of her. She couldn't wait to tell him who she had run into today. She wondered if he had heard the news that Deborah was back in town.

———————————

After working at the Worldwide Travel Agency for about six months answering the phones and running errands, Mr. Mitchell approached Deborah about learning the new, recently installed computer system. She was a little surprised, but excited about the opportunity. Most of the restaurants and clubs she had worked in over the last few years had been computerized and she had always enjoyed learning the new systems. Truthfully, she had been amazed when she had started at the Agency that they were still operating without computers. "Only in Deerfield," she thought.

After only a few months, she was nearly running the entire office herself. It felt good to be needed and the Mitchell's trusted her more and more every day. Something in her didn't want to let them down.

She was grateful that, though they were Christians, Harold and Helen Mitchell never had made her feel guilty about not going to church. They never preached to her so in the safety of the Worldwide Travel Agency, she began to gradually let down her guard. The Mitchell's generously gave her a fifty cent hourly raise when she began to do more than just answer the phones. Perhaps now she could get her fines paid off quickly.

Deborah remembered having mixed emotions the first day she saw Anne again. She had always liked Daniel's younger sister, but there was still so much shame surrounding her relationship with Daniel, it left Deborah feeling awkward. However, Anne's genuine warmth and happiness to see her that first day caused her to look forward to Anne's to pick up her airline tickets.

Deborah's wandering thoughts suddenly shifted back to her present situation. She realized the sun was now much lower in the Florida sky than when she had arrived; time had slipped by quickly. She gathered her things to head back to the house on Magnolia Street; the house which had become her home for the past couple days. She loved its Bed and Breakfast feeling.

Deborah had committed herself to do some work on a few tape assignments her counselors had given her and she still had a couple of ungodly beliefs that they wanted her to work on by herself. As soon as she got back she was going to take a shower and catch a little nap. Even though she had dozed off here and there lying on the beach, she still felt sleepy. "Getting out all this emotional stuff has worn me out. No telling what tomorrow will bring," she mused. She tried to dismiss any thoughts of tomorrow as she walked from the beach to her car. The sun had felt wonderful and Deborah didn't want to lose the relaxation she captured on the beach this afternoon, "God only knows how hard it is to find," she thought to herself. Perhaps tomorrow morning she would wake up early enough to catch a sunrise walk along the beach.

As she got in the car to head back, her thoughts drifted back to Anne. It was Anne who had first approached her with a brochure about the *Restore Your Soul Ministry* in Palm City. Anne never pushed; she simply and lovingly encouraged her to take a look at the information and testimonies. Something had stirred inside of Deborah after she read the brochure. It had taken more than nine months to save up the money and make the arrangements, but something had told her that this was part of the answer she had been searching for. She owed this whole trip to her.

Anne wasn't the only one who befriended her. The whole Erickson family had shown her what real Christianity was supposed to look like; she would be eternally grateful to her for that, and so much more. Within just months after her first dinner invitation, she had begun to feel a part of the Erickson family. They had captured Deborah's attention and then her heart. She could still vividly remember the day when her heart opened up to the idea of maybe being married and having a family, too. The possibility seemed so far away but she found herself looking at Anne's life with different eyes.

Anne's husband, Robert, seemed to receive Deborah with the same gracious hospitality as his wife. The children, Joanna the oldest, Joshua the middle child, and Jacob the youngest, were all in love with Deborah. The feeling was mutual in spite of Deborah's past reservations about children. She enjoyed the attention she received every time she walked into the Erickson household.

One day Anne finally asked Deborah about her relationship with God. She poured out her confusion and frustration with the hypocrisy she had grown up with in the Noble family home; though she still did not divulge anything beyond the generalities of what had happened to her during her childhood years. She loved and trusted Anne but she had vowed years ago that no one would ever know the truth of what had really happened. So far, she had even managed to evade probing looks and questions from Lydia and Joyce. Deborah was glad there were so many other issues for them to look at in her life. She knew that before tomorrow morning, there was a major decision to be made. Would she finally tell them what she had never told anyone before?

The day Anne had ministered to her; Deborah found herself praying along with Anne and asking Jesus to forgive her of her sins and become Lord of her life. As she rose from the chair in Anne's cozy family room, she felt a hundred pounds lighter.

That same day, Anne invited her to join the women's Bible study held once a week in her home. She hesitated before responding-an AA meeting was one thing, but getting together with a bunch of church ladies was quite another. She had told Anne that she would think about it and then quickly made her way out the back door. She needed time to process what had just happened.

As she crawled into bed that night, Deborah knew she felt different. True, there was still a great deal of turmoil in her mind and in her heart, but something had changed after praying with Anne. She fell asleep still wondering, "Is it just wishful thinking, or has something great and wonderful really happened to me today?"

The following morning, she came into the kitchen and found her mother humming as she prepared their evening meal in a crock-pot. For the first time in a long time, the sight of her mother didn't annoy her. Maybe something really had happened yesterday.

Deborah wasn't sure what finally convinced her to begin coming to Anne's weekly Bible studies. She remembered how uncomfortable and awkward she felt the first evening; however, the majority of the women were as warm, kind and genuine as Anne. The others, she found out later, were just as uncomfortable on their first night as she had been. The Bible study was so different than the cold, formal church services, she remembered attending as a child. These women were actually had fun as they studied and shared. She became fascinated with how they applied the Word of God to their everyday lives. It wasn't long before she found herself doing the same thing. It was more than a little disconcerting to Deborah that she was becoming something she had hated for so long. Before she even realized it, Deborah had become one of "those Christians."

As she stepped out of the shower and began to dry off, Deborah thought to herself, "Yes, the day Anne Erickson walked in to the Worldwide Travel Agency had truly been a divine appointment!"

Chapter Nineteen

Reflections

જે જ

Deborah closed the blinds and climbed into bed. The sheets felt cool against her sun-drenched skin. She hoped she hadn't gotten too much sun, even with her liberally applied sunscreen. As she closed her eyes, Daniel, Anne's brother, came to mind. She remembered the first time she had run into him at Anne's house after returning to Deerfield. He had seemed surprised, as if suddenly, and without invitation or permission, she had invaded his personal world. Previously, she had only seen him once before. It was at the local hardware store downtown.

Mr. Mitchell needed a kit to fix the toilet that continued to run unless you jiggled the handle up and down. Jiggling had finally quit working so she had stopped by Brown & Son's Hardware Store on the corner of 7th Street and Main.

Deborah immediately recognized Daniel Worthington from the back as she walked into the store that morning. Startled, she reacted like a scared rabbit whose best course of action was to run. Before she could turn around and head back out the door, Mr. Brown had said, rather loudly, "Good morning." Daniel turned around and saw her for the first time since she had returned back home. Anne told him that Deborah Noble was back in town, but this was the first time he had actually run into her. He remembered that Anne had casually mentioned to him that Deborah was working at the Worldwide Travel Agency only a few blocks from the hardware store. The minute he turned around to say hello, she dropped her head and found herself counting the tile squares on the floor as she mumbled, "Hi, Daniel," and headed toward the plumbing aisle.

"Well it's obvious, nothing's changed. Deborah Noble still can't stand me," how quickly and unexpectedly the feeling of being abandoned in the middle of a dance floor returned to him. "OK, get a grip. That was the past and right now I've got to pick up a gallon of paint and some brushes or the new offices will never get painted." He wondered if Deborah was aware that he no longer worked for someone else, but now owned his own ad agency. Daniel shook his head fuming, "What difference does it make? Why do I still have some sick need to impress a woman who obviously doesn't care if I exist or not?"

Over the next year, Daniel found himself running into Deborah on several occasions as he picked up his kids from Anne's. They had little but pleasantries to say to each other. There were times when he'd arrive to get the kids and Deborah would be in the kitchen helping Anne get supper ready or playing in the back yard with the children. It appeared that she was trying her best to avoid any direct contact and that was okay with him. He always felt an invisible wall go up every time he was in her presence-it had been the norm ever since that prom night when everything had changed between them. After awhile, he just shrugged it off. Anne was very good about keeping the confidences of the women to whom she ministered. Daniel had learned not to ask any questions. Besides, he had enough on his hands; raising two children without their mother was a full-time job. He didn't need to know what Deborah Noble's problem was and he really didn't have time to care.

Daniel's wife's illness and subsequent death had come quickly. She was diagnosed with ovarian cancer but the diagnosis had come only after the disease was in the advanced stages. Before anyone in Deerfield knew it, Susan was gone. The news had shaken the town and Daniel's own faith. He continually found himself asking "Why?" Their oldest son, David, was eight at the time; he would be turning ten in just a couple of months. Aimee had only been five and a half at the time of her mother's death. He didn't know what he would have done without Anne and her husband. Thank God, Robert had never complained about the extra responsibility Anne had taken on by helping him with the children. He was more than grateful to have had the steadfastness of Anne, her husband, Robert, and Pastor Harrison in his life during this time. The whole church body had been there for him, as well, with food, prayer, and comforting hugs. While he truly appreciated everyone's concern and care, it could not bring back his wife.

Daniel knew that he wasn't supposed to blame God for what had happened to Susan, but it was a struggle. He was aware that the Enemy had in some way been given access to bring premature death. He often regretted the times he had not prayed for his wife and wished he had expressed more concern for her well-being. Regret was no fun to live with, so whenever he had the chance he did his best to encourage other men not to take their wives for granted.

Susan had never complained. They had assumed that most of her female problems were due to difficulties she had experienced with her two pregnancies. "Why didn't I get her to a specialist sooner?" was the question he went to bed with and woke up with. Months after her death, Daniel realized that it wasn't God he blamed, but himself. Tired of dealing with the torment, he had finally made an appointment with the new pastor.

Pastor Harrison had recommended several books related to the grieving process and the loss of a loved one. Just facing the issue and talking aloud to someone had helped. They had scheduled several subsequent counseling appointments and eventually, the guilt and condemnation did not seem like it overwhelmed him anymore. He was working on forgiving himself.

Pastor Harrison had also opened up a whole new spiritual horizon for him when he began to discuss generational curses and the need to repent of generational sin. It was something Daniel had never really thought about previously. He knew that the Bible said that Jesus had redeemed us from the curse of the law but had never really thought about what that meant to him and his family. Pastor Harrison gently reminded Daniel that everything that Jesus had done on the cross had to be appropriated at a personal and individual level. He showed him a number of scriptures where people in the Word had stood in the gap for the proceeding generations and had repented of family sin. It had given Daniel a great deal to think about at the time.

Pastor Harrison also shared that healing and deliverance had also been completed on the Cross by Christ. Even though Jesus had died for everyone's salvation, each person still had to personally, by faith appropriate the Word of God in order to receive what Jesus had already done. He quoted Isaiah 53:5: "By His stripes, we are healed," and then had gone on to explain that the scripture was the truth, yet each person still had to appropriate by faith and do the Word of God related to healing. Redemption was no different. Even though Christ redeemed us from the curse of the law by becoming a curse for us, each person had to appropriate His blood and apply it to the generational sin that allowed the curse to be there. That was done through repentance. The only antidote to sin was repentance and instead of the blood of bulls, sheep, or other animals being applied to the sin as it was in the Old Testament, the Blood of Jesus was applied. It had the power to wipe away sin and bring redemption from the curse. It took away the legal right of the enemy to continue to perpetuate the curse.

Several days after the conversation, Daniel had an eye-opening revelation. A number of Susan's ancestors had died prematurely either of cancer or heart disease. There had also been varying degrees of occult involvement in her family; her grandfather and great-grandfather both had been dedicated members of the Masonic Lodge, and Susan's mother was always off on some New Age adventure. Her father had been an atheist. It was a miracle that Susan had found faith in Christ at all.

Daniel began to realize that his neglect as a husband may have not been the only cause of her early death. Pastor Harrison had reminded him that the Enemy was always seeking an open door so that he may enter our lives and cause destruction; his job was to "kill, steal and destroy." He would use any avenue to complete his mission. Daniel could now see that there were spiritual doors opened that could have allowed the Enemy to perpetuate the generational curse of premature death. It helped to make the scripture in Hosea even clearer, "My people are destroyed for lack of knowledge." He also was well aware of the Scripture that said how the Lord would work all things to the good for those that loved Him and were called according to His purpose. Daniel was more than intrigued to find out how the Lord could work this one to his good. The death of his wife had left him shell shocked and examining his faith.

Daniel had met Susan in college. Daniel had attended Ohio State where he had received a degree in business and marketing, and Susan had been an English major. She had a passion to teach school and also wanted to write Christian novels during her summers off. Susan always had everything planned out, right down to the last detail. Daniel had felt comfortable with her right from the start.

Admittedly, in the beginning of their courtship, Daniel had often found himself comparing Susan to Deborah. From the time he was ten years old, Deborah had been the yard stick by which he subconsciously measured every other woman. The habit was hard to break. But as time went on, thoughts of Deborah began to fade. He grew to accept Susan for who she was and fell in love with the heart and soul of this unique woman. She was gentle, yet she possessed a special, quiet, inner strength. Her faith ran deep, despite her family background, and she had a way about her that calmed Daniel's soul. As their friendship grew, one day he realized that he couldn't imagine his life without her. It was then that he decided to propose. He was thrilled beyond measure when she actually said, "Yes!" He remembered how in the last stages of her illness, she made him promise that he would find a wife and remarry after she was gone, "Promise me, Daniel, it's one of the ways that I'll be at peace with my dying." She wanted to know that he and the children would be taken care of when she was gone. "Did she have any clue how difficult it was to watch her suffer while promising that he would find another wife and mother for the children?" Susan had even made him promise that he wouldn't wait too long, reminding him how the formative years were too important for the children to be without a mother for a very long time.

He had never known anyone as self-sacrificing as Susan. Even in death, her concern was for everyone around her. As he left her bedside, Daniel knew keeping the promise to remarry would be easier said than done. It certainly was a promise that he had no desire of even considering at this moment but it was obvious that his answer brought Susan peace. She had closed her eyes after he had responded "yes." Suddenly her breathing became less labored and it was as if she had fallen into a deep, peaceful sleep. Only two days later, she was gone.

Susan's dream of teaching school had never been realized. She had graduated from college shortly after their marriage and then became pregnant with their oldest son, David. Just a few short years later, Aimee arrived. Susan had suffered from complications with both pregnancies and had needed a lot of rest during and after the birth of each child. Although Susan worked part-time during part of both pregnancies, they had made the conscientious decision that they would sacrifice her income so that she could stay at home and care for the children. The year that Susan had become ill, Aimee had just begun pre-school.

The next year both she and Aimee were planning to start school together; Aimee as a first grade student and she as a teacher.

After Deborah rekindled her relationship with Anne, she was introduced to Susan through the pictures of family gatherings hanging on the living room walls. She had learned that Daniel and Susan had gotten married when he was twenty-four, and vaguely remembered a phone call from her mother around that time. She remembered having heard the news that he was getting married and so she went out and got high that evening. The cocaine wiped away any of the emotional sting she felt when she had heard the news.

From the pictures, Deborah saw that Susan had been a pretty woman with sandy-colored hair and dark brown eyes. It was clearly obvious from the pictures that Susan adored her children and her husband. She was rarely captured looking at the camera; her attention was usually on her family and her expressions were ones of pride, fulfillment and joy all rolled together. In the past, Deborah had always looked at marriage as a form of imprisonment. She had seen her mother live in that prison for nearly thirty-five years-it was something that she had previously wanted no part of. But as she looked at the photographs, she found herself thinking of how lucky Susan Worthington had been. Susan had enjoyed what Deborah knew she would probably never ever find-a Godly husband and a family.

Deborah always exercised restraint when Anne talked about her brother and his family, never asking too many questions, but deep within there was a longing to know more. She was aware from Anne, and little things that Andrea Kline said at the Bible study that the woman had set her sights on Daniel. Andrea always came early and left late. She assumed Andrea's lingering was in hopes of catching Daniel at his sister's house. The woman had made it apparent to everyone that God had told her Daniel was going to be her husband-she had actually expressed her decision to be patient until he realized that she was perfect for him. It was obvious to Deborah that Anne was extremely uncomfortable at times with the things Andrea said about her brother and his children.

Chapter Twenty

The Dream

Deborah rolled over in bed and looked at the clock. Thirty minutes more and then she would get up, have a snack and finish her assignments. She didn't want to face Lydia and Joyce in the morning without doing what they had asked. Today, they had assigned a tape on "shame" and a video called "Restoring Sexuality" for her homework. The title of the second one caught her interest. It seemed a little unusual, maybe even unnatural, to be talking about God and sexuality in the same breath. Normally, she would have considered those two topics to be worlds apart. But Lydia and Joyce both seemed very comfortable with issues of sexuality, even when she had talked rather graphically about her own sexual issues. It was going to be interesting to see what the tape had to say about the subject. "God only knows if anyone's sexuality needs restoring, it's mine!" she whispered to herself as she closed her eyes for just a few more minutes of rest. She quickly dozed back off.

A couple of hours later, Deborah woke with a start. Rather than simply enjoying the comfort of her bed for a few more minutes, she had actually fallen into a deep sleep. It was already quite dark outside. A little disorientated, she got out of bed, still re-playing in her mind the dream that she had just had. She reached for her journal resting on the edge of the small lamp table beside her bed. It was Anne who had encouraged her to start journaling, and then Lydia and Joyce had asked her to do the same thing when she received things outside of her session. They had prepared her for the possibility that God might even speak to her in dreams while she was there this week.

Deborah opened the journal and began to write. The first scene in the dream had opened in the Noble family home. She was about six or seven years old and she was searching for something, something lost. First, she looked in the basement of the house; it was cold, dark, and frightening, and she didn't know exactly what it was that she was looking for. In the next scene, she found herself in the kitchen searching through the cupboards. Still empty handed, Deborah found herself upstairs where the family had always slept. Now, however, she was about twelve or thirteen years old and she was looking through the bedroom closets.

As she opened the first closet door, she found Justin crouched inside. As he reached out to grab her, she quickly shut the door. In the next closet, she found her former pimp and drug dealer, Moses. She shuttered as she slammed the closet door before his clutching fingers could grab her. In every room and on every wall, there were more closets. In every closet there was another man. One closet held Tommie Lee-he had murder on his face when he saw her. She gasped and quickly slammed the door. There were countless closets containing countless other faces. Some faces had names to go with them, others were just nameless faces.

Deborah searched through closet after closet. She was finally in the last room opening the last closet door when she realized that the door was stuck. She couldn't get it open no matter how hard she pulled. She continued to pull on the closet handle with such a force that it finally came off in her hands. Somehow, in the dream, she just knew that she had to get into that last closet; however, her efforts seemed fruitless. Then a most peculiar thing happened: she clicked her heels together like Dorothy from the Wizard of Oz (it had always been one of her favorite movies as a child). Suddenly the closet door sprung open, but this closet wasn't like the others. There were no men, no faces. She slowly walked into it wanting to see what was inside, scared of what she might find. The closet transformed into a tunnel. Carefully, Deborah began to feel her way deeper into the dark abyss that lay in front of her. Her heart was pounding rapidly and so loudly that it seemed to echo off the walls around her. She continued moving forward, deeper and deeper into the darkness. Her eyes began to adjust to the black world she had entered as she grasped for clues along the way, but there were none.

Without warning, Deborah came to the end of the tunnel. She found herself in a room with a coffin in the center of it. Ever since she had attended her great-grandmother's funeral as a little girl, she had always hated anything associated with death. But as frightened as she was, Deborah knew she had to open the lid. Cautiously and hesitantly, she made her way toward the coffin and slowly opened the lid. There was no one in it; the coffin was empty. Suddenly she felt a tap on her shoulder. She screamed and jumped! The fear she felt was overwhelming. She turned around to see who it was. Her father reached out, grabbed her, and pulled her to himself. Then she awoke.

It didn't take a rocket scientist to discern what this dream was about. She knew God was telling her that she had to face her issues with her father. She instinctively knew that the other closets and the other men represented the fact that, in the past few days, she had already opened up and freely and honestly talked about many of the issues related to them enabling God to close the emotional doors.

Clicking her heels meant two things. First, she was going to have to call on a spiritual power other than her own natural ability to be able to open up to Lydia and Joyce tomorrow.

Second, that the power to open up was actually already resident within her. It was amazing how fast the interpretation came to her.

The tunnel represented the realization that she was going to have to dig deep and go to some frightening and dark places in order to face what her father had done. The fact that her father was not in the coffin meant that her issue was still alive-it was at the root of all her other problems with men.

The interpretation came effortlessly and stopped as quickly as it began. Deborah took a deep breath. She certainly was going to need all the help she could get if she was going to open up to her counselors tomorrow. She thought about her homework assignments, maybe they could help prepare her. She could already feel the shame start to rise within her just thinking about what she would need to talk about tomorrow. Deborah decided to just listen to the tape in her room and then go to the study to watch the video. She was relieved as her focus began to shift to her assignments so she could get her mind off the dream. With deliberate diligence, she completed all of her assignments; she finished the rest of her ungodly beliefs, listened to the tape, watched the video, and took several pages of notes. She was still a bit shaken by the dream, but found some comfort when she realized that the information on the tapes would make facing tomorrow a little bit easier. "God is continuing to give me exactly what I need precisely when I need it. He's never late and not a minute too soon!" she thought to herself.

As Deborah prepared for bed she thought, "Anne would love this place. Maybe someday we can take a trip to Florida together." She was already mentally making a list of the other women in the weekly Bible study that she wanted to tell about the ministry in Palm City. Who knew maybe it was something that could even help Andrea. She had actually even considered suggesting the ministry to her own mother and even her sister,

Mary Rachel.

Mary Rachel! Now there was a whole other topic that she hadn't begun to get to yet. After finishing college and getting married, Mary Rachel had moved to South Carolina. Deborah barely knew her husband, Jonathan, or their only son, Nathan, though it was not for lack of effort on Mary Rachel's part. Deborah had only seen her sister a couple of times since she had left home at seventeen. Mary Rachel on the other hand, had faithfully sent Christmas cards, birthday cards and pictures of her son whenever she had an address to reach her.

Now that she was living back home, Deborah had seen Mary Rachel and her family on several holidays. She and her sister acted interested in each other's lives and the whole family was secretly thankful for Nathan's ability to become the center of attention-it helped relieve the discomfort of trying to make conversation. Family time together was usually painfully strained.

Mary Rachel and Jonathan did everything methodically, precisely, and on schedule. They had been married for several years and had actually paid off their home before she became pregnant with Nathan, who was now five. Deborah had never dared ask her sister if another child fit into their long-term plan.

Jonathan was a financial planner whose decisiveness and precision seemed to spill over into every area of their lives, which actually, suited Mary Rachel just fine. All of her life she battled fear. Her philosophy was simple: the more controlled and ordered her life was and the less she had to worry about, the better. She and her husband were occasional church goers but it appeared that Jonathan's god was money. His parents divorced when he was only seven and Jonathan's mother had never forgiven God for the fact that her husband ran off with her best friend. Consequently, Jonathan had not been raised in church and had the same disdain for God as his mother did. Mary Rachel, on the other hand, went to church out of duty, fear, and habits formed in childhood.

Tonight, Deborah decided that on her next long weekend, she would make a visit to her sister's home. Maybe she would even have an opportunity to witness to her. She laughed to herself, "Now that would be quite a switch."

Deborah pulled her pajamas from the hook on the back of her bedroom door and slipped into them. Her assignments were completed and, even after her afternoon nap, she was still fatigued and ready for bed. Going through this stuff really was draining! She reached for her Bible from the nightstand and began to read Psalm 142. The counselors had suggested it to her this afternoon to prepare her for tomorrow's session. She loved the raw, emotional honesty that David expressed through song. "Yes, Lord," she thought, "I need you to bring my soul out of prison just like David." A scripture came to mind that Anne had shared with her last year, it had become one of her favorites; "He, who is forgiven much, loves much." Boy, wasn't that the truth!"

Only someone like herself, someone who knew what it was like to be imprisoned by so many prisons, could appreciate the freedom she was discovering. Each time the bars of another prison that surrounded her came down, she fell more in love with Jesus. Suddenly Deborah heard the gentle, loving voice of the Holy Spirit, "I've not only called you to be free; I have called you to be a 'freedom maker'." She lay trembling in her bed. She wasn't sure when she had heard the Lord's voice more clearly. "Exactly what did You mean Lord? What is a freedom maker?" thoughts raced through her mind. Whatever He meant by it, there was an excitement and a fire spreading through her body. "Could this be what the prophet, Jeremiah, meant when he had said that there was fire shut up in his bones?"

Deborah was so grateful that Anne had taught her how to listen to the voice of God within her. Before, she had always waited for the Lord's voice to boom out of the sky just like in the movie, "The Ten Commandments," with Charleston Heston. Anne had been so patient when explaining how most of the time, when the Lord spoke, a person would hear Him within their own mind and heart-it was that inner, still, small voice. If you weren't careful, you could miss it, thinking that it was your own thoughts or emotions. Because of Anne's instructions, her prayer time consisted of praying to the Lord and then listening for His response. All those years in church as a child and she never had really experienced or understood true communion with the Lord until now.

"A Freedom Maker." It sounded noble and full of adventure. She couldn't wait to tell Anne what she had heard when she returned home. Maybe Anne would know what the Lord really meant by it. As Anne had previously explained to her, the prophetic voice made everything seem very immediate, as if whatever the Lord spoke would happen the very next moment. Anne had helped Deborah understand that even though the Lord had spoken, it could take years for His Words to be fulfilled in someone's life. Prophecy she called it; God foretelling and speaking to His children. Anne had given her such a sensible explanation. She had used the example of a good father who desired to communicate to his children on a regular basis. She pointed out the scripture, "My sheep know My Voice;" and she had also shared that throughout the Bible, God spoke to His servants through visions, dreams, angels and with His own voice all of the time. Suddenly she felt the witness of the Holy Spirit run over her body. "Yes, the Lord wants me to know that was Him speaking to me." The very thought gave her what she had come to jokingly call "God bumps." She lay quietly waiting to see if there was anything else the Lord wanted to say but all she could hear was the swish of the paddle fan overhead. She closed her eyes and was soon fast asleep.

Morning came all too quickly. Deborah had set her alarm

for 6:00 a.m. in order to have enough time to take an early morning walk. She quickly threw on her shorts, t-shirt and sneakers, got in her car, and headed the short distance to the beach. The parking lot was nearly deserted; only a few other early-birds were on the beach, some walking, some enjoying their morning coffee on the public benches placed at the edge of the parking lot, and some taking pictures of the beautiful sunrise. It was a glorious spring morning and she was glad that she had pushed through her grogginess and got out of bed. It was good to be alive. Last night, before falling asleep, she had a moment of fear that she would have another dream about her father, but her sleep had been peaceful and deep. Actually, she felt quite rested this morning.

Deborah was going to miss Florida when she went back to Deerfield. She walked along the beach as rays of the morning sun pierced through the finely-misted haze. Rich hues of red, orange and gold swirled in the Eastern sky. She began to think about what she was about to face in the morning's ministry session.

Deborah wasn't sure what had happened during the night but she woke up resolved to face the issue with her father. She was still apprehensive about the morning session. Feelings of anticipation were mixed in with the fear but for the most part she was ready. Part of her knew that the counselors already suspected she was withholding something. Pretty hard to hide much from those two! She caught a couple of knowing glances Lydia and Joyce had exchanged when they thought she wasn't looking. Deborah had determined that today she wasn't going to make them pull it out of her. She was just going to walk into the room this morning and tell them. Tell them everything!

As she continued to walk, she couldn't stop the flood of memories. Thoughts of what had happened the very first time her father had crossed that invisible line of what was right between a father and a daughter came to her mind. The very first time her father had touched her where he shouldn't have happened the summer right before she turned thirteen. She was just beginning to develop and was extremely self-conscious and a little uncomfortable, with the changes happening in her body. Her mother had gone to early morning prayer and Deborah was still in her bed. Her father came into her room and sat on the edge of her bed. She remembered the strange almost tortured look in his eyes. His voice was almost a whisper as he told her what a beautiful woman she was becoming. At first she was pleased that he had noticed, but as he continued to look at her, a panicky feeling deep in the pit of her stomach began to stir. She realized that she was holding her breath.

Then it happened. Her father asked if he could touch her breast to see how much of a woman she was becoming. Everything in her had wanted to scream "No" but instead she had remained silent and frozen in the bed as her father slowly lifted her pajama top and touched her breast. As quickly as he came in, Daddy left the room. It had happened so fast that for days she thought it might have just been a dream-until it happened again. Deborah suddenly experienced that old familiar nauseous feeling rise up in her stomach as she walked along the beach. "Not now," she thought, "there's plenty of time this morning to face this." As she continued her morning walk, she tried to find distraction in the beauty around her but it wasn't easy. It was if a dam had broken and there was nothing left to hold back the memories.

Deborah could hardly wait to get back to *His House* and get into her morning session. Her counselors had called it the *Healing Session*. Tuesday had been the *Redemption Session* when they had dealt with generational curses and yesterday had been the *Transformation Session*. She knew, without a doubt, that God had prepared her for today through the previous sessions and through her time alone with Him. Lydia and Joyce must have been praying. She could hardly wait to get in that room and spill her guts; it was hard to believe that the secret she had so closely guarded most of her life had now turned into something she couldn't wait to tell.

Over the past few days Deborah had come to appreciate Lydia's and Joyce's steady demeanor. They never appeared shocked or disgusted even when she had told them shocking and disgusting things. She would often glance to check and see if their eyes had changed but they remained the same, full of concern and care. They had been like two angels; they were there but not obtrusively there. It almost felt like she was having a private audience with God and they were simply His Ladies in Waiting. Always ready to serve both her and the King, they were able to stand by quietly as the Lord Himself worked on her heart. Deborah realized how precious they had become to her in such a short time. She hoped the Lord had prepared them for the rest of the story.

Returning to her room, Deborah quickly showered, dressed, and then grabbed a piece of fruit, a muffin, and some juice from the common kitchen. She wasn't necessarily hungry but knew she needed to have something in her stomach. The quiet ticking of the kitchen clock announced it was almost nine o'clock-time to get her things and walk next door.

She was still riddled with anticipation and dread as she headed out the front door and down the brick path which connected the two houses. Lydia was just pulling into the parking lot. She parked next to Joyce's car which was obviously empty. "Joyce must already be inside," Deborah thought. She was thankful for the distraction. Lydia waved hello as she got out of the car and Deborah climbed the steps and waited on the front porch for her. Together they walked into *His House* and down the hall to the Restoration Room. The light conversation they shared helped give her mind a short respite from what she had to face this morning. Lydia inquired about her night's sleep and homework assignment as they entered the room. Joyce looked up and asked her if she had made it to the beach this morning. The women seemed rested and ready to go.

"How and where will I start?" Deborah mused to herself as the two women settled into their chairs and got their paperwork organized. She sat down on the couch that had become an old friend over the past few days and quickly reached over, grabbing a pillow and immediately hugging it to her chest. In that moment, it was of little consequence to her whether Lydia and Joyce saw or noted the movement. All that mattered was covering herself from the feelings of nakedness and vulnerability overwhelming her at the moment. The pillow gave her a limited sense of protection and she was glad to have something to hold on to as the session began.

Chapter Twenty-One

The Fourth Day

‪ ‪

After the prayer, Lydia began to share scriptures related to the day's session. Deborah tried to focus and listen but the deafening roar inside her head was totally distracting. She had been so confident this morning that she was going to be able to do this. Why was that old helpless feeling suddenly overtaking her once again? Just as she was about to succumb to the sense of panic and anxiety, Joyce intervened, "Deborah, are you okay?"

Deborah shook her head, "No. I don't know if I can do this." She leaned forward and put her head in her lap and began to rock herself in an almost child-like fashion.

Joyce said, "Would it be okay if we lay hands on you and pray? The enemy is trying to attack you. He wants to stop what the Lord desires to do for you today."

She shook her head, "Yes" hoping it would make a difference but not really believing it. Nothing had ever been able to help when she felt like this-it was like sinking into a dark pit and being smothered by something that she could not fight her way out of by herself. Most of the time, she would have to fall asleep to get out of it. In the past, she would run to the drugs every time this feeling got close to her.

Her spiritual counselors simultaneously got up and began to lay hands on Deborah. They prayed in tongues-something

Deborah had heard before but had never really understood. As they prayed, the roar in her head began to lift. The pit of panic and despair which would have normally swallowed her, eased and Deborah felt like she was standing on solid ground again. "Maybe there really is something to this praying in the Spirit," she thought.

Immediately, as if she had read Deborah's mind, Lydia asked, "Can we talk about the Baptism of the Holy Spirit and speaking in tongues? The Lord impressed on me last night that the power of the Holy Spirit is crucial for you to be able to withstand the power of the enemy. I believe it's vital in helping you get through today's session."

At that moment, Deborah was ready to try anything, "Sure," she answered, "but I want to know what it really means. I think I know, but some of it's still pretty confusing."

Lydia reached for her Bible and over the next ten minutes she shared scripture and testimony about the Baptism of the Holy Spirit. Both she and Joyce talked about their experiences and what a difference it had made in their own Christian walks. Deborah could feel the same electric feeling in the air that had been present when Anne had shared her testimony about accepting Jesus as her Lord and Savior. Lydia explained that the Holy Spirit was a gift from God to the believer, a promise of what was to come. Moreover, this gift contained the Power of God so that when it was accepted by a believer, he or she would have power over sin and the Enemy. "Now it makes sense why the roar in my head went away," Deborah thought. "All this time, I was being attacked by Satan and I thought it was something I had conjured up myself. If speaking in tongues can prevent those awful feelings, I'm ready for it!"

Lydia shared scripture of when the disciples spoke in tongues on the day of Pentecost and how, when the Apostle Paul and other believers laid hands on people, they would begin to speak in tongues also. She continued to share out of 1st Corinthians 14:2 where it explains that when people speak in tongues, they speak mysteries directly to God.

Joyce interjected, "It's a heavenly language and a private language just between you and the Lord."

"Yes," Lydia said. "And 1st Corinthians 14:4 says that you edify or build yourself up spiritually when you speak in tongues. It is one of those foolish things that the Bible talks about. It feels foolish to your natural mind but once you see things change in your life and feel the power of the Holy Spirit, you won't want to be without this gift of God."

Joyce added, "The Word of God in John 7:38 also tells us that rivers of living water will flow out of our bellies, and in verse 39 it goes on to say that by this He meant the Spirit who they would receive later. Your spiritual language will not come from your natural mind. It will flow out of your spirit and that's why it's so pure. It's not contaminated by your own understanding, past experience or theology." Deborah was once again feeling a mixture of anticipation and fear as the two women continued to share.

Lydia said, "You still have to cooperate with the Holy Spirit. You have to open your mouth and begin to speak. Some people are under the misconception that the Holy Spirit will just take over and speaking in tongues is out of your control. The Holy Spirit will not overpower you-He is gentle like a dove and will work with you and through your own spirit."

Joyce continued to share, "Everyone feels awkward in the beginning but once you get past the first few syllables, you'll feel a release. It's like priming a well that has not been used for a long time; the water begins to trickle up at first and then, as you continue to pump, the flow becomes stronger and stronger.

"It's also different than normal speech which is formulated in our minds. Speaking in tongues comes out of your spirit, out of your innermost being, or belly, as the Word says. You just have to relax and let it flow," Lydia said. "Are you ready?" Deborah nodded, unable to speak. She was already starting to tremble all over. Joyce and Lydia each began to both pray in the Spirit at the same time. Then Lydia said, "I take authority over all fear, religious spirits and self-consciousness and bind you in the Name of Jesus."

Then Joyce encouraged her and said, "Ok, now its time to ask the Lord for His Holy Spirit as the scripture said in Luke 11:13.

It took a moment for her to find her voice. Softly Deborah whispered, "Jesus, I ask you to baptize me with your Holy Spirit. I want all of you and I need all the help I can get."

They continued to lay hands on her while praying in tongues. Lydia prayed, "Lord, we ask You to baptize Deborah with the Holy Ghost and with power just as your Word says. Let rivers of living water begin to flow out of her spirit now." She reached down and gently laid her fingertips on Deborah's stomach. Deborah felt herself shaking even harder as a warm heat began to spread from her head down and throughout her entire body. She still didn't know what she would say if she opened her mouth.

Joyce kept encouraging her, "The power of God is here, Deborah. Just open your mouth and see what comes out. Focus on the Lord and your desire to communicate with Him, and then let your heart speak. Just don't use your English language." Deborah closed her eyes and tried to concentrate. She had to admit that something seemed to want to come out of her, but it seemed stuck right in her chest.

At that point, Lydia declared, "We bind every occult spirit from hindering Deborah, in the name of Jesus."

Immediately syllables and words that were foreign to her ears began to pour out of her. It felt as if a dam had let loose. A deep sense of joy and relief began to fill her from the inside out as tears poured down her face. She felt certain that everything she had ever wanted to tell God was being released deep from within her and could feel the Lord's presence surrounding her. It was peaceful, yet powerful, and contained a sense of freedom she had longed for but had never personally experienced. Now, she understood what made Anne so different from so many of the other Christians she had met.

Lydia and Joyce both began to experience the joy of the Lord, also. So, they all laughed, prayed, and cried together, but these were tears of joy. Deborah was almost afraid to stop praying in the Spirit.

Lydia, led by the Spirit as to what Deborah was thinking said, "Don't be afraid, Deborah. This is not going to go away. The Holy Spirit is here to stay. Any time you desire, you can begin to pray in the Spirit. The more that you use your prayer language the easier it will be. At times your prayer language will even expand and change, just as a child's vocabulary increases as they mature."

Joyce exclaimed, "You will never be the same! Now Lydia and I can feel more confident about your well-being once we send you home. We know that you're going to need the Holy Spirit to help you walk out and hold the freedom and ministry that you're receiving this week."

Deborah realized that in all the excitement she had actually forgotten what she had come intending to do this morning. "Maybe now it will be easier," she thought.

"We have one other prayer that we want to go over before we start today's session," Lydia said. "It's a prayer to break ungodly soul ties, but first let me explain. We can have ungodly soul ties with people, places or things, even with our own pain or emotions. Whenever someone or something has more influence or effect on us than the Lord, it represents an ungodly soul tie."

Joyce interjected, "We can have good Godly soul ties like David and Jonathan in the Bible, but ungodly soul ties control us and affect us negatively. We can have ungodly soul ties even with our family, friends or church."

"In your case, you probably have ungodly soul ties with bulimia, food, alcohol, and nicotine as well as the men you were involved with sexually," Lydia added. "Just like during the other portions of ministry, we're going to ask the Lord to speak to you and to us in order to reveal every ungodly soul tie you need to break agreement with today."

So many people were already flashing through her mind that Deborah thought to herself, "This could take all day!"

Lydia added, "This is a good time to exercise your prayer language. If you get stuck and can't think of anymore, pray in the Spirit and see what else the Lord shows you. You'll also want to always include your immediate family members in the list. Remember, you're not breaking off all relationships, just ungodly soul ties. Many times our relationships are actually better after we have broken the ungodly soul ties."

Joyce handed her the prayer and she began, "Lord I renounce and break agreement with every ungodly soul tie with my mother and father, and with Paul, Tim and Mary Rachel." Suddenly Deborah stopped, "What if I can't remember all the names of the men?"

Lydia could feel the cloak of shame trying to come back over Deborah. "God already knows, this is no surprise to Him. Simply say the names that come to your mind and then just say, 'and any other men I was involved with emotionally or sexually'."

She breathed a sigh of relief and continued on, "I break soul ties with Justin, Tommie Lee, Roy, Hootch and the Renegades." She felt sick to her stomach just thinking of all the men who had had a piece of her soul. Tears welled up in her eyes.

Lydia quickly came over and put her hand gently on her shoulder and said, "Just forgive them, Deborah, forgive them all."

Over and over Deborah began to say, "I forgive them, Lord, I forgive all the men, all the men." Suddenly and unexpectedly another level of pain began to flow out of her as she cried out, "Forgive me, Lord, forgive me. Forgive me for all my sin. Restore my soul, restore my heart. I'm so sorry, Lord."

Lydia and Joyce looked at each other and nodded. The Lord was breaking through. This was true heart repentance. It was difficult to watch someone being so broken, so contrite. But it also was part of the path they had traveled down with so many others. It was the path of healing.

As the pain of brokenness and Deborah's sobs began to subside, Lydia said, "Just take your time, its good to get in touch with your pain. That's what this is all about. And don't forget to forgive yourself, too."

It took her a moment, but finally Deborah was able to forgive herself. Then she reached for some tissues and began to wipe her face. A slight smile even broke through as she picked up the prayer and continued breaking soul ties. It felt so good when she finally finished the list and prayed, "Lord, I charge Your angels to retrieve the pieces of my soul and bring them back so I can be whole."

"Good job," Lydia quickly said. "You're really learning to get in touch with what the Holy Spirit is showing you. That's going to help as we move to the next part of this session. Today we're going to ask the Lord to show you other broken or hurt areas that He wants to heal, along with any areas of unforgiveness you might still have towards others. Let's take a short break before we get started. I have to make a phone call so give me at least ten minutes."

Lydia picked up her cell phone and went into the office to make her phone call. Meanwhile, Deborah sat glued to the couch. Joyce asked "What's wrong? You look like you are about to get your teeth drilled without Novocain? Didn't you feel good about what just happened this morning?"

Deborah replied, "It's not that. What happened already was great. I just don't know if I'm ready for what's going to happen next."

Joyce said, "All you have to do is trust the Lord. Hasn't

He been faithful in giving us the grace and wisdom to deal with everything that's come up so far? And He's been very faithful to do so in right timing, don't you agree? I just want to encourage you, don't hold anything back. Sooner or later, God will need to do this work in you so don't take any unnecessary baggage home with you."

Deborah looked into Joyce's soft blue eyes wondering if she already knew the secret that she was about to unfold. They were kind eyes, with a touch of sadness behind them. "I really want everything the Lord has for me. Please pray for me, Joyce. I know what I have to do."

That morning in Ohio, as Anne was out doing her weekly shopping and errands, a sense of urgency came over her with a deep desire to stop by her brother's office. Unsure why but feeling the prompting of the Holy Spirit, Anne directed her car in the opposite direction from the grocery store and headed toward Daniel's office.

As the Worthington Marketing and Advertising sign came into view, she immediately felt a witness of the Holy Spirit all over. "I wonder what's up," she thought to herself as she got out of her van. "Maybe Daniel has a big deal that just needs a little extra prayer." Now that Susan was gone, Daniel no longer had the prayer of agreement with his wife so he would often turn to her for prayer for his children and the business. She had no problem partnering with Daniel in prayer, but God had already been putting it on her heart to pray for a wife for Daniel and a mother for the children, even though she didn't dare tell him that. Anne just had a sense that he needed earnest and fervent prayer to step into marriage again. To her, it was a privilege to pray for the whole family, and Robert was very understanding and supportive. What her brother had gone through with Susan's death had been heartbreaking but she knew that God could heal all things, including his broken heart. All in God's timing, of course!

"Hi, Irene, is my successful, good looking brother in at the moment?" She already knew that Daniel was in because she had seen him through the window in his office sitting at his desk working diligently on one of his projects. He grinned at his sister as he stepped out from behind his desk and walked to the open doorway. "What are you buttering me up for, Sis? Do you and Robert need a babysitter for Friday night?"

"That's not a bad idea," Anne said. "But, actually, to be honest, I don't know why I'm here. I was on my way to the grocery store and just felt like the Holy Spirit wanted me to come by your office. You tell me why I'm here."

He replied "Well, maybe it's about my meeting tomorrow morning with Pastor Harrison. Everything is going well in the business right now. I was concerned about the Sergio deal a few days ago but everything's smoothed out beautifully on that front. Why don't we go in my office and see what the Lord is up to. Hold my calls, Irene. This shouldn't take too long."

As they walked into the office together, Irene thought to herself that working for a boss who was a Christian was one of the best things that had ever happened to her. Now, she too was wondering what the Lord wanted them to pray about. "Whatever it is, Lord, I agree with Anne and Daniel," she said softly to herself.

Anne and Daniel sat down on the "thinking couch" as Daniel called it. Located in the corner of his office, the slightly worn, dark green, suede sofa didn't quite match the otherwise professional office look. Anne remembered Susan trying to get him to toss it when he first moved in to his new building but he had just chuckled and refused, saying that he had gotten some of his best ideas on that couch. As they sat down Anne said, "Let's just pray in the Spirit for a little bit and clear our minds so we can hear what the Lord is speaking to us." They had barely begun to pray when Daniel was surprised to get a picture of Deborah in his mind. It wasn't her as the adult she was now but as an adolescent, perhaps around the age of twelve or thirteen. He continued to pray wondering what Anne was receiving from the Lord. Immediately Anne stopped praying and looked at him, "This is so strange but I'm seeing Deborah. She looks so frightened. I wonder what's happening in Florida.

"Well, maybe I'm not crazy after all," Daniel thought. He then looked at Anne, "I just saw a picture in my mind of Deborah when she was just a young girl. What do you think God is saying, Sis?" he asked.

"Obviously she needs prayer, but I wonder why I had to come here. Maybe there's something really big about to happen and it needs the power of agreement. I could have just called one of the ladies in my Bible study but I really felt led to come here, Daniel. I hope you're not upset with me for interrupting your day."

"Absolutely not! I'm sure the Holy Spirit has a very good reason for bringing you by today. It's the least I can do after all the praying you've done for the kids and me," Daniel replied.

As they continued to pray for Deborah there was a feeling of oppression and heaviness in the air. Together they warred against the demonic fear which they felt was attacking her. Finally, the atmosphere began to change. They were getting the breakthrough. "I'm certain this has something to do with Deborah when she was younger," Daniel said, "I keep seeing her getting on the bus with that empty, hurt look in her eye. I wonder what happened to her that summer." Suddenly he got a sick feeling in the pit of his stomach, "I feel like throwing up. Whatever happened must have been something really bad."

Anne immediately began to pray that the trauma would be revealed and healed. As she did, the nausea he was experiencing began to lift. He prayed, "God give Deborah the grace to face whatever she has to today for her soul to be restored. Help her to not run from Your Presence. Restore her ability to receive the Your love." As he continued to pray, he suddenly he saw her again. This time, however, there were two Deborah's in his vision, both a younger and an older version. He began to describe to Anne what he was seeing, "I see her at the age she is now, but there's a radiant light all around her and a kindness in her eyes. She turns toward the young girl and opens up her arms. The young Deborah begins to run towards her and then the grown up Deborah embraces her and suddenly they become one person. And now I see the Lord's hands reaching down from heaven and putting a new heart into the one person. I believe God is giving her a new heart and reconciling the past for her." He didn't know if he had ever received such a clear picture from the Lord before.

By the time they were done, Anne and Daniel both had tears running down their faces. The presence of God had filled the office. Whatever was happening in Florida, God was pleased with their prayers.

Chapter Twenty-Two

The Secret

ॐ ॐ

After Joyce and Deborah left the counseling room together, Deborah walked next door to get another bottle of water. As she reached for the handle on the refrigerator, there was an inexplicable sense of peace which settled over her entire being. At the same time, she heard a quiet voice inside of her say, "The victory has already been won."

She wasn't sure what it meant but she was beginning to recognize the voice of God and realized that it made her feel better. She thought to herself, "I better be careful who I tell or people will really think I'm going crazy. Now I'm hearing voices and I believe God's talking to me! Well, whoever is praying for me, bless them, Lord." Thoughts of Anne suddenly filled her mind. "Thank you for Anne, her friendship and her prayers. It means so much to me to have someone in my life that hears Your voice and knows how to pray." She was convinced that Anne had once again been faithful to pray for her and that's what helped release the peace she was experiencing. Deborah didn't know how Anne kept up with her family, church activities and all the people she prayed for. It had to be the grace of God. "Bless her today, Lord and her family," she whispered as she closed the refrigerator door.

Deborah walked back into the counseling center right as Lydia was exiting the office. "Perfect timing," Lydia exclaimed, "I just finished up my phone call. It was another minister who needed a little advice and the Lord gave me a word of wisdom for him. I wouldn't have thought of it in a hundred years... God is so cool. He never fails to amaze me. I feel so sorry for Christians who live all their lives without ever tapping into the supernatural power of God!" She had to admit, Lydia's enthusiasm for God and what He could do was contagious. The whole atmosphere at *Restore Your Soul Ministries* was life changing. She wished there was some way she could bottle it up and take it home with her.

Once again, before the thought was out of her mind, Lydia exclaimed, "You know, you're never going to be the same. Now that you've received the Baptism of the Holy Spirit you're going to begin to move in the gifts of the Spirit and experience the supernatural just like we do."

Deborah and Lydia walked back into the counseling room together. Joyce was already sitting in her chair, praying softly in the Spirit. As Lydia sat down, she reached for her Bible. "I would like to share a few more scriptures before we begin," she said. "First of all, we need to understand that forgiveness does not make what someone did right or justified. It simply means we choose to release them into God's hands. We will let Him be the judge, not us. God's Word tells us in Matthew 18:34 that if we don't forgive others like God forgives us, we will be turned over to the tormentors. Some translations use the word jailers. The tormentors or jailers represent demonic oppression," Lydia continued. "You see, unforgiveness is like an umbilical cord. It keeps us connected to our past and it doesn't allow us to move forward into the healing and blessings of the Lord." "Forgiveness, on the other hand, gives us a right to access God's healing virtue. It is like a password that gives us access to the throne room. It is not healing, but it's our first step towards healing."

Lydia then got up and walked to the closet door. "I like to illustrate it like this," she said. "Let's look at the closet door as forgiveness. As we open it, we have access to the closet. Let's say that the healing presence of God is in the closet. Opening the door of forgiveness gives us access into the presence of God for healing. You may swing the door of forgiveness all day long. I forgive my mother, I forgive my mother, I forgive my mother," she repeated as she swung the closet door open and closed again and again. You can forgive and forgive, and yet still wonder why you're not healed."

Joyce interjected, "Once we forgive, it's our responsibility to invite the Lord to bring healing into our lives. For years, I just thought all I had to do was forgive people. I had never even thought of asking Him to really heal me. Once I got a hold of this truth, Jesus became my Healer not just theologically but experientially!"

Lydia added, "That's when scripture is no longer just words on a page but a living reality. So today, you're not only going to forgive, you're going to ask the Lord Jesus to visit you and heal the wounds." Lydia could see that Deborah was listening intently and taking everything she was saying all in. Deborah was very perceptive and it was a joy ministering to her. She was definitely a sponge willing to absorb the water of God's Word and His Spirit.

Then Lydia, reading from Isaiah 61:1, talked about how Jesus came to heal the brokenhearted and from Psalm 23:3 where it says that He restores our souls. "Now let's read all of Psalm 142. It's where David pours out his complaint and trouble before the Lord:

I cry out to the Lord with my voice; with my voice to the Lord I make my supplication. I pour out my complaint before Him; I declare before Him my trouble. When my spirit was overwhelmed within me, then You knew my path. In the way in which I walk, they have secretly set a snare for me. Look on my right hand and see, for there is no one who acknowledges me; refuge has failed me; no one cares for my soul. I cried out to You O Lord: I said, "You are my refuge, my portion in the land of the living. Attend to my cry, for I am brought very low; deliver me from my persecutors, for they are stronger than I. Bring my soul out of prison, that I may praise Your name; the righteous shall surround me, for You shall deal bountifully with me."

As instructed the day before, Deborah had read that very psalm last night before bed. Now, it suddenly came to life! God was telling her it was not only alright but even necessary that she pour out her pain to Him.

Lydia continued in a soft tone, "Today, as the Lord shows you areas of past hurt, it's important that you pour out the hurt to Him. It's like cleansing all the infection and pus out of a natural wound. It can't heal until it's cleaned out. God wants to pull the scab off of your heart and reveal to you its true condition."

Deborah winced at the thought but nodded her head in understanding and agreement.

Noting the nonverbal communication, Lydia went on, "Once the wound is identified and the pain is poured out, the next step is to forgive those who created it in the first place. You'll have to forgive others and then at times yourself and sometimes even God. Even though we're not in the position to actually forgive God, sometimes we have to release the anger, hurt and pain we've held in our heart towards Him."

Suddenly Deborah saw herself lying in bed as a young girl praying, "Make it stop! Make it stop!" Tears filled her eyes; she knew that was the point when she began to harden her heart against God. "It hadn't stopped, not then. Not until I took it into my own hands," she thought. A wave of unbelief began to swell over her and pull her under once again. Sensing something was awry both Lydia and Joyce began to pray in tongues simultaneously.   Rather than overtaking her, the wave diminished. Deborah took a deep breath and also began to pray softly in her new found prayer language. She felt calmness surround her again.

Lydia continued, "After you've forgiven everyone, then we're going to ask the Lord to come into the memory and minister to you. Sometimes He'll speak to you or show you something. Other times, you may just feel His presence as peace, joy, comfort or whatever else He might bring to you."

Joyce interjected, "Once the Lord touches you with His healing, that memory will never be the same and you'll never have the same pain or trauma associated with it."

Lydia added, "This session is different for everyone. We just allow the Holy Spirit to totally lead us. We have no specific prayers to help assist you like the past couple of days. Our job is to be your intercessors. Sometimes we may have a word of knowledge about what the Lord wants to heal. When we do, we'll share it with you and ask you what it might mean to you."

Joyce added, "I just feel we need to bind up all shame and emotional control. It's so important that you let yourself feel in this session." She prayed aloud, "Lord, I take authority over all shame, fear and control that would try to block or hinder Deborah in this session."

"Are you ready to begin?" Lydia asked gently.

Deborah took a deep breath and said, "I already know where God wants to begin. He showed me yesterday in a dream. I'm not sure how to start. This is something I've never told anyone." Her voice began to crack.

They knew this was the moment they had both been waiting for all week. Everything else, as important as it was, had been a preparation for Deborah to be able to share what she was about to share. Neither woman knew what it was exactly. What they did know was that the Holy Spirit had shown them that something had devastated the woman's soul as a child, something that, up to now, she had been unwilling to share with them.

They sat quietly, virtually holding their breath as they waited for her to continue. "I haven't told you everything. I just wasn't ready. I'm really sorry," she said while trying to evaluate their response. She sure didn't want them upset with her, not at this point.

Lydia immediately reassured her, "That's okay, Deborah. It usually takes a few days before people begin to trust us and the Spirit of God in us. I want to remind you that anything you share with us will be kept in strict confidence."

"It started the summer between sixth and seventh grade," Deborah plunged in, "It started with him touching me." Lydia and Joyce instinctively knew she was referring to her father. This wasn't the first time they had heard stories of incest and sexual abuse. Immediately, all of Deborah's life made sense: the promiscuity, the unworthiness, the addictions and bulimia–all were rooted in the story they were about to hear.

"Are you talking about your father?" Joyce asked carefully.

Deborah nodded, "He would come into my room and talk to me about how I was developing. He wanted to see and then he touched me. We were all so scared of him. I didn't know how to say 'no'. I know it sounds stupid now, but then I didn't really even know if it was wrong or not. It felt wrong, but it was my father, the one who was always telling us right from wrong."

They simply nodded in understanding.

"I would just lay there frozen. I never said a word. I would just close my eyes and hope he'd go away. Sometimes it would happen so fast, I would think maybe it was just a dream. I've always felt like it was all my fault. I just laid there. I should have done something to make him stop." Even as the words were coming from her mouth, Deborah realized that she had never been able to say "no" to any man. No matter how they had abused her or used her, she always felt as helpless as she had when her father had started touching her.

"When I started school that fall, he stopped. I was so relieved. It was like it was all a bad dream. But then I got busy in school and just tried to forget about what had happened. I began to have trouble falling asleep and I never relaxed when I knew my father was in the house. I was always on guard. I started staying away from home as much as possible. I'd find any excuse not to come home."

Lydia said, "Did the abuse just stop then?"

A scream deep from within came rising to the surface; it almost slipped out of Deborah before she could swallow it back down. She looked at Lydia and sadly shook her head from side to side.

"It started again the next summer. But this time it was different; he said I was thirteen. According to the Bible, I was a woman now. He said it was his job to teach me the things a woman needed to know." Suddenly, the thirteen-year-old trapped in the trauma emerged as she began reliving the whole experience. It literally felt like she was back in her bedroom at the Noble family home. Deborah remembered now so clearly her father sitting on the edge of her bed saying, "Your mother is not doing her job as a wife and it's not fair to me. I feel like I'm being forced to sin with other women like my father did and I'll never do what he did. It's up to you to help me." Deborah was no longer looking at Lydia and Joyce. Her eyes were focused off in the distance, as if watching a movie that only she could see.

"I've tried so hard to forget, but yesterday all the memories came back." Deborah began to whimper like a little wounded girl. "It hurt, it hurt so bad. I wanted him to stop. He kept saying I was a woman now; and that God gave women to serve men, and that one day I'd thank him. I was going to help him and he was going to help me."

The counselors looked at each other and just shook their heads. No wonder she had been running from God. It was a miracle she was there at all. Deborah continued "I couldn't breathe. I thought he was going to crush me. I wanted to scream but I couldn't. Nothing would come out of my mouth." Deborah's eyes filled with panic. "The first time it happened, I had blood between my legs and I couldn't tell anyone. I didn't know what had happened; I was so afraid I was going to die." She began to sob into the pillow that she was clutching tightly in her hands.

"I was so confused. I honestly didn't know what had just taken place. I had actually just lost my virginity and I didn't even know it." She sobbed louder. "I felt so dirty and so bad. I finally got up and took a shower, and another one, and another, and another. I just wanted to wash it all away," her voice trailed off into a near whisper.

Lydia asked gently, "Did it happen just that once?"

She shook her head. "No, it continued throughout the summer. I could hardly wait until school started. I was hoping it would stop again but it didn't. It would happen at least once a week, sometimes more if my mother was out of the house a lot. It was so awful. I never knew if it was going to happen at night or in the morning. That was when I really began to have trouble sleeping."

She choked, "Sometimes it would happen before I went to school, and I wouldn't have time to shower. I felt like everyone who looked at me knew. I couldn't concentrate in class. I started skipping school and pretending I was sick so I didn't have to go." All of a sudden she exclaimed in anger, "That son of a bitch used me until I was sixteen years old!" Quickly, she caught herself. "Oh, I'm sorry for swearing; it just slipped out."

Actually the women were relieved to see some anger. Up until then, Deborah hadn't demonstrated any. They knew it had been repressed and she would have to get in touch with it in order to truly be healed.

"Once I started my periods, my father had me go to the doctor and tell them I had a lot of pain and that my cycle was irregular. It wasn't even true, but they immediately put me on birth control pills. He knew what was going to happen before I went. He was constantly asking me if I was still taking my pills."

"I can't tell you what it was like to have to go sit in church and watch my father pray and worship knowing that sometime during the next week, he would be forcing himself on me. I started realizing how wrong it was as I got older and older. I don't know who I hated more, him or myself for allowing it to continue. I just figured God couldn't be real or He would have sent a lightning bolt one Sunday morning while my father was sitting so piously in his pew."

Then out of nowhere Deborah burst out in exasperation, "Was my mother blind? Couldn't she see what was happening? Did she just not care as long as he wasn't bothering her?" She went on, "I finally confronted him the summer I turned sixteen. The summer before that, I had actually tried to use the Bible to make him stop; I showed him in Leviticus where it talks about sexual sins with family members. He just said that was Old Testament and we were living under grace. God had given him a beautiful daughter so that he would not have to disgrace the family the way his father had. God understood his needs and it was really my mother's fault for not taking care of him. She was the one who needed to repent."

"No wonder Deborah had been so angry at her mother and women in general," Lydia thought. "It was just like the enemy to take the truth of God's word and twist it. Yes, we're living under a dispensation of grace, but it doesn't give us license to sin." Nothing made her angrier than religious spirits, and it was obvious Theodore Noble had been controlled by a big one. How else could he have sat in church with the daughter that he was molesting?"

Deborah went on, "Finally I made a decision in my heart to kill him rather than be raped one more time. I don't know what your opinion is but I think anytime a woman feels forced to have sex, it's a form of rape. She looked intently at Lydia and

Joyce, looking for affirmation.

They both nodded in agreement.

"I finally went to a store where they sold hunting supplies and bought a knife, a large knife. I told the clerk I needed a knife that could gut a deer. I told him it was a birthday present for my father. I said that he was a hunter. That night when he entered my room, I reached under my pillow and pulled out the knife. I told him that if he ever touched me again I would use it on him. I thought there might be a fight, but there wasn't."

"What did he do?" Joyce questioned quietly.

"I couldn't believe it," Deborah answered, "He walked out of my room and never touched me again. From that day on, he acted as if it had never happened. I was so relieved but I was still so mad at myself. Why hadn't I put a stop to it sooner?"

Lydia gently explained, "It's very common for sexual abuse victims to blame themselves. You were the child, Deborah. Your father controlled you and your whole family through intimidation and abuse. You saw what he had done to Paul. It's totally understandable that you felt helpless to put a stop to it."

Joyce added, "Actually, some women are so helpless, the sexual abuse can continue into their adulthood, sometimes even after they're married."

Deborah looked surprise, "You mean I'm not the only one who felt it was impossible to make it stop?"

Lydia said, "Actually, sexual abuse breaks down your ability to set boundaries; it takes away your ability to say 'no.' Just so you know, sometimes sexual abuse and incest victims often feel like they're the only ones. In fact, this is something that happens all too often in our society. Many of the women who come here for healing have suffered from some form of sexual abuse or damage, and so have many of the men."

It would not surprise me at all if your father had been sexually abused, also. Looking at his physical abuse of Paul, and his sexual abuse of you, it's a very good possibility," Joyce said.

Still Deborah felt like crying. At least the nausea had subsided; she had felt like throwing up earlier but now all she felt was a tremendous sense of relief after finally sharing her secret. She was a little astounded that they were sitting so calmly talking about it. Deborah didn't know what she thought would happen when she finally told them the truth. She checked Lydia and Joyce's eyes for any sign of disgust; instead all she found was compassion.

Chapter Twenty-Three

The Healing Balm

ॐ ॐ

"Deborah, we're so proud of you for being able to share with us today-we understand how difficult it had to be for you. Remember how I shared earlier that we help clean out the wound when we pour out our pain and trouble to the Lord?" Lydia asked gently. "Now, I need you just to talk it out to the Lord."

Joyce added, "Just share from your heart. Let Him know how you felt as a young girl when all that was happening. Our job is to pray for you as you talk it out to the Lord." Even though she had shared her story, Deborah still had a very real fear of losing total control if she really got in touch with the pain. Her eyes were filled with apprehension as she looked at them.

Lydia said, "We know it's scary, but it's the only way, Deborah. This pain has been inside of you all these years and nothing you've done has ever been able to make it go away. It's time to give it to the Lord."

"I know sometimes it feels like if you start to let out your feelings the pain or anger will never stop. But, there will be a bottom to your pain. We promise," Joyce interjected. Deborah was trying to trust them but was torn with the desire to just run out of the room, rather than face what was being required of her. Lydia and Joyce both immediately began to pray simultaneously in the Holy Spirit in soft voices.

Deborah said, "I don't know where or how to begin."

"Just try to put yourself back into that memory and get in touch with what that young girl was feeling and thinking," Lydia replied.

Deborah closed her eyes and then slowly began, "Lord, the first thing I felt was dread. I dreaded going to bed. I dreaded the bedroom door opening. I dreaded seeing my father. I began to even hate the smell of him."

"That's good," Lydia said, "just continue talking it out."

Tears began to slowly run down Deborah's tanned face. "I felt like I was living in a bad movie that just wouldn't stop. In the beginning, I would wake up and just tell myself it was a bad dream. But after awhile, only the drugs and alcohol would make the pain go away. Even then it would never totally go away. I felt so naked, so exposed. It felt like everyone who saw me 'knew.' I hated getting on the school bus and sitting in class. I used to love school and learning but after awhile I just hated even being around people." Her eyes were still closed as she continued, "I wanted to run as far away as I could from what happened. I felt so ashamed and dirty. I would want to just stand up in church and scream, 'Can't you people see, are you blind?' At first, I would go to church and pray believing that, somehow, God or someone would make him stop. Then I just got mad at God and gave up. God, I was so angry with you!"

Deborah suddenly opened her eyes, now full of anger, and exploded, "So just where was this God of yours who is supposed to love me and protect me? Why didn't He stop my father? Why didn't He take care of me?"

Lydia and Joyce had both been through this more times than they could count. People who had been abused as children often wrestled with questions like, "Where was God and why didn't He stop the abuse?" These questions always masked the real accusation: God must not love me or He would have stopped the abuse. Lydia spoke softly, "Deborah, God ordained children to be loved and protected by their families. When families choose to sin, their sin damages their children. Originally, God ordained your life and knew you before the foundation of the earth. That means your life was chosen before sin entered the earth. He created families in the beginning to be a source of His divine love, protection and provision. It was man's choice to sin and let the evil into the earth that set you up for abuse."

"Generational sin opens the door for the Enemy to have legal ground to kill, steal and even destroy your life until that sin is repented of and taken to the cross of Jesus Christ," Joyce said. "I really wrestled with feeling bitter about the family I had been born into, also. Once I realized it was sin and the Devil that had perverted my family and caused my pain, and not God, I was able to direct my anger in the right direction. That's why I enjoy spiritual warfare so much now."

Lydia continued to share, "God loves you, and we can trust that He was looking for someone, anyone, who could help you. Many people live their lives so far from God's ability to speak to them or direct them that they are unable to help others in trouble. When God isn't able to find someone He can work through to rescue or stop the abuse, then He protects our spirits until we find our way back to Him. The problem is that, because we're angry with God, the journey takes a lot longer than it should. Do you know that God has been waiting and longing to comfort you and minister to you ever since it first happened?"

Deborah could feel a sense of calm spreading through her as she began to come into agreement with the truth, "Yes, God does love me. After all, He led me here didn't He?" she thought.

"It's normal for you to be upset with the Lord," Joyce added. "A child doesn't understand how God works in the earth. She only knows that God is big and powerful, and she wants Him to rescue her just like superheroes do on television. It's okay to express your anger with the Lord. We've never ministered to an abuse victim yet who wasn't angry," Joyce said.

"There are actually five areas of forgiveness related to abuse," Lydia said. "First, the victim has to forgive the perpetrator. Then, they have to forgive the people who should have protected them and didn't. Next, they have to forgive God, themselves, and finally anyone else who re-victimized them. Sometimes it takes a while to work through the list. Occasionally, it works in a slightly different order, but for true healing to happen each area of forgiveness needs to be touched at some point. But let's continue sharing with the Lord how you felt."

"I hated my father!" Deborah exclaimed. "I knew it was wrong, and I hated him for it; but eventually I grew to hate my mother, too. I hated her for being so stupid, so not there, so blank!"

"You actually hated their sin," Joyce said carefully and softly. "It was what your father did and what your mother didn't do that you hated. They sinned against you. You hated their sin." Joyce reiterated.

Once again, she nodded her head as she was receiving the truth. "Yes, I hated the sin. And now I realize it was okay to hate that. The Word says I can hate evil. Their sin was evil. I was just too young to know the difference." Suddenly the guilt that she had carried for years of being a bad daughter began to lift. Another heavy burden was literally being taken from her, a burden she had carried since she was thirteen years old.

"I never wanted to hate them. I always felt so terrible for hating my mother and father, but now I can see it differently. If my mother's sin of passivity had not been there, and my father's sexual sins and religious bondage had not been there, I would have loved them. I guess I really always did love them, that's why it hurt so much." Now, the little girl's pain came bubbling to the surface too quickly for Deborah to swallow it back down. She began to cry out, "I did love you, Daddy. You were so strong and handsome and I thought you could do anything and knew everything. I miss you, Daddy. It was as if you died when I was thirteen and I was on my own. I did love you and I'm so sorry for everything. You were just as tormented then as I've been since. I just know that someone hurt you, too. You were confused. I forgive you, Daddy. I forgive you." She could hardly believe the words and feelings that were coming out of her. After all this time the bitterness, anger, hate and hardness had all melted down and at the bottom of it all was a little girl who simply loved and needed her father.

Lydia and Joyce continued to sit quietly while they prayed softly. They did not want any demonic activity to rob this precious moment. Not only was Deborah's heart being reconciled back to her Heavenly Father, but it was also being reconciled back to her earthly father. They had seen it so often how, despite all of the abuse, people still had a desire and need to be able to forgive and love their parents. Patiently, the counselors waited until the sobbing quietly subsided. Lydia finally said, "Now that you've shared your pain with the Lord and you've forgiven your mother and father, let's ask Jesus to reveal Himself as your Healer in that memory."

Joyce added, "Sometimes it's difficult to allow Jesus to come to those painful memories because we feel so ashamed about what happened, but He already knows. He was there, now you need to allow Him to reveal Himself to you."

Lydia said, "Once Jesus truly comes into a memory, it can never be the same. The Word says that He is the Alpha and Omega, the beginning and the end. We're bound in time, but He is not. Just ask Him to bring His healing and truth into the painful memories of your father abusing you. The Enemy has lied to you all of your life and told you it was your fault, that no one would love you if they knew. The Lord wants to bring truth and healing to you today."

She winced at the thought. "It's too hard to imagine seeing Jesus in my bedroom while my father is molesting me. I don't think I can do that!" she exclaimed.

Lydia said, "You can't do this with your own mind. This has to be done by prophetic anointing. It's not about your ability to imagine or create something on your own."

Taking a deep breath Deborah finally prayed, "Jesus, I need you to heal the pain of what my father did to me. I need you to speak truth to me." As she closed her eyes, she saw herself lying in her bed the morning her father first penetrated her body and her soul. She looked so young, so innocent, and so afraid. She wanted to run from the scene that was playing out in her mind, but she knew she had to face it. "Jesus, help me," she said softly.

Immediately, Deborah saw the Lord standing in the corner of her room with tears slowly slipping down His face. In the picture, she turned her face toward His and their eyes locked. "I will never leave you nor forsake you. We'll get through this, you and I, together." The words were spoken directly into her mind from His mind.

The next scene was her father walking out of the room after he was done with her. She lay shaken and bleeding in the bed. The Lord quickly moved to her bedside, gathered her in His arms, and rocked her gently as He told her that this was not her fault.

As He rocked her and spoke to her in His soothing voice, the fear and shame began to vanish. "Jesus knows; He still loves me and now He's letting me know that He does not want this to ruin my life. If I'll just give it to Him, He'll take care of everything." The truth began to penetrate her heart. In the picture in her mind, Deborah began to sob heavily in the arms of the Lord, just as she had sobbed earlier in the counseling room.

As He comforted her, the terrible aloneness she had felt most of her life started to leave. It was the feeling that there was no one she could talk to, no one to care, no one to comfort her and no one to tell her what she should do next. She remembered lying in bed at night as a child gripped by the fear and panic that she was on her own. There was no one to take care of her! The verse from Psalm 142 came to mind, "Refuge has failed me, no one cares for my soul," Deborah realized, "Jesus did care. He had cared all along. The Devil lied to me; he told me that God didn't love me and that He wasn't there for me, but He was." It was too difficult to explain or to put into words but the loving presence of Jesus was changing everything. Rather than feeling abandoned Deborah felt comforted. Rather than feeling hopeless, she felt hope in her heart. Rather than feeling bitter and angry, she felt the peace of forgiveness. "Yes, my father robbed me of my innocence and the incest stole many years from my life, but now I know the Lord will redeem everything. I'm not going to let what happened rob anymore of my life," she declared out loud.

Then Deborah began to share with them everything that she had seen and heard as the Lord ministered to her. They sat and listened, but the main thing they cared about was that Deborah had been touched by God. And that had been apparent; they had seen the glory of the Lord on her face as He was ministering to her.

As Deborah finished recounting what had transpired between her and the Lord, Lydia said, "That's wonderful! Your countenance is totally changed. I don't want to rush you. Do you feel ready to go on?"

She nodded. Slowly that afternoon, step by step, the women helped her walk through a lifetime of pain. As the Holy Spirit brought up memory after memory, the ministers allowed Deborah to pour out her troubled heart to the Lord. The Lord continued to reveal Himself as her Healer time and time again over the next few hours.

To Deborah, Lydia and Joyce had somehow faded into the fabric of the room as she had continued to get in touch with the pain of the past. She knew the counselors were there, but they were held in the distance as the memories and the presence of the Lord surrounded her. After her father, the men in her life lined up as if in a parade. One after another, she forgave them; Justin, Tommie Lee, Roy, Hootch, the Renegades, Moses, every man who had every used or abused her.

It was hard to describe the love that surrounded her as she

moved through the memories. As the Lord's unconditional love penetrated her shame and pain, it felt as if a hand had reached through the dirty mire of her heart and wiped it clean and made it whole. She could feel God's grace enabling her to forgive people whom she had vowed she would never forgive or forget what they had done to her. Much of the anger and hurt with her mother had already been dealt with on Tuesday when she worked through the generational sins, but the Holy Spirit continued bringing to the surface more of the pain related to Deborah's mother and her brothers and sister. For someone who had tried to sell herself for years on the notion that she really didn't care about the things that had happened to her, Deborah realized that she had cared; she had cared deeply. Those things had mattered, and because they did, she had to continually harden her heart in order to survive.

Her memories of sexual abuse by her father had been a dam that had held back a river of other emotions. Now, the river was unleashed and it continued to flow for several more hours. Initially, the memories came fast and furious, but then they slowed until finally she stopped and said, "I'm not getting anything else."

Lydia said, "Let's take another minute or two and be quiet before the Lord. We don't want to miss anything else that He may want to do." She nodded in agreement. Even though Deborah's eyes were swollen, and she had used nearly a half a box of tissues, releasing all the pent up emotions was feeling too good to stop. She prayed softly in the Spirit with them.

Joyce said quietly, "I'm just getting one more person that you need to forgive."

She looked surprised and thought to herself, "Could there possible be anyone else?"

Lydia nodded her head in agreement as Joyce said, "Deborah, you've forgiven everyone but yourself." At that moment a wave of pain and shame came out of nowhere and caught Deborah off guard. She put her head in her hands. The only way to describe the pain was gut wrenching.

"I can't, I just can't," the words were out of her mouth before she knew it. "I've been so stupid and I've done so many bad things. I just can't."

Lydia said firmly, "But, you have to. Jesus has forgiven you and you've forgiven everyone else. If He gave you the grace to forgive all of those people, surely He can give you the grace to forgive yourself."

Deborah swallowed hard, choking back the tears. "Jesus, I can't do this without your grace, help me! Please help me!" No sooner were the words out of her mouth when she saw herself as a child, a young girl, a teenager and a young woman. The four Deborah's looked back at her, each with a sadness that penetrated her heart. "How can I not forgive them? They hadn't known anything different." Tears slowly found their way down both cheeks as she studied the images in her mind.

Slowly, and quite deliberately Deborah claimed, "I forgive myself. I forgive myself. I forgive myself. I forgive myself." As she did, each of the Deborah's gave her a shy, little smile. They moved the tips of their fingers slightly to wave goodbye as each one melted into the next; the child into the young girl, the young girl into the teenager, and finally, the teenager into the young woman.

The young woman, who looked like Deborah in her twenties, then opened up her arms. As she did, Deborah saw herself as she was today, stepping out of the shadows to embrace the young woman. She too melted into the adult Deborah during the embrace.

In her spirit, Deborah felt herself tap into a pool of deep, calm, pure water. This was not just a surface peace, but a peace deeper than she had ever felt in her entire life; it filled her soul beyond measure. She was whole again, no longer fragmented by the dissociation that helped her deny the pain of the past. She felt put back together again, and it was wonderful.

Lydia and Joyce watched the miracle with joy. Even

though they didn't know exactly what was happening, they could tell by the anointing that filled the room that it was something incredible and special. Suddenly the sound of laughter began to fill the room as the joy of the Lord came bubbling up from the depth of Deborah's spirit, "I'm going to be alright. I really am healed. God really does love me! I don't have to be scared anymore. I can't believe this. I have never felt so good in all my life!"

Laughter began to overtake Lydia and Joyce as they shared in her joy. "God is so good!" No matter how many times they had experienced the Lord healing someone; it was still a joyous miracle when it happened again. It was like being at the birth of a baby, where each time, you're still captured by the awe of God's creation. No matter how many newborn babies you saw, birth was a glorious sight and so was watching the Lord bring healing to a broken spirit.

"Now, I know I'm done," Deborah said. "There really is a bottom. Actually, I thought I was just one of those bottomless pits-just a black hole of pain. But I was wrong and I'm so glad!" Her radiant smile filled the room and despite the make-up that had run off, she looked beautiful. It was amazing how pain and bitterness could distort people from the inside out.

Lydia said, "You look so beautiful." For the first time in her life, Deborah was able to receive the compliment and believe it.

"Thank you. I feel beautiful! What an incredible feeling. I can't explain everything right now, but the best way to describe it is that I just want to live. I want to enjoy my life and all the people God has put in it." A saying, which she had always thought was so corny, popped into her mind: "Today is the first day of the rest of your life." Now she understood exactly what the saying meant and why it was so special. She just knew that the person who had coined the phrase must have had an experience with God just like she had experienced today. "Today is the first day of the rest of my life," she said the phrase out loud and laughed. "Now I know what it means!"

The women smiled with her. Joyce said, "We're so proud of you. You did an excellent job today in allowing the Holy Spirit to lead you. It took a great deal of courage to face some of the things you had to face today."

Lydia added, "You really have a strong prophetic anointing and your ability to communicate and receive from the Lord is very keen. I want to encourage you to develop your gifting; I believe God wants to use it to bring healing to others, even as He used it to heal you today."

Deborah's green eyes were like crystal clear pools as she looked deep into Lydia's eyes. Just as deep calls unto deep, Lydia's exhortation to embrace her prophetic call rang true in her spirit. Something rose up in Deborah as the giftings inside of her cried out, and with it came a hunger to know everything there was to know about God and the purposes for which she had been created.

Lydia's words acted like a spark, lighting a flame of fire in the depth of her being. Scripture Deborah had heard years ago came to mind: "My ministers are as flames of fire." Then a quick picture followed on the heels of the scripture. She saw herself again, but his time she was much older. She was standing in a pulpit before a large group of people. The picture left as quickly as it had come; she squinted just a bit trying to hold onto it, but it was gone.

Lydia said, "What did the Lord just show you?" Deborah described the picture to her. "I believe the Lord is showing you that one day you'll preach His Word," Lydia responded.

Deborah nodded slowly as Lydia confirmed what she already knew deep inside. The thought was a bit overwhelming. God sure didn't waste any time; one minute she was a mixed up mess and then right after she felt whole and healed for a moment. God was showing her how He was going to use her in the future. "Are you sure it's not just my imagination?" she asked, still questioning what she had just seen.

"I don't think so," Lydia chuckled as she answered. "But don't worry; God always confirms His call. If He wants you to minister for Him, He'll make it absolutely clear. Let's take a moment to pray and seal all the healing the Lord has done for you today," Lydia said as she and Joyce stood up. After three and a half hours of sitting and barely moving, it felt good to stand and stretch.

Joyce began, "Heavenly Father, we thank you so much for all of the healing that you poured into Deborah today. We seal it by the Blood of Jesus. Holy Spirit, we ask You to take care of anything left in its time. We pray that Your prophetic healing anointing would dwell richly within her."

Lydia had one hand on Deborah's forehead and another on her shoulder, "Lord, you have healed this special one. Now, I pray you use her for Your glory. Make her a flame of fire and do not let her flame go out." Deborah couldn't believe her ears, it was the same scripture that had just come to mind moments earlier. She had shared the picture with Lydia but not the Scripture. She was amazed by how sensitive the counselors were to the Spirit of God. It could be almost scary if she didn't know the source was truly the Lord.

When Deborah stood to her feet after the prayer, she felt as if she might just float away; the heaviness was gone. Instinctively she reached out to hug both of her counselors asking, "How can I ever thank you? I could never have done this without you!" It occurred to her in that moment-this was the first time she had reached out to anyone since she had been a child and had hugged her Grandma Ellen. Just the fact that she had initiated the advance was a miracle and a real victory.

"All we did was pray," Lydia said. "It's the Lord who did the work. Just seeing the radiance on your face is reward enough."

Joyce nodded in agreement as Deborah reached the door. "Don't forget. Tomorrow is the day we do deliverance. If the Enemy tries to harass you tonight, simply bind him in the name of Jesus and plead the Blood of Jesus over yourself. Get a good night's rest." Deborah had almost forgotten that there was more. "Well, if it's anything like the last four days I'm ready. Even though it's been a little scary facing the unknown, each day has been special in its own right," she thought to herself. Deborah assured them, as she went out the door, "I'm ready. I'll see you two in the morning at ten. I can hardly wait to see what the Lord is going to do next."

Lydia and Joyce smiled to themselves as they watched her skip, dance and glide down the sidewalk to the house next door. Lydia asked, "Can you get the paperwork done for tomorrow's session?"

Joyce shook her head in agreement, "Sure, is there anything else I can do for you?"

Lydia replied, "No, that should do it. I'm going to grab a quick sandwich and then I have two more appointments this afternoon. I'll see you tomorrow morning. I think I'll fast. There's a lot of occult in Deborah's background and even though things went real well today, I don't want to take any chances or give the Enemy any opportunity."

Joyce agreed, "I'll fast with you and I'll be praying for your afternoon. I know it's going to be a long day for you."

"Thanks. Right now I'm just blessed by the goodness of God but I'm sure, by the end of the day, I'll be glad you're praying. I have a family that I've never met with before coming in for an evaluation. I have a feeling it's going to be a little messy," Lydia shared as they both headed out the door themselves.

What neither of them could see as they walked to their cars was a great cloud of witnesses rejoicing in the heavens. Nor could they hear the command, "Angels, go forth and prepare for battle. My daughters will need you tomorrow." The voice of the Lord was uttered and the heavens shook as the warring angels were dispatched to earth.

Chapter Twenty-Four

The Fifth Day

ટ્ય∾ ∾ટ્ટ

Deborah was up before the alarm. She had fallen asleep early and had slept a solid nine hours. As wonderful as yesterday had been, she had felt pretty drained by bedtime. But this morning was different. "Can I really still be alive and feeling this great?" she hummed as she made the bed. It was the song that had been playing in the front room the day she had arrived, *"Amazing love, how can it be, that You my King would die for me?"*

She continued to get ready while reflecting on the day before. "How can I ever possibly put into words what happened?" She wanted to be able to tell Anne everything when she got back to Deerfield. Yesterday, she had been too worn out to journal, but this afternoon she would try to write down the events of yesterday so that nothing would be forgotten. Following yesterday's session, Deborah had driven down to one of the little hole-in-the-wall seafood places right where the inter-coastal river and the ocean met. It was an odd time of day, between lunch and supper, so there was only one other customer. She had decided to eat out on the deck, intending to enjoy the water and sunshine as much as she could before returning to Ohio. She was surprised that she had an appetite after what had just taken place.

The service at the restaurant was slow and laid-back, but today Deborah didn't mind. There was nothing on earth that could bother her, not when she felt so good inside. When the food finally did arrive, the fish was fresh and delicious. She took her time eating, savoring both the food and the fresh salt air. It turned out to be such a pleasant afternoon and evening.

After returning to the house, Deborah finished up her homework and ran into Maureen. They spent some time talking and sharing, and she had learned that before becoming a part of the ministry team, Maureen had been through her share of problems, too. As the two women sat in the study, sharing conversation over a cup of coffee and some chocolate chip cookies that Maureen had baked earlier, Maureen began to share her own story of how she had arrived at *Restore Your Soul Ministry*.

"I was consumed by my career and drove myself into a nervous breakdown by the age of 39," she told Deborah. "I'm 43 now. I actually ended up in a mental ward for six months and then lived with an aunt for six more months. Fortunately for me, Aunt Mary was a Christian and eventually led me to the Lord. It was through her that I actually ended up finding this place. Here, I discovered I wasn't crazy at all-I just had been driven all my life and had totally missed all the indicators that I was suffering from burn-out. I was an attorney and practiced business law."

Deborah couldn't help it, she almost spit out her coffee as she laughed at the thought. "I'm so sorry; I'm not laughing at you. It's just that you seem so domestic. I would have never thought..." She broke off her sentence, knowing that anything else she said could only make her reaction worse, possibly even offensive.

Maureen chuckled at her response. "Amazing isn't it? Now, I'm happy for the first time in my life. I went through the ministry and spent a week here just like you. A month later, Lydia called me to tell me that they had an opening for a hostess and caretaker for *His House*. I couldn't believe my ears. At first, I was sure she had to be crazy. But my aunt and I prayed and we both felt it was my next step."

"But you're perfect for the job," Deborah exclaimed.

Maureen replied, "Getting perfected *in* the job would be more like it. The transition was really difficult; I was not used to serving others. Before I had the breakdown, I had a full-time office staff that served me, and my own housekeeper. Then I found myself in this place, making beds, making cookies and wondering how I had got here."

"That had to have been challenging," Deborah replied, her face still expressing some of her shock.

"It wasn't easy, but I discovered the Lord's grace is sufficient for every occasion. When I first started, each day seemed like an eternity. Eventually, I found myself enjoying the guests. And then, I found myself praying for them, interceding for their ministry times. I also got involved with the church. The days kept slipping by until now its three years later."

"How long do you plan on staying?" Deborah asked.

"As long as the Lord wants me to be here-I'm in no hurry. I believe I'm ready for whatever He has for me. During the past three years I've had a lot of physical and emotional healing; I hadn't realized the wear and tear my lifestyle had put on my soul and my body. I lived on caffeine and cigarettes for years."

Again, the picture caught Deborah off guard, "Saint Maureen, who would have guessed?" she thought to herself. "It's still so hard to picture," Deborah said shaking her head. "You seem like you've always been here; patient, loving and gracious. You're like part of the house. I can't imagine it without you."

"Thank you, Deborah. I'll take that as a compliment. No, I'm not the same woman I was and I'm thankful for it. I do believe one day I will practice law again but a different kind of law, and at a much different pace. Still I will always cherish these years."

"What kind of law do you want to practice?" Deborah asked. "My grandfather was a judge. Actually, I've always found myself on the wrong side of the law."

"I believe the Lord has been speaking to me about going into child advocacy law. Someone has to defend the children. I would be defending those who are unable to defend themselves." Maureen paused a moment. Deborah thought she saw a tear in her eye as she continued on. "It's funny, I was too busy for a marriage and children of my own, but now the Lord wants me to dedicate my life to helping children. He sure does use the foolish things. Next fall, I'm going to be taking some classes part-time to brush up on that area of law. I'll be here for at least another year."

"This place is like no other place," Deborah thought as she got ready for bed that evening. She was still amazed at her conversation with Maureen. "No one is who they seem to be around here, are they? It's just like in the Bible days. Simon, the one who denied the Lord, became Peter the Rock. Saul, the murderer, became Paul the Apostle. David, the overlooked shepherd boy, became a king. There's no telling what God will do if I just give Him the chance." She drifted off to sleep thinking of the possibilities.

Before she knew it Deborah's alarm was ringing and her morning thoughts picked up right where she had left them last night. As she showered and got ready for today's session, she wondered who she would be after God got through with her. She smiled again as she tried to picture Maureen as a hard driving attorney living on caffeine and cigarettes. "What a transformation!" she thought to herself.

Lydia and Joyce both arrived at *His House* a few minutes early. Unbeknownst to each other, they each had decided to take the few extra minutes they had due to fasting breakfast and decided to get there a little early to pray.

Lydia called out, "Good morning! Looks like the Holy Spirit has a plan."

As Joyce locked her car she replied, "It sure feels like it! I felt prompted to get here a little early to pray." They both walked into the house together, praying in the Spirit as they went. Together they spent the next ten minutes interceding earnestly for the morning's session. As they prayed, another meeting was just getting under way.

Pastor Harrison's secretary, Sophia, escorted Daniel and Anne into his office. "Pastor will be with you in just a few minutes. He was at the hospital this morning and is running a few minutes late." Anne was relieved because it gave her and Daniel an opportunity to talk. They had driven separate cars this morning. "I hope we're doing the right thing," she said.

Daniel smiled at his sister, who could be so confident when she heard from the Lord, but so insecure when she was in the flesh. "Yes, Anne, it's the right thing. You know the Lord showed you that we needed to meet with Pastor Harrison. Don't start back pedaling on me now!"

"I don't have any sense of where we should begin," Anne said. "Even though Andrea makes me so angry on the one hand, on the other hand, I still feel sorry for her."

"I do, too, but we have to be honest with Pastor Harrison and tell him everything," Daniel said as the door to the office opened again.

Pastor Harrison came in, quickly apologizing for being a few minutes late.

Daniel reassured him without hesitation, "That's no problem at all. We're grateful you were able to meet with us on such short notice."

"Let's pray before we begin," the pastor said as he bowed his head and prayed for God's wisdom and insight. Anne and Daniel bowed their heads also and both gave a hearty "Amen" as the pastor concluded.

"Let's cut right to the chase," Pastor Harrison began.

"It's about Andrea Kline, isn't it?" Daniel and Anne nodded in unison, though they were both caught off guard at how quickly he had gotten to the point.

"I don't think she's ready for marriage, yet," the pastor said "and I'm concerned that this relationship is premature."

"What relationship?" Daniel questioned sharply.

Anne looked at the Pastor in shock. "Pastor Harrison, what are you implying?"

Seeing the look on both of their faces, Pastor Harrison said, "What's going on here? Isn't this meeting about you entering into courtship with Andrea?"

Daniel's face was turning red with frustration. Anne reached out her hand and touched his arm and said, "Wait a minute, are you joking? There's some kind of mistake here, Pastor. We're here to discuss Andrea, but not in that way."

Pastor Harrison had a concerned look on his face, but was nodding his head slightly. "Now, it makes sense. You two don't even know what I'm talking about, do you? I knew things didn't feel right when Andrea was in here last week. Still, when you called for an appointment I thought I must have been mistaken. I just couldn't see the two of you together, so I figured I better slow things down a bit."

"Slow things down?" Daniel sputtered. "The woman is practically stalking me. Are you telling me she met with you to discuss the possibility of marriage with me? I can't believe the nerve of that woman!"

"Pastor Harrison, that's exactly why we're here today," Anne said. "Andrea has gotten totally out of hand. She has become obsessed with my brother and is telling everyone that he's supposed to be her husband. Something has to be done!"

Pastor Harrison was shaking his head. "I knew my spirit did not bear witness in the meeting, but I thought it was because I just couldn't see the two of you together. She was very convincing. Andrea said that God had been speaking to both of you. She shared several dreams with me and said that you had been spending time together so she could get to know the children; she said you wanted to begin to prepare their hearts…"

Anne had heard enough and interrupted the pastor in mid-sentence, "Prepare the children's hearts? That's it! I can't handle hearing another word. The woman is delusional! Pastor Harrison, you have to do something-this has gotten way out of hand. My brother is an honorable man and I know he has not given Andrea any encouragement. Daniel's only fault is that he's too nice!" Pastor Harrison was surprised at Anne's outburst. It was out of character for her. He knew she was taking this matter very seriously for her to respond in such a manner.

"Anne and Daniel, you have every reason to be upset and concerned. I want you to know that I will have a meeting with Andrea as soon as possible, and I *will* get to the bottom of this. Daniel, I want you to know I believe you. I know you are an honorable man and that you would not lead a woman on." Pastor Harrison continued, "It's obvious that the sudden break-up of her marriage has left Andrea more emotionally devastated than any of us knew. The circumstances surrounding it were pretty ugly, too. However, that's no excuse for her behavior."

Anne and Daniel looked at each other with relief. The matter was now in Pastor Harrison's hands. It was good to have a pastor who was willing to get involved when necessary. The three prayed together. As they stood to leave, Pastor Harrison said, "Just one word of advice. Keep a low profile with Andrea. Be polite but be firm with your boundaries. Don't try to confront her on your own. Let me help you get to the bottom of this."

Lydia and Joyce heard the front door of *His House* open right after they finished praying that morning. Deborah was humming as she came down the hall. That was a good sign. Obviously, nothing bad had happened during the night. They were relieved. One never knew what the enemy might try to stir up right before deliverance.

Because of a good night's rest and the ministry she had received the day before, Deborah looked like a younger version of herself. She even carried herself differently as she walked across the room and sat down on the sofa. "I'm ready to go," Deborah said smiling broadly at them.

"Well, let's pray before we get started," Lydia suggested.

Once they had finished, Joyce handed Deborah a piece of paper. "Normally, we would've had you read your true identity yesterday before we started the healing session, but things just worked out differently. So today, that's where we want to begin. Please read it out loud to us."

Deborah began to study the paper in front of her. She had only seen a few lines before tears began to fill her eyes. "I can't believe it. I thought I was all done crying," she said.

"Remember, it's okay to express your emotions," Lydia said encouragingly, "You're crying because the words carry the anointing of God and they touched your heart. That's good."

Joyce added, "I cried just writing it. I could feel the presence and affirmation of the Lord as I put it in my computer. It was like He was saying, 'Yes, that's my girl.'"

At that, the tears streamed even harder down Deborah's face. "I don't know if I can get through this," she said.

"Just take your time," Joyce said gently.

As Deborah composed herself, the sun broke through the morning haze. The room suddenly brightened and was full of color and light. It was as if the glory of the Lord was making a special visitation. She began to read out loud tentatively; her voice getting stronger and stronger with each sentence, *"I am free to be me, a **unique, beautiful** creation fashioned by the Lord. The love of God is **transforming** me into a **secure, righteous, Godly woman.** Because of the Blood of Christ, I have been washed **clean; purity** is my portion. I am **intelligent, discerning** and have **the mind of Christ.** I have been **forgiven** and am able to freely **forgive** others with a **merciful** heart.*

*Because I am **mended** and **healed**, I am **self-nurturing, warm, trusting** and have **healthy interdependent relationships**. I am able to set **boundaries** and say **"no"** when necessary. Because I have been **humbled,** it's easy for me to be **submissive** and **obedient.** I am an **anointed, cherished, daughter of a King,** accepted, loved and **worthy** to receive **double honor.** I embrace my **life** and **destiny** with **courage, creativity, commitment** and **grace.***

As sunlight continued to bathe the room, the words that had been written on the whiteboard on Wednesday now jumped off the page at her. Joyce had typed them all in bold type so it would be easy to remember them. As Deborah finished, she clutched the paper to her breast. "Joyce, it's so beautiful. It's just right." Tears filled her eyes again. "Thank you so much. I know this hasn't been an easy week for either of you but I hope someday you will see it was worth it."

Joyce replied, "It already is. You've been so refreshing to minister to and we know that you're well on your way to becoming everything you just read. It's all there in seed form. Now it simply has to blossom. Your job is to water it and keep the soil of your heart cultivated by the Word of God."

Smiling at Deborah, Lydia reached for her Bible and said, "We still have a lot more to complete today. We better get started." She then carefully began to lay a scriptural foundation for deliverance. As she shared, it all made more sense to Deborah. Before talking about deliverance seemed a little mysterious and scary, but Lydia presented it in a very practical and simple manner so that Deborah was able to understand. Lydia shared, "Mark 16:17 states that 'these signs will follow believers, in My name they will cast out demons.' His name represents His authority. As believers Jesus gave us His authority over Satan. Today, we will simply be exercising that authority. In Matthew 12:28 Jesus set the example by saying, 'But if I cast out demons by the Spirit of God, surely the Kingdom of God has come upon you.' The Bible says the

Kingdom of God consists of righteousness, peace and joy in the Holy Ghost. So as believers, if we don't have all of the righteousness, peace and joy we're entitled to, we need to cast out the Enemy who is trying to rule us with fear or anger or bitterness or hate."

Lydia continued, "In the Book of Isaiah, chapter 61, it shares that the Lord was anointed to set the captives free and 1 John 3:8 says, 'For this purpose the Son of God was manifested, that He might destroy the works of the devil.' Deborah today is the day of the vengeance of your God. All the enemies that have harassed, tormented and brought destruction, robbery and death to you will be defeated. Now you'll still have to deal with your carnal flesh, but it's a whole lot easier to crucify the flesh once the demonic has been taken care of through deliverance. Actually, it's much easier to cast a devil out rather than to crucify the flesh daily. Sometimes Christians are embarrassed to think they might be oppressed by a demon, but it's always best to start there and cast them out. We have a motto around here, 'When in doubt, cast it out.' In other words, you can't go wrong by exercising your authority. The worst thing that can happen is that you cast out a nonexistent demon. The best thing that can happen is that you get free. There's no way to lose."

As Lydia shared the Scriptures, Deborah remembered that she had seen the movie, the *Exorcist,* when she was younger. "No wonder I've been feeling a little uncomfortable," she thought, "that movie was so gruesome and scary." When she shared the fact with her counselors, they immediately reassured her that it would not be anything like that.

"Satan has no more legal ground," Lydia said firmly. "We have dealt with the open doors of generational curses, unforgiveness, vows, judgments, soul ties, and spirit/soul hurts. Now the Enemy simply has to leave. He has been rendered powerless. Remember, a Christian cannot be possessed by a demon because they have already been possessed by the Lord. However, they can be oppressed in unredeemed parts of their soul and body. We are saved, but we're also being saved. That means our spirit is saved, but then we have to work out our salvation with fear and trembling. 2 Corinthians 7:1 says that it's our responsibility to cleanse ourselves from all filthiness of the flesh and spirit."

Deborah smiled at both of them and said, "Ok, what are we waiting for? Let's get started."

Chapter Twenty-Five

Freedom

෮෭ ෭෮

Next door, while Maureen was finishing up her morning chores, the Holy Spirit began to nudge her to pray. As she prayed in the Spirit, thoughts of Deborah began to fill her mind. Maureen realized that today was Friday, and that Deborah's deliverance session was probably ready to begin. Sharing her testimony with Deborah last night had been enjoyable. She chuckled to herself as she finished emptying the dishwasher, remembering the surprised look on her new-found friend's face when she shared that she was an attorney. Maureen continued to pray throughout the morning as the Lord led her. She always felt like a part of the ministry team even if she wasn't next door in the counseling room itself.

Meanwhile, Lydia and Joyce completed some last minute instructions with Deborah. Though she was still a little nervous on the outside, Deborah was feeling a little more peaceful on the inside. It occurred to her that she was actually beginning to discern the difference between her spirit and her emotions. Before, everything had always felt like a jumbled up mess inside. Now, she finally understood what Anne had tried to explain to her, "God wants to separate your spirit and soul so you can be led by your spirit."

Deborah's thoughts came back to what Lydia was saying, "We want you to keep your eyes open during the deliverance because the eyes are the windows of the soul. Sometimes we can actually see demonic activity through the eyes. Don't let that scare you; it just helps us to do a better job."

Joyce said, "Also, the Greek word for spirit is pneuma, which means breath. We have found that many times spirits will leave as we breathe out. So if you feel anything inside, simply breathe out."

"We'll remind you to breathe as we go," Lydia interjected. "Also, sometimes you may have the urge to cough or burp. Don't hold back. This is not a time to be polite; this is a time to get rid of anything inside of you that no longer has a right to be there."

Joyce added gently, "Don't worry, though. We bind up all excessive manifestations. The Enemy has brought enough destruction into your life. Now, he's going to be evicted and evicted immediately."

Lydia added, "One more thing. Give us feedback on anything out of the ordinary that you hear in your head or feel in your body. Sometimes the Enemy might say things like 'this isn't working' or 'you really don't want that to go.' Those aren't your thoughts and we need to know what's happening. Also, sometimes you may feel things in your body like tingling sensations, numbness or a pain. Just tell us, don't get scared; it's just the Enemy being stirred and having to leave."

"When I went through my deliverance, the demons kept trying to put me to sleep," Joyce shared with a chuckle. "I felt so drowsy. I found out later that that's very common with religious spirits, and I had a few of them!"

Deborah was once again amazed at the transparency of the two women she had been with this past week. It certainly made it easier for her to do the same. Because secrecy and walls of separation had been her fortress for so long, she wondered what life was going to be like when she returned home now that the walls had fallen. She knew that she wanted to tell Anne everything, but how would she handle her mother and some of the other people in her life. Or maybe the question should be, "What could they handle?" She acknowledged that her mind had wandered, "Lydia, can you please repeat that?"

"Yes, I was just saying that this is going to be like the rest of the week. You'll experience the gentleness, faithfulness and joy of your God. We'll continue working together as a team as we pray and intercede. Our job is to help lead you through the process but we need you to rise up in the spirit of His Might and take your authority. If we find any blockages or hindrances, like some unforgiveness still left in place, we'll just stop and deal with them."

Joyce stated, "Our strategy is to confront the spirits through strongholds and related demons. First, we'll have you renounce and break agreement with them, and then together, we will all command them to leave in the name of Jesus. That means we're doing this through the authority which He's given us. The Word says His Name is above every other name and we definitely see that when we do deliverance."

Lydia was positioning her chair in the center of the room, "We're going to move you over here so it'll be easier for us to pray and lay hands on you while we're ministering. That's okay, isn't it?" Deborah nodded affirmatively as she got up from the sofa and repositioned herself in the chair that had previously been Lydia's. It felt warm and very safe as she sat down. It sounded a little strange, but she was glad she was going to deal with the Enemy from Lydia's chair. She could tell that the Devil didn't scare her. She prayed that the Lord would give her the same courage. "Any other questions before we get started?" Lydia asked. Deborah shook her head "no" in response.

As Joyce got up from her chair to stand next to Deborah, she said, "Deborah, you operate in the gift of discerning of spirits, also. So if you get a name of something related to the stronghold we're on, make sure you tell us. Remember, we do this with you, not to you!"

Lydia directed, "Remember we're going to deal with things even if they were only seen in the past generations. I feel that the strategy the Holy Spirit is showing me is to first deal with the occult stronghold. Satan is called Beelzebub or lord of the flies. One characteristic of a fly is that they lay dormant in the winter season; you don't even know they're there, but once spring time comes, they start stirring. So we're going to do this deliverance based on what might have had the legal right to be there from the past, not just what we see right now. Just pray after me, I renounce and break agreement with the stronghold of the occult and the demons of divination, palm reading, astrology, superstition, witchcraft, masonry, drugs, rebellion, sexual sin, nature worship, idolatry, virgin sacrifice and Belial."

As Deborah said the word, Belial, a cold chill went down her spine and the hair on her neck stood up. "What's Belial?" she asked. "That name doesn't feel good."

Lydia responded, "Belial is an ancient generational spirit. The word is found throughout the Bible. Some of the new translations use the word 'evil' when translating the name Belial. In 2 Corinthians 6:15, it says, 'What accord has Christ with Belial?' In several passages, like Judges chapter 19, you'll find the sons of Belial involved with sexual perversion, rape, homosexuality, murder, and apostasy. The word Belial in the Hebrew also means unworthiness. We always want to do deliverance for Belial when we find incest-especially related to religious homes. In 1 Kings 21:13, the sons of Belial conspire with Jezebel in the murder of Naboth so Ahab could get the vineyard he wanted. Jezebel is a very religious spirit and so are those who co-labor with her."

Joyce interjected, "That was the magnetic attraction you found with Tommie Lee the first night. I'm sure he was a carrier of the spirit of Belial. Do you remember in the Bible when Mary and Elizabeth were pregnant with Jesus and John the Baptist?

John leaped in his mother's womb as the two women greeted each other. That was the Holy Spirit in one recognizing the Holy Spirit in the other. Demonic spirits can also recognize and be attracted to each other. It always brings destruction to the people involved, but the demons are happy."

Deborah shuddered at the thought and felt that same cold chill again. A sense of urgency that she hadn't felt all week came over her. "Can we hurry up? I just want this thing gone," she said in a strained voice.

"Absolutely, renounce Belial and we'll get started on the occult stronghold."

"I renounce and break agreement with the spirit of Belial and I want nothing to do with you for the rest of my life," she adamantly declared.

Lydia and Joyce immediately began to pray in the Spirit and then began to command the occult stronghold and all the related demons to come out. One by one they called them out in the name of Jesus. Deborah joined in while still trying to breathe out as she had been instructed. As they began to call out the spirit of Belial, Deborah immediately began to choke a bit and a look of panic crossed her face.

Lydia said, "Don't be scared. Just fight, tell Belial it has to go. Draw on the Lord's Spirit of Might inside of you."

Deborah could feel a much bigger battle going on within her than with some of the other demons that had been called out previously. Suddenly, she felt a power bigger than herself rise up within her and a new authority came through her voice. "Belial, leave me now in the name of Jesus Christ!" she commanded. It was as if a log jam broke inside of her. She began to cough from a very deep place. For a moment, Deborah felt like she was being turned inside out. And then, as suddenly as it came the moment passed, and she felt a sense of freedom inside that she had never known. A small surge of tears surfaced, but this time it was tears of relief.

Lydia and Joyce were rejoicing. "Great job, Deborah!

We're so proud of you. The rest is going to be easy."

Lydia declared, "I just love deliverance and the freedom it brings!"

Deborah now understood, for the first time in her life, what deliverance was and she loved it, too. Well, maybe not everything you had to go through, but she certainly loved the results. "Let's do some more," she said, eager to receive everything she could.

The counselors looking over the top of Deborah's head, smiled at each other knowingly. What a delight it was to minister to someone who was so eager and open. Shelly, the last person they ministered to had had such a religious spirit that most of the session was spent with her defending why none of the stronghold list applied. Deborah was so refreshing!

"We're going to do the stronghold of abandonment next. So renounce and break agreement with the stronghold of abandonment, and spirits of rejection, orphan, neglect, isolation, loneliness, self-sufficiency, independence and insecurity," Lydia said slowly so that Deborah had time to respond. Together, they began to command abandonment and each of the spirits to leave her. Again, Deborah felt like she wanted to cry; a deep pain was beginning to rise from within. At first, she tried to hold it back.

Joyce said, "Just let the pain come. Sometimes in deliverance, the pain of what we went through also comes out. That's a good thing so don't hold it back."

With that little bit of encouragement, Deborah broke down and began to sob. In between sobs she said, "When you said that word 'orphan,' I felt so horribly alone. I really have felt like an orphan taking care of myself all of my life." As she cried out a lifetime of pain related to this stronghold, Deborah also began to experience another response: her heart began to melt like wax near a flame. She felt herself reaching out to God the Father like never before. The words of Jesus, "Abba, Father," whirled through her mind. Now between sobs, she kept repeating, "I have a Father. I have a Father." Lydia and Joyce knew what was happening. With that particular stronghold out of the way, Deborah's heart was finally able to feel and receive the love of the Father. Although she had been loved by the Father all along, the Enemy had fought her ability to experience God's love. Another huge battle was out of the way! God was doing a deep and quick work in her today. Joyce reached for more tissues and tucked them into Deborah's hand. Once Deborah had wiped her face, she looked up at both of them and smiled. Her entire countenance had changed again. The radiance and joy reflecting on her face was virtually indescribable. "For the first time in my life, I really feel loved," she said. "And I really think I can love other people now."

Deborah reached out and grasped each of Lydia's and Joyce's hands in hers and held them tightly for a moment. "That's a good sign!" Lydia thought excitedly. "She really is getting connected."

"I would have started with deliverance on the first day if I had known it would feel this good!" Deborah exclaimed.

"Oh no, you wouldn't have," Joyce laughed. "We would have had such a battle on our hands if we hadn't dealt with all the generational sin, ungodly beliefs, unforgiveness and spirit/soul hurts first. That's why we love this process; it makes deliverance so much easier for everyone involved."

"Just kidding," Deborah said. "I know you're the experts and that's why I'm here."

Lydia replied, "The only expert we know is the Holy Spirit. Our part is to listen for His instructions. When we do that, everything works. And what I hear Him saying now is that we need to take care of the stronghold of unworthiness next."

A couple of hours and a number of strongholds later, Joyce said, "This is the last one and then we're done." By now, Deborah and her two ministers were beginning to feel tired and hungry. It had been a productive but long morning. They concluded with the stronghold of physical infirmities.

"Let's take a moment and see if the Holy Spirit has

anything else to say to us," Lydia said.

As they were praying softly in the spirit, Deborah thought to herself, "What could possibly be left? It had felt as if they had covered everything imaginable; they dealt with strongholds of anger, rebellion, addiction, fear, shame, control, sexual sin, depression, escape, rejection, strife-the list had gone on and on."

Joyce interrupted her thoughts, "The Holy Spirit just said we need to deal with a spirit of gypsy. It came down from your European ancestry and has kept you from ever settling down or owning anything. It was also part of the drawing you had to fortune telling and divination."

Like a pro, Deborah immediately said, "I renounce and break agreement with the spirit of gypsy and any related demons. Gypsy spirit, I command you to go in the Name of Jesus." After a couple of deep breaths, she looked at them and said, "It's gone now."

Joyce knew exactly what Lydia was thinking, "Deborah had not only been ministered to, but it was clear she was now equipped. She had just ministered to herself with no help from them. She took responsibility for her own deliverance and owned the process. This would prove helpful to her and those she came in contact with for the rest of her life." Joyce knew Lydia's heart and the five-fold ministry calling on her life; she understood how important it was to Lydia that people went home, not just ministered to, but equipped. That was Lydia's purpose: to train and equip the saints. She loved the healing ministry, but was truly fulfilled when people began to internalize the process for themselves and were able to minister to others.

Next door, Maureen felt a peace descend as well. She intuitively knew the deliverance session must be over. She sensed that God was well pleased with what had happened next door. It was going to be exciting to see Deborah this afternoon; she loved to see how clear and bright people's eyes looked and how joyful their countenances were after deliverance.

Maureen thought about how much money she had spent on face creams, make-up and anything else that would make her feel better about the way she looked. After all of that, all it really took was one good deliverance session. When the beauty of the Lord was able to shine through, everyone looked better. "Wouldn't that make an interesting commercial!" she chuckled to herself.

Lydia said, "Before we lay hands on you and release a fresh anointing, we want to pray for your sexuality, if that's alright? Did you get a chance to listen to watch the video we assigned on Restoring Sexuality?"

Deborah nodded, "Yes, it really helped me to understand and build my faith. I'd love for you to pray for me in that area."

Joyce replied, "We've had so many wonderful testimonies of what the Lord has done to restore people's sexuality. It does make sense that if He can make everything else brand new, He can heal and make our sexuality brand new, too." Both Lydia and Joyce put their hands gently on her. "I just want to make sure your heart is clear. Have you forgiven everyone who damaged you sexually?"

Deborah thought for a moment and then said, "Lord, I forgive myself for the times I exploited myself and allowed even more abuse. Okay, now I'm ready."

Lydia began to pray, "Lord, we bring Deborah's sexuality before Your throne. We ask you to make all things new; send Your refiner's fire and purify her spirit, soul and body, and cleanse her of all sexual imprinting. We pray that you would restore her spiritual virginity."

Joyce continued, "Lord, we pray that when she gets married and walks down the aisle, she will feel holy and pure. Until then, we pray that she would not awaken love before its time. Restore her passion and any desires that have died within her." As the women continued to pray over her, she felt a warmth and heat begin to flow from her head down through her entire body. It felt like warm honey. At first she thought it might just be her imagination, but then she realized the Spirit of God was truly touching her and making the restoration real to her. A picture began to form in her mind: she was in a full length, white dress standing at the threshold of a church. As she stepped through the doors, there was a man waiting in the front of the sanctuary. Just as she began to focus on his face, the picture lifted. "Was that real?" she asked herself. "Did the Lord just show me that I'm going to be getting married? And not just married, but married in a church with a wedding dress and everything?"

"Are you alright?" Joyce asked. "What's going on?"

She said, "I think I'm actually feeling the fire of God and I just saw myself in a white wedding dress in a church."

Lydia noted, "You're very prophetic, perhaps God is giving you another peek at what's to come. Don't be alarmed, He's simply revealing His will to you. You don't have to worry; it's not going to happen to you tomorrow. God will do it in His perfect timing and, when He does, you'll be ready."

Deborah nodded, "It just caught me off guard but I'm okay." Actually, she wasn't ready to admit it aloud, but the vision had created a bit of excitement, which was strange for her. She had said she would never get married. "Oh, my gosh! I found another vow," she said aloud.

After she prayed and broke the vow that she would never get married, and released that portion of her life to the Lord, Lydia continued to pray, "Lord, we also ask that You would release a new and fresh anointing to Deborah, fill every dry and empty place with the river of Your Spirit. We pray a hedge of protection around her and command all demons that have been cast out to go to the dry places never to return."

Deborah had finally come to the end of her five days of restoration ministry, well aware that, in reality, it was just a beginning.

Tommie Lee walked out of court still hand-cuffed yet grinning from ear to ear. He had turned State's evidence not against his buddies in the outlaw club, but against their supplier. It had made the D.A. very happy and as a result, he had only six more months of his sentence left to serve; he had already done nearly two years of time and with the deal his attorney had got him, he would be out by Thanksgiving.

Now, all he had to do was track Deborah down. "Won't that be a lovely Christmas present, me under her tree!" he chuckled to himself at the thought. Even the deputy responsible for returning him to prison said, "What are you so happy about? I'm taking you back right back to where you came from."

"But I'm not going to be there for long and when I get out I've got a date with a good looking brunette," Tommie Lee responded with a smirk on his face. As he re-entered his cell that afternoon, Johnson was waiting for him.

"What happened, man? Did the Judge approve the plea deal?" he asked, even though the look on Tommie Lee's face had already given him the answer.

"He sure the hell did. I'm going to be out of here by Thanksgiving! And then, I'm going to give Deborah the best Christmas present she ever had-the bitch always wanted to die, so I'm just going to put her out of her misery!" he said with a mixture of glee and bitterness in his voice. Now, if he could only remember the name of the town in Ohio that she was from, he was sure he could persuade one of her family members to talk. Knowing he would be out in just six more months created an urgency within him to track her down. He didn't want to waste any time once he got out. The sooner he found her the better!

Chapter Twenty-Six

Saying Good Bye

ॐ ॐ

It was always difficult to say good bye to the special guests the Lord invited to *His House* but this one was particularly challenging. Both Lydia and Joyce were thankful that Deborah had Anne to support her when she returned home. They had been praying all week that the Lord would soften her heart toward the idea of involvement in a church. She was going to need Godly people to love her and pray for her as she walked out the next phase of her healing.

As they stood up to hug her for the last time in the safety of the counseling room, they felt like two mama birds preparing to push their young one out of the nest. Joyce said, "We'll be praying for transition grace. Sometimes it's a little frightening to leave the safety of this room. I remember the day it was time for me to head back home-I felt like a new person but I knew I had an old life to return to. However, God had many surprises waiting for me. Look at my life now. I'm right back in this room, just on the other side of the couch. Just trust God over the future."

"We know Anne will be there for you, but we want to encourage you to visit some churches and find one that you can be a part of. All of us need that place of spiritual covering and fellowship," Lydia suggested. She knew that a church family would be key to Deborah's continued growth in the Lord.

"I promise," Deborah said. "I just pray that I can find a place where there's as much of the presence of God and love as there is here. Then it won't be difficult at all to be a part of a church."

"You definitely want to feel the presence of God wherever you decide to go, but most of all you need to simply trust the Lord. His Word says that He sets the solitary in families. Just pray that He shows you your spiritual family."

"I know I've already said it," Deborah told the women, "but I don't know how I can ever thank you enough for all your time and the love you've shown me this week. I left my offering in the sowing box next door, but it seems so meager compared to what I've received this week. I want you to know that I will send more as often as I can, not just for the ministry I've received, but to bless the future of this ministry," Deborah said. Tears began to slip out of the corners of her eyes.

Lydia and Joyce each grabbed a tissue at the same time. They, too, were feeling the emotion of saying good bye to her. "Remember we're here for you. If you find you really need prayer for something, call one of us and we'll get back to you. Most of all, keep meditating on your new Godly Beliefs and True Identity and continue to let the Holy Spirit minister to you," Lydia said. "We also want to bless you by sowing into your life with a set of our *Journey to Freedom* tapes."

Deborah beamed, "Thank you so much! It will be like taking you home with me." She had listened to many of the cd's during the week for homework assignments and had been disappointed that she hadn't had time to listen to all of them.

Lydia stood to her feet first, "I have another appointment this afternoon, so I have to get some lunch. I don't know about you two but I'm famished."

Joyce and Deborah laughed and stood as well. It was obvious that the anointing was lifting and Lydia was on to other things. The women hugged one another. "I don't think this is the last time we'll be seeing each other," Lydia said.

For a moment, Deborah was caught off guard by how much it hurt to think of never seeing these two women again. She was equally surprised that she was in touch with what she was feeling. "I don't think so either," she said.

As they walked out of the room together, she paused for a moment, and looked back, as if to say good bye to the room itself. The afternoon sun left a golden glow on the yellow walls. What a special place it had become to her. Her throat caught as she said, "I'm going to miss this place."

"It's like leaving an anointed cocoon isn't it? But every butterfly has to come out and spread its beautiful new wings," Joyce said.

Deborah smiled at the thought and walked out of the room and down the hall. Lydia already at the front door reached out for one last hug from Deborah and then headed toward her car.

Joyce continued, "I'm going to finish up the paper work and just eat my lunch here."

Deborah gave her another quick hug and said, "Maureen and I agreed to have a late lunch together and then I have to pack. I'm going to miss you, so I guess this is good bye, for now at least." With a lump in her throat, she nodded as Joyce opened the door for her.

Tomorrow morning Deborah would be heading back to Ohio. It was hard to believe the week was over already. So much had happened and here it was Friday already! She wondered how Anne was doing.

Actually, Anne was doing much better after the meeting with Pastor Harrison and Daniel. She was so relieved to know that the Andrea matter was in the pastor's hands.

Pastor Harrison himself had been so disturbed by the meeting that he had called his wife directly after they had left his office. "Honey, please be praying. You know I had a meeting with Daniel and Anne today but you won't believe what happened. It appears that the whole 'relationship' is really a figment of Andrea's imagination. Be praying because I suspect this is not the end of it. I'm setting up a meeting for next week and I would really appreciate it if you would be there, also."

The pastor's wife, Christina, answered, "Sure, just have Sophia let me know when it's going to be."

"I hope we've caught this thing soon enough. It has all the makings of a stalking situation. Andrea has been coming by Daniel's house unannounced and has been telling everyone that the Lord has shown her that he's supposed to be her husband."

"Well Mark, I know if anyone can handle it with Godly wisdom, you can. From the first time I met Andrea, I just felt uncomfortable around her. She always says all the right things, but something in my spirit does not feel at peace when she's around," Christina said. Over the years, Mark had come to rely on his wife's discernment. Her giftedness was like having a secret weapon.

"I've got to get back to work, honey. Thanks for the input. I'll see you this evening. I'm looking forward to a nice, quiet dinner with you and the kids. I should be home by 5:30. Love you."

As Christina hung up the phone, she prayed that her husband's day wouldn't get robbed by this issue. "Lord, give Mark peace today and let his mind be focused. Give him wisdom for this situation. Also Lord, please make Your true will known to Andrea."

Anne and Daniel continued their conversation on the way to their cars. Anne suggested, "I think it's important that you go back and document any unusual visits or comments by Andrea and keep a journal. I don't know why, but just in case you have to take legal action I think it's important that you have a record of the facts. I hope it won't go that far, but I'm starting to get seriously concerned about her mental health."

"I know, Sis. At first I thought it was just an infatuation, but for her to have already talked to the Pastor as if we're actually thinking about marriage-that's more than just wishing and hoping. Thanks for the great advice; I will jot down a few things. I really appreciate that you came with me today. I know how busy you are with the kids and everything."

"Truthfully, it feels good to have a bit of a break. I'm actually going to do some shopping once I leave here," Anne replied. "Robert's birthday is coming up and I want to find something special for him."

Daniel turned and gave his sister a quick hug before going to his own car. He hoped she really knew how much he appreciated her support. He felt so much better now that he had spoken to Pastor; however, it was time to get back to work and the Sergio account. He called Irene from his cell phone as he headed back to the office to inform her of his imminent return.

Unaware of all that had taken place in Deerfield that morning, Deborah was freshening up before she and Maureen went to lunch. She had cried every bit of make-up off during her final session. But when she looked in the mirror, she was surprised to see that she actually looked better than she had before the session began this morning. "Freedom is a wonderful thing!" she thought to herself. After a second look, she decided to simply brush her hair and put on some lipstick.

Maureen had promised to take her to one of her "special" places and she was looking forward to it. It had been difficult to say good bye to Lydia and Joyce, and she was glad that she had lunch to look forward to. Deborah suspected that it was no accident that Maureen had suggested they go to lunch together; she knew what Deborah would be feeling once the sessions were over. One part of her felt like celebrating, the other was a bit sad that the week was coming to an end. For the moment, she was going to focus on having a good time with Maureen. She grabbed her purse and headed to the front room; she found Maureen already waiting for her there.

Maureen had suggested a quaint restaurant on beachside. The food was absolutely heavenly, but for Deborah, nothing compared to the fellowship and getting to know Maureen a little better. She decided to take a risk and share some of her testimony with Maureen, watching carefully to see her reaction. If Maureen was shocked at anything, she certainly never showed it. Actually, Deborah had reacted with more surprise last night when Maureen had shared her background as a hard-driven attorney. The women laughed and talked as if they were old friends.

When they arrived back at Magnolia Street, Deborah was faced with yet another good bye. Maureen had to prepare for a cell group meeting that evening so Deborah would be on her own. As the two women hugged, Deborah again felt a twinge of pain stab at her heart. Though she had only begun to get to know Maureen last night, she already was missing their friendship. As they said their good-byes, the women promised to keep in touch through e-mail.

"Thank you so much for all you do here," Deborah said. "You really help make this place feel warm, inviting and so special."

"Thanks, Deborah. Please, don't forget to sign our guestbook before you leave. I'll be praying for your safe journey home. I know that you're planning to leave quite early tomorrow morning, so I guess this is goodbye. I really enjoyed lunch and getting to know you better. Just remember, God has a special plan for your life. Just relax and let it unfold."

Deborah reached for the guestbook and said, "I'll take this to my room so I won't forget. Thanks again for everything." She walked down the hall to her room. It was tempting to lie down and take a nap, but she knew if she did she might not be able to fall asleep tonight. She sat on the bed and decided to write in the guestbook before she did anything else. She wrote: *"Words can't describe what this past week has meant to me-this house has been a special part of it. Having a safe, homey place to come to every night made everything feel better. I pray that everyone involved in this ministry would receive a special blessing from the Lord. I came here a hurt and broken woman, but today I'm leaving full of hope knowing I'm forgiven. Thank you for everything, Deborah Noble."*

As she closed the book, tears welled up in Deborah's eyes. Saying goodbye was harder than she thought it was going to be. She pulled her suitcase from the closet and began to pack. It took so little time that she decided to make her way to the study to watch one last video before she left.

When she dropped the guestbook off on the table, Deborah noticed Maureen had left a little note telling her she had put the electric teapot on and there was hot water and cookies in the kitchen. "How thoughtful, that's just what the doctor ordered," Deborah thought as she headed into the cozy kitchen.

Deborah brought her tea and cookies back into the study and put in a video entitled, *A Life Worth Living.*

It hadn't been an assignment, but when she asked Lydia if it was okay if she watched it, Lydia's response had been very positive. Lydia had said, "Actually, it would be a great video for you to watch. We just didn't want to overload you. It's all about destiny, vision and purpose. I highly recommend it. I think you'll really identify with it." Deborah adjusted the sound and picked up her tea cup.

Deborah's attention was immediately captured by the woman saying, "If you want to die, it's because you just haven't really learned how to live!" She went on to say that God had created life to be a great adventure with Him. Her testimony was quite similar to Deborah's, and she was fascinated by it. The woman, Rebecca Barret, was an excellent speaker. She, too, had gone through a life of abuse, addiction and everything else that went with it until she found Jesus. She had been molested by a family member just like Deborah, but it was an uncle, not her father. Deborah had never heard anyone openly share a testimony like Rebecca's. As she listened, it gave her a glimmer of hope that God could use her. Still she didn't know if she was ready to be that open. Rebecca, on the other hand, was being used by God all over the world. Rebecca Barret had developed a special program used to disciple women who were going through recovery. At the end of the video, Deborah grabbed a piece of paper and pencil and jotted down the information to contact her ministry for more information. Rebecca's forthright style and boldness to speak the truth had both inspired and motivated her. She prayed that God would reveal His purpose for her life and that He would give her a special vision. So much of her life had been wasted, but now she was ready to pursue her destiny in Christ.

Deborah thought about the video all the way back to her room. While preparing for bed, a chill of excitement coursed through her body. She was able to think about her future, rather than just how she would get through the next day or even just the next hour. Her thoughts wandered to the vision she had had this afternoon of herself in a wedding dress. She tried to bring it back hoping that she might be able to see the face of the groom, but nothing happened. Obviously, it wasn't time yet for that to be revealed, or had her imagination simply ran away with her this afternoon? "I wonder, is my destiny is somehow connected to my future husband?" Deborah questioned as she climbed into bed. It surprised her to even be entertaining such an idea. Thinking about it now, however, brought a strange sense of contentment to her.

As she shut her eyes, the presence of the Holy Spirit settled upon her. Deborah realized that she had one more goodbye to say: it was time to say goodbye to Debbie Lynn Webster-the identity she had created when she was seventeen-for good! She knew that she would be going home as Deborah

Noble. Softly, she spoke to herself, "Goodbye Debbie Lynn. I'm sorry for everything I put you through. Please forgive me." A gentle sense of completeness filled her heart.

This week, Deborah had reconciled with God, her family and now herself. From this day forth, she was Deborah Lynn Noble. "Lord, please help me get a good night's sleep tonight, I have a lot of driving to do in the morning," she prayed drawing up the cover's around her. Delight filled her soul as she realized no "goodbye" had to be said to the Lord. He would be going with her. Contentment surrounded her as she drifted off to sleep.

From His Heavenly vantage point, the Lord looked down with pleasure as His daughter slept peacefully. For years He had wanted to get close enough to her to heal and restore her wounded soul. He had interceded and wept over her pain, but she had kept running and running from Him. Finally, she had run into His arms.

Chapter Twenty-Seven

Going Home

ॐ ॐ

Saturday morning, as Deborah stepped outside the door of the wonderful old house that had been her refuge of healing the past week, the warm Florida sunlight hit her face. She felt like hugging the whole world, the house, the people in it, even the big beautiful oak tree that stood so majestically in the front yard. It was a tower of strength. Years and years of growth gave the tree an aura of ancient wisdom within its giant limbs while providing refuge from the hot Florida sun. Everything around Deborah reminded her of the God with whom she had reconciled with after so many years of wrestling with Him.

Deborah finally realized what it felt like to embrace God and to embrace life itself. "The prodigal has come home," she thought. Suddenly the parable of the prodigal took on new meaning: The world is everyone's pigpen and each one of us has to make the journey back to the Father's arms. That's what life is all about. Sin has caused us all to leave the inheritance of God and the safety and comfort of a loving relationship with Him. Now, each one of us has the choice of making the journey back home."

For the first time she saw it so clearly. Phrases of Scripture heard long ago began to fill her heart with new meaning: *"You are in the world but not of this world; I have come to give you life and life more abundantly; Receive the joy of your salvation; Whom the Son sets free is free indeed; I have come to give you beauty for ashes."*

How quickly the Scriptures came back to her! No searching her memory, they were just simply available when she needed them. No longer were they dead words scrawled across pages, nor did they intimidate her or made her feel like she could never measure up. These words were alive in her.

As she moved slowly toward her car, wanting to savor this wonderful moment, Deborah also had an urge to turn around and run back to the safety of the place that had been her home for the past five days. How unbelievable! Only five days. And yet it seemed like she had been on a long, long journey. The urge, passing as quickly as it had come, was replaced by the excitement of her new life set before her. Another scripture came to mind, *"The Word is living and powerful."*

"I'm actually excited about being alive," she acknowledged aloud. Deborah knew it was something that she hadn't felt since she was a very little girl-and then only on rare occasions: Christmas morning, a day with her grandmother, a few moments when the beauty of nature had captured her heart. Each of those moments had always been short lived and then followed by incredible disappointment. Fear crept in. What if this feeling disappeared as quickly as those moments had and she could never find it again? She took a deep breath as she heard the Holy Spirit whisper in her ear, *"This isn't just a feeling. This is a revelation. A revelation can never be stolen. The enemy may try to cloud it with circumstances, but the light of true revelation will always shine forth. Fear not Daughter, this is yours to keep!"* God was talking to her within her thoughts and she knew it was Him. It was actually happening just the way the way Lydia and Joyce had promised her. Deborah's confusion was gone. She realized that there had still been a little fear. Could she be able to hear from God outside the anointed counseling room without the two women praying for her? They seemed to do it effortlessly, and now she had experienced it for herself with a clarity and ease she had never known before. She could hear God's voice!

Truth had become revelation knowledge. Deborah now realized that it was all simply relationship, just like Joyce and Lydia had said. She hadn't asked God anything, hadn't even prayed; yet, He was there with the answer to her fear. He truly did know what she needed before she prayed.

The parable of the prodigal son flooded her heart and mind yet again; she could virtually feel a robe being wrapped around her shoulders and the ring being placed on her finger. "Yes," she thought, "an inheritance can't be stolen, it's mine. Mine to keep!" Excitement rose within her.

Driving up the I-95 ramp, as she headed out of Palm City, Deborah almost boasted aloud, "Look out life, I'm ready to merge!" The humorous thought brought a grin to her face as she began to accelerate. Even driving felt good. Everything looked different, clearer and brighter somehow. The sky was bluer; the trees were greener; even the colors of the cars in traffic were more vibrant. The gray haze of shame and depression that had clouded her spirit had been lifted. Her vision for life as it could be had returned. This was something she had not felt since she was a little girl.

Deborah drove down the Interstate, a constant smile on her face. She was actually excited to get home to see her family another feeling that she hadn't experienced in a very long time. For just a brief moment, a little of her old apprehension crept in as she wondered how her family would receive her. Deborah had brought so much pain and heartache into their lives over the years. Tears welled up in her eyes and she had to blink them away in order to see the road which had become a blur in front of her. Then, one of her new Godly beliefs rose up from within without warning, "As I embrace the people in my life with forgiveness, mercy and unconditional love, God will soften their hearts toward me. When a man's ways please God He makes even His enemies to be at peace with him," (Proverbs 16:7). This is certainly a whole new way of looking at life. The power of rejection was no longer everyone else's weapon to wield against her. The power of acceptance was within her. Again, she realized her life was beginning to unfurl and blossom just the way her counselors had said it would. She had not even had time to memorize her Godly beliefs; yet, when she needed truth, the Holy Spirit had brought it back to her remembrance. Once again, another Scripture came alive. "I really do have the mind of Christ," she thought to herself. "So, I can just relax and rest in the faithfulness of the Holy Spirit to help me walk out the precious treasures of revelation I received during the past week." A wave of peace gently washed over her.

A large part of her wanted to go and shout to the whole world about what God had done for her. The old things had passed away; she was truly a new creature. She knew, however, that she had to be a living epistle-a testimony of grace fit to be read by all men. Because she had broken her family's trust so many times, Deborah realized she would have to give them time-time to see that something truly had changed on the inside of her-time to accept that the changes were genuine. "They'll just need time," she thought, "time for trust to be rebuilt."

As she continued her drive North, Deborah set her heart on embracing the process of restoration with her family, especially her mother. No matter how long it took, no matter what circumstances happened along the way, her heart was settled. She had chosen to love them, and love them she would, right where they were at. She was ready to give them the same love she had received from the Lord-an unconditional love, full of forgiveness.

Thoughts of Mary Rachel and other family members

filled her mind as she passed a large tractor-trailer. "Mary Rachel," she said her name softly to herself. How she hoped one day she and her sister would really be able to talk-not just about day-to-day surface things-but about their hidden secrets of the past. Deborah had always wondered if she had been the only one that had experienced the uninvited touches of their father.

There were so many things that had been left in silence; a kind of silence that was cold and dark, silence that had slowly separated the Noble family. There were things she longed for Mary Rachel to understand, like why she had acted as she had when they were younger, why she left home at such a young age, and why she had kept her distance for so many years. She knew her sister had always felt abandoned by her, and she had carried a great deal of guilt about it for many years. At one time, she and Mary Rachel had been quite close.

Deborah wondered if her sister ever had any of the same thoughts or regrets that she had. She immediately prayed, "Lord, open my sister's heart. Help us to be able to communicate. Give me patience, Lord, as You restore what was lost and stolen from us."

Two middle children, never being able to compete with the oldest and the baby in the family, Deborah thought about her relationship with Mary Rachel in the early years. Thoughts of drawn out summer days, communicating through their imaginary family of dolls, filled her mind; they had often found solace in hours of uninterrupted play together. How sad it was that it had been an imaginary family who had sustained them rather than the real one God had intended. Deborah had never seen it quite that way before. How sad, but yet how true.

It was hard to believe, but Deborah was especially excited about the prospect of seeing her mother. After all, they did live together and their relationship would surely test all that she had received. This past week had given her a new perspective into the kind of pain her mother had lived with and what she had done, or not done, to cope with it. She had a new sense of compassion for her mother, which until this week, had always been overshadowed by the wounds and anger of a childhood gone wrong. Would God ever open a door of opportunity for her to tell her mother what had happened to her? She knew that only God could prepare her mother's heart for a conversation like that. However, she also realized that she could be content if He never opened that door. Whether her mother knew of the abuse or not, she had found healing and peace this week and that was enough for her.

Regardless of the fact that some of her greatest hurt and disappointment had been with her mother, Deborah wondered if something similar had happened in her mother's life which caused her not to be able to even mention the word 'sex.'" For now, she had to trust God with the answers to those questions. "Yes, there's still a lot of work for the Lord to do in this relationship, but I'm so grateful that in my own heart the work has already begun," she thought to herself.

Without warning, the faces of her brothers, Paul and Tim, flashed before her. Paul and Tim, Biblical names, like Mary Rachel and Deborah. Everyone in her family had a name from the Bible. It used to make her so angry. Bible names, Bible do's and don'ts. Truth be told, whether it was names, rules, or church going, it didn't matter, everything that related to family, religion, or life itself had made her angry in those days. She chuckled and admitted to herself that she had just plain been angry and had projected it on the entire world around her. "I really can change my world by changing what was inside of me, just like Lydia said," she thought.

Deborah came back to the moment and noticed that she had driven miles without once being angry with another driver. Now that was a miracle! Since the day she had started driving, the highway had been a great place to vent. She thought of all the innocent people who had gotten in her way and the wrath she had cursed them with while being in such a hurry to get nowhere as fast as she could. Looking back now in the light of revelation, it seemed so ridiculous to her; but at the time it was deadly serious. Who would have thought that even driving could be fun? It was no longer another battle that she always seemed to lose. Happily cruising along, Deborah caught the Welcome to Georgia sign on the border. She breathed a silent goodbye to Florida and began to look for a place to pull off for a quick break.

Florida, which had once been a place of cruelty and abuse, would now always hold a special place in her heart. For many, it was the Sunshine State, but for her it had become the Sonshine State. Deborah laughed softly to herself as the thought crossed her mind. She made a mental note to remember to include that in the thank you note she would send to the precious women who had laid down their lives for her the past five days. She knew Lydia and Joyce would appreciate the thought. "How will I ever thank them enough?" Again the voice of the Holy Spirit spoke to her heart, *"By walking out your freedom in ways that will capture the hearts of others."*

Deborah pulled off the Interstate in search of gas and a good cup of coffee-decaf naturally! No more artificial stimulants for her; thinking about all the past drugs and alcohol she had consumed in her lifetime, it seemed almost humorous that now she was even concerned about putting caffeine in her body. She thought about the lectures her father had given her when she was a teenager and how she was "slowly killing herself." If only her Dad could see her now! Old feelings of regret began to surface, especially concerning how their relationship had been left torn and broken when she had left home. Later, cancer had invaded his body and had taken his life quickly. Dad, Mr. Health Nut, dead at 59. That had become a great excuse to continue with her abusive lifestyle. After all, she'd rationalize that he took care of himself and it hadn't helped him. Now of course, Deborah could see the open door for premature death caused by generational sin. She also knew that her father's guilt and inability to forgive himself for the things he had done had slowly eaten him alive.

Immediately, the Holy Spirit gave her something with which to fight the regret. "Wait a minute!" she realized. "He can see me now! I'm surrounded by a great cloud of witnesses!" She twirled in the parking lot just as a little girl would spin around for her daddy while showing off a new dress. Then she saw them, her heavenly Father and her natural father embracing each other as they said together, "Yes, we can see you now!" She could feel a father's pride turned toward her. It felt strange, even foreign, yet quite wonderful. Not only had she forgiven her father, but obviously God had forgiven him, too. There was a time, not that long ago, when that thought would have made her really angry. She had always hoped he would rot in hell and suffer for what he had done to her, her mother and her brothers. "Well, he must have made it right with the Lord even though he never had the chance with me," she thought.

Deborah wondered what her father had been like in the last years of his life. If she had gone home during those years, would they have had the talk she had always wanted to have? Would he have broken down and wept for the pain he had caused her? Those kinds of questions weren't necessary. The pain of the past was gone. She could accept that however her natural father had made peace with her heavenly Father, it was alright with her.

Deborah walked into the door of the coffee shop, enjoying the aroma of freshly brewed coffee and humming the words of the song that kept playing through her mind:

I'm forgiven because You were forsaken.
I'm accepted, You were condemned.
I'm alive and well, Your spirit is within me, because You died and rose again.
Amazing love, how can it be, that You my King would die for me?
Amazing love, I know it's true and it's my joy to honor

you. In all I do, I honor you.

The song, "You Are My King" by the Newsboys had captured her heart.

The counter clerk, clearly annoyed, looked at her as if to say, "What are you so happy about when I'm so miserable?"

As she ordered her cup of decaf and an egg croissant, another significant realization occurred to Deborah. She was actually enjoying time by herself. In the past, time had always been an enemy that had to be filled. The tormenting thoughts and memories always seemed to overtake her whenever she was alone. She had learned to fill her time with friends, lovers, drugs, and the constant companions that came on every time she turned on the television. From the newscasters to the sitcom stars, they had always been there for her and took her mind off of what she had vowed to forget. Even as a child, time alone had been something to avoid at all costs. Deborah remembered the torment when her bedroom door finally closed at the end of every day and she was left alone; all alone in the dark. Fear and torment would often overwhelm her. Deborah remembered that Lydia and Joyce had gently pointed out that much of her promiscuity had come from avoiding those feelings of being left alone at night. Rather than facing her fears and allowing God to deliver her, she had created her own answer: seduce a man and she wouldn't have to go to bed and face a night alone. It seemed so simplistic but obvious to her now. She was reminded of how many times the light of morning brought an overwhelming urge to push a man out of her bed or to run out of his. Now it all made sense. She had used men to avoid her fears, rather than face them. She had convinced herself that it was simply her inability to make a commitment or to accept the responsibility of a real relationship that made her the way she was. Yes, that was part of her explanation, but how much deeper than that it had all gone.

As she sat down to enjoy a late breakfast, Deborah's thoughts turned to Daniel. She reminded herself to remember to thank him along with Anne. After all, Anne was the one who had heard about the *Restore Your Soul Ministry* in Palm City and had encouraged her to check it out. She remembered feeling Anne's prayers on the long ride down to Florida. Funny, now the trip down seemed like light years away.

Deborah couldn't even count the number of times she had been tempted to turn around and go back. Panic and fear had tormented her mile after mile, even right as she was pulling into the parking lot of *His House*. It hadn't stopped until after her first session. How glad she was that she had not missed what the Lord had prepared for her! A swell of gratitude rose in her when she realized that it had taken the prayers of a number of prayer warriors to keep her on that path. Daniel and Anne were two of them.

There were others that also needed to be thanked for not giving up on her. Her great aunt, Liberty, was one. Born on July 3rd, Liberty had been named in remembrance of the Fourth of July. Growing up, Deborah had always loved that name and her aunt who claimed it. Even as a little girl she used to think, if only she could have only had a name like that, perhaps she would be as free and as bold as her aunt had always been. Of course, she knew now that it wasn't in the name, but it was in her relationship with God that her aunt Liberty had truly found her freedom. Interestingly, Liberty had escaped the snares of religious bondage that had entrapped the Noble family. "How had she done that?" Deborah wondered, "What was it which made her aunt so different from the rest of the family?" She remembered how she would put up walls of cold indifference every time her aunt would try to talk to her in the past, yet she always admired her from afar. Yes, it was definitely time to pay Aunt Liberty a call, also.

Chapter Twenty-Eight

The Vision

ॐ ॐ

On the road again, Deborah continued to alternate between prayer, worship and the thoughts that kept coming to her as the miles clicked by. She was actually glad to have this time alone; time to reflect on the past; time to be grateful for the ministry that she had received; time to dream about the future and all that it might contain; and surprisingly, time to think about Daniel.

During the spirit/soul hurt session, the Lord had brought back to mind Deborah's junior prom night and what she had done to Daniel. She had decided that when she got home she was going to face that part of her past and ask him to forgive her. What had transpired that evening had been another thing left untouched; it was never discussed after it had happened. Deborah was fully aware that prom night had created an invisible wall between the two of them for over twenty years. Until the Lord brought the memory back, it had lay hidden under layers of time, drugs, alcohol and a need to forget. She remembered clearly the hurt look on Daniel's face when she had seen him at church the Sunday after the prom. Even at sixteen and hung-over, her father still had the power to get her in a pew every Sunday morning. Sometimes she went just to avoid another sermon, and other times it was to protect her mother and the rest of the family from her father's rage. Whatever the reason, it always worked. That Sunday she would have done anything to avoid facing Daniel Worthington!

In Deborah's mind, Daniel had always seemed too good for her. However, now she knew there had also been a fear that he was just like Daddy-someone who looked spiritual on the outside but really didn't know God on the inside. Daddy who was always an elder; Daddy who was always at church; Daddy, who was always quoting the Bible; that same Daddy had abused her; and that the same Daddy left those awful marks on Paul's back.

This week Deborah realized that she had decided as a young girl it was too risky to take the chance on Daniel being like her father. Consequently, she gravitated toward men who didn't put on a show. They were sinners and they didn't try to hide it; the more outrageous they were the better she liked them and the more honest she thought they were. Those circumstances and Deborah's train-of-thought motivated the events which happened that prom night

Both Deborah's and Daniel's parents had arranged the night for them. Deborah had felt forced to go along with the whole idea just to keep everyone happy. Halfway through the prom, however, she had caught wind that Justin had scored some coke. In Deerfield, Ohio, especially twenty years ago, that was quite a feat, unlike today where hard drugs are available even at the middle and elementary school levels. She had dumped Daniel that night, looking for a high she had never experienced before; she had left him and the dance. She had simply walked out of the prom and totally out of his life without a word.

Now, Deborah saw that night as a crossroad in her life and she had definitely taken the wrong road- the one that seemed to have no way back. She had met up with Justin and the "cool" gang in the school parking lot and had partied all night; ultimately losing what little bit of dignity she had left. Though, Deborah had already lost her virginity to her father, she had convinced herself that it had never counted and had made a conscious choice to keep herself from further sexual involvement with any of the boys she dated. Now even that was gone, and she felt dirtier than she ever had in her entire life.

To make matters worse, when her parents found out that she had walked out on Daniel, her father became livid and her mother just looked at her with a pained expression and deep grief in her eyes. There was no use trying to explain anything. How could they have understood that she was really doing him a favor by getting out of his life? Then came the whole issue of having to face the Worthington family on Sunday morning. Deborah was so angry just at having to attend church at all, much less feeling so defiled and totally different than everyone around her.

Deborah remembered vowing that, as soon as she left home she would never darken the door of a church again. "Wow, another vow uncovered! Lydia and Joyce were right; the Lord will continue ministering to me." She prayed the prayer the counselors had taught her to release that portion of her life back to God. How grateful she was to have the Lord uncover yet another vow that kept her in bondage. She breathed another sigh of relief. If the Holy Spirit kept helping her as He had already this morning, this wouldn't be so hard after all.

Walking into church that morning Deborah remembered the look of hurt on Daniel's face quickly turning from pity to disgust, or had she completely misinterpreted what she had seen? Perhaps it wasn't pity at all, maybe it had been compassion and sadness all along and she just hadn't been able to see it then.

She had never given him another chance after that fateful night and had never looked Daniel Worthington in the eye again. She hadn't spoken to him the rest of her high school days and she certainly never tried to explain her actions. Daniel respected the defensive wall Deborah had built around herself and the two hadn't had another conversation until a year and a half ago, when they had run into each other at the hardware store downtown.

Remembering how uncomfortable and awkward she felt

still caused Deborah's face to flush as she continued on her drive back home. She pulled into the next rest area to make a pit stop but she still couldn't shake her thoughts of Daniel. As she got back into the car, she said aloud, "Okay God, what do you want me to see here?" Instantly she saw it: a vision of her and Daniel standing at the altar of a church-actually the church that they had both grown up in-his two children sitting on the front row and the church full of family and friends. Deborah was wearing a beautiful, long white flowing dress. She couldn't believe her eyes. Forgiving the past and renewing a friendship was one thing, but this was something else entirely. She didn't know if she should rebuke the thought or what. "Could that be the same dress I saw myself in yesterday afternoon? This is crazy! Where are Lydia and Joyce when you needed them?" she quipped half-jokingly, half seriously to herself. Unsure of what to do, Deborah simply gave the thought back to the Lord. Intuitively she knew it had touched her deep inside.

Deborah had no way of knowing that as she was driving, Daniel was sitting at Anne's kitchen telling her of a dream he had the night before. It had shaken him to the core and, because he trusted his sister's spiritual discernment, he wanted to talk it over with her. In the dream, he had been standing at an altar with Deborah. He knew that as a teenager, it had once been his dream to marry his childhood sweetheart, but now too much had happened in both of their lives. Losing his wife, Susan, had been anything but easy, and raising his two children alone for the past two and a half years had changed him. Besides, Deborah herself had been through so much. Just looking into her troubled eyes when she came back to Deerfield told him that she was not the same young girl he had given his heart to over twenty years ago. He reminded himself that she was the same girl who had stomped on his heart and hadn't even bothered to hand it back to him when she was done. The prospect that this might be God's will for his life scared him, but he was, even when fearful, an honest man. And, if he was going to be honest, especially with himself, the morning after the dream, he had felt more alive than he had in several years.

Anne and Daniel began to pray together about the dream. They asked the Lord to confirm it if was truly His will for his life. They also prayed that the Lord would also bring a witness to Deborah's heart as well. He had to admit that ever since she had moved back to Deerfield he had experienced a certain desire to help her or to make sure she was okay. Initially, he assumed it was because of his sister's relationship with her, and another case of his big heart getting him in trouble again. Today, he and Anne prayed fervently about the dream and then released it into the Lord's hands. That was all they could do for now.

Chapter Twenty-Nine

The Arrival

ॐ ॐ

It had been a long day of driving and Deborah was tired. She started looking for a motel room for the night, good supper, a good night's sleep. She would be ready to finish her drive in the morning.

She wondered how she would sleep tonight. This would be her first night outside of the safety of the ministry house where she had slept like a baby for the first time in years. The insomnia she had fought ever since she was a child had simply disappeared once she had gotten so much out that first day of ministry.

She remembered falling into bed from sheer exhaustion that Monday night; how delightfully surprised she had been when she didn't wake up until early the next morning. It had felt wonderfully delicious-what a rare treat it was to sleep the whole night through. What amazed her even more was that it continued throughout the week. Tonight would be a true test.

Tomorrow morning was Sunday. Deborah had made a decision that she would get to bed early and wake up in time to drive straight to the morning church service. She hadn't been to church in years, but this was a new beginning. As close as she had become to those who were part of the women's Bible study that met at Anne's house. She still had felt too dirty and too different to allow herself to think about being part of a church body. But things had changed; she realized that she had finally been able to receive what God had been trying to give her all along: forgiveness, mercy, grace, healing, and restoration. They were no longer words that simply sounded good. Now, they were her experience, her reality.

Deborah checked into a motel located off the highway and went straight to her room. She took a quick shower and then went out to find herself a good meal. As she sat down in the small country restaurant which boasted of good old-fashioned home cooking, Deborah realized just how hungry she was. The waitress came over with her water and took her order; the special sounded good so she ordered the meat loaf with mashed potatoes, gravy, green beans and a salad. Within minutes, a piping hot meal was served, all of its aromas blending together to entice her taste buds. As she ate, she contemplated what her arrival back home tomorrow morning would be like. As much as she hoped no one would make a big deal of her being back in church, somehow she really wanted everyone to notice the changes that had taken place in her. She finished eating and pushed back her plate, fully satisfied. She tipped the young waitress real well and headed back to her motel room.

Once she got back to the room, it dawned on Deborah how good it felt to have her appetite back and how good it was to eat and hold down an entire meal without a thought of throwing up. Ever since she had given her heart to the Lord, the bulimia continued to have less and less hold on her but it had still been a battle at times. Now the desire to binge and purge was completely gone.

Bulimia was one of the first shameful secrets Deborah had ever shared with Anne. Anne had purchased some books for her that had helped but occasionally, she still battled the temptation. It usually surfaced when she was angry with herself, ashamed or fearful. Now when those feelings rose within, she had learned to call Anne and they would pray and talk. Usually, after the phone call, she would be able to resist the temptation. But now, the battle that had raged within her for so many years was totally gone. She prayed that it would stay that way.

Deborah went into the bathroom to brush her teeth. It still surprised her when she looked in the mirror; the pain was gone from her eyes, the wear and tear of many years of hard living had somehow been lifted from her face, and she looked like a younger much happier version of herself. She grinned at the image staring back at her. "No makeup in the world is that good!" she thought. And she actually felt younger, too. It was all so amazing. Here she was, 36 years old and God was giving her a new beginning. "So that's what the scripture means, 'I will renew your strength and you shall mount up with wings like eagles.'"

She clicked on the TV in search of the weather channel. When she finally found it, she learned that the weather was going to stay clear and sunny for the rest of her journey home. That was good news.

Eventually, Deborah changed into her pajamas and then reached for her Bible. She pulled out from between its pages the sheets of paper containing her new Godly Beliefs and her True Identity. She read them out loud just as Lydia and Joyce had instructed her to do; hearing what God had to say about her and her life made her feel good. Then, she opened up her Bible to Isaiah 61 and read the whole chapter again. How amazing it was to really believe what she was reading! Her soul had finally truly discovered salvation. She closed her Bible, closed her eyes, and was asleep in minutes.

Before she knew it the alarm rang at 6 a.m. and Deborah bounced right to her feet. It was time to get up and on the road if she was going to make it to church. What she didn't know was that Daniel had put a fleece out to the Lord as he had left his Anne's house the day before. He had asked the Lord to confirm his dream from the night before by having Deborah come to the Sunday morning church service. He knew it was a long shot, a real long shot, and he also knew Anne wasn't too big on fleeces. However, he knew it would certainly get his attention. If Deborah Noble darkened the door of Deerfield Family Worship Center, it would definitely be an act of God!

After visiting the drive-thru of the only fast food restaurant in the little town that had sprung up around the Interstate exit, Deborah was back on the road humming once again. This time it was the words of the old hymn, "Amazing Grace." She couldn't believe it-this morning she was actually anxious to get to church, "I don't know if I've ever felt like this before, even as a child."

Sunday mornings had always been such a tense situation at the Noble house. Out of his fear of what the pastor might think if they were a minute late, Deborah's father would run from room to room screaming at her mother to get the kids ready or they would be late again. He never once helped her with the task while continually lashing out at her. Even as a child she knew none of the chaos made sense. Inevitably, Mary Rachel or Tim would have torn something, spilled something, or in some way messed up their clothes. Cleaning up a mess or a clothing change would be the last straw for their father. He would be out the door, storming off to the car fuming all the way. Then he'd sit in the car, his anger boiling to the point of rage. When he could take the delay no longer, he would lay on the horn. The sound of the car horn was always a clear indication to the family that things had gone from bad to worse. The ride to church service would be silent, cold and icy. Mother had failed again and someone would have to pay. The second they drove into the church parking lot, however, her father's countenance would change as he lovingly escorted his family into the church sanctuary.

Even now it made Deborah angry just thinking of it, but that was okay. Lydia and Joyce had helped her understand that some things were supposed to make her angry and that some things even made God angry. Yes, her anger was legitimate, but she just had to be careful not to sin with her anger. "Ah," she thought, "one more thing on my list that I hadn't had time to forgive last week. Would the list ever come to an end?"

Driving up the Interstate, Deborah kept her eyes on the road, but in her heart she chose to forgive her father for all those Sunday mornings that had produced dread in her heart and a knot in her stomach.

With only an hour left to go, Deborah turned off the Interstate onto a smaller highway which would take her directly into Deerfield. Suddenly, out of nowhere, traffic began to slow down in front of her; there had hardly been a car on the road just a few minutes ago. She wondered what was happening as she continued to ease her car forward. Now the traffic was totally stopped. She pulled over to the shoulder a bit to trying to see what was up ahead. Deborah could see a construction worker standing with a stop sign while others were working on the bridge up ahead. Traffic was down to one lane. She couldn't believe it! "On Sunday morning?" she exclaimed to no one. She let out a sigh and then began to ask the Lord to remove any opposition that might be preventing her from getting to church this morning. She could sense that the enemy was working in the atmosphere around her trying to stop her from making it to Deerfield on time. As quickly as traffic had stopped, it started once again. Breathing a sigh of relief, Deborah said a quick "thank you" to the Lord, and slowly accelerated her Honda Civic. "Ah, back on the road again." Just as she started to make up time, nature called and she realized that she would have to find a bathroom. "Not now," she thought. "Well, I need some breath mints any way, maybe there'll be a convenience store in the next town." Sure enough, as she pulled into Scranton there was a little store on the right. She made her way quickly out of the car and into the store. The clerk seemed to take forever ringing up her roll of mints and the Sunday paper, but soon she was on her way again. She was once again lost in her thoughts until she suddenly saw the *Welcome to Deerfield* sign upon entering the city limits.

Pulling into Deerfield, the small town Deborah had grown up in seemed different too. Normally, it felt like a death trap to her-a place that would suck the life right out of her if she wasn't careful. Today, it felt different; there was calmness and tranquility in the air. "Has it always been here and I just missed it? Or was God doing something new in Deerfield?" she questioned.

The streets were quiet. Most of the people were still sleeping or on their way to church. Deborah shrugged. Right now the state of the town didn't really matter; she had more important matters to concentrate on this morning.

The temperature in Deerfield was much cooler than it had been the past week in Florida; the April morning air was crisp and cool, it felt good and fresh upon her face as she drove through the sleepy town with her window down. She knew she was probably going to be late for church. At first, the thought disturbed her, but then she realized that being late would allow her to slip into the back of the church unnoticed.

Daniel had glanced at his watch and looked around the church for what seemed like the hundredth time. Obviously, his fleece had given him his answer: apparently the dream had not been from the Lord. He had to admit that, while he felt a bit of relief in that deep down place inside, there was also a sense of disappointment. "Twenty years and I still haven't gotten that woman out of my system. What is wrong with me?" He tried to shake it off and listen to the announcements but he really wasn't absorbing much of what he was hearing. Daniel took one last glance around the church; still no Deborah. That's it! I'm not going to let the enemy distract me from turning my attention toward worshipping the Lord," Daniel almost blurted out loud.

Deborah reached for the large brass handle of the church door, took a deep, calming breath and entered into the foyer. She was glad to have a minute to collect herself before walking into the back of the sanctuary. She was relieved remembering that Pastor Buckley-who had pastored the church since the Dark Ages-had finally retired two years ago. As a child, she had lost all respect and confidence in the man who had not discerned, or even seemed to care about, the person her father really was. "Was the pastor blind, too?" she wondered. "How could he have not seen the true condition of the Noble family? My angry, older brother, Tim and Mary Rachel who were scared of their own shadow, and me, the rebellious black sheep of the family, couldn't he see we were a mess. All of the family symptoms seemed so obvious now. How did Pastor Buckley avoid seeing the weariness and lack of joy in my mother?" It seemed like all he had ever really cared about was what Theodore Noble could do for the church or for him personally. She caught herself, "This isn't the time to stir up a wound God is still healing. And I sure don't want to rebuild the stronghold of bitterness that kept me bound for so many years. No, freedom feels too good. I just need to walk in forgiveness." Deborah reminded herself that she had forgiven the man last week and had repented for the judgment she had held in her heart all those years; however, it was still comforting to know that the First Assembly of Deerfield-which held so many painful memories-had evolved into the Deerfield Family Worship Center under the leadership of a new pastor.

Deborah had heard some good things about Pastor Harrison from the women in Anne's weekly Bible study. At first he and his wife had ruffled some feathers, but now the church was growing and thriving. She took one more deep breath and slowly opened the door of the sanctuary.

As the praise and worship filled the sanctuary, Daniel entered into the presence of God: soon the thoughts of Deborah and his fleece fled from his mind. He became so focused on his communion with God that he didn't even notice the doors open, or Deborah slip into the back of the church. She was nearly fifteen minutes late.

Apologizing to God with every breath for being late, Deborah was thankful to find a seat near the aisle in the second to the last row; she felt like the Lord had reserved it just for her. After settling into her seat, she looked around the sanctuary. It looked so different from how she remembered it as a child; new paint, banners on the wall, and modern chairs made the church feel fresh and inviting. Gone were the old wooden pews that were so uncomfortable and hard as a child. Everything was lighter and brighter than it had been years ago. She stood to her feet to join the rest of the congregation in worship.

Worship was certainly livelier than she had ever remembered it being as a child. How good it felt to lift her hands in praise with her new found freedom. The upbeat praise became a little slower and quieter as the musicians and singers began to move from praising the Lord to worship. Worship felt like a fresh shower. Deborah tilted her face toward heaven and could virtually feel the drops of mercy and grace resting like the morning dew upon her face. As the music slowed into a melody that she had never heard before, the singers became still, and Pastor Harrison got up from his seat and walked to the pulpit. He was fairly young, probably in his early to mid-forties-not at all like Pastor Buckley who had seemed ancient to her even as a child. She hoped he wasn't going to bring the time of worship to a close.

Chapter Thirty

Forgiven

ॐ ॐ

Sitting in the front of the church, Daniel was having the same thoughts. He was relieved when the Pastor quietly announced, "The altars are open this morning," and then sat back down next to his wife. Even though Pastor Harrison had been there for two years, he was still called the new pastor. What Daniel loved about him was that he was a man led by the Spirit of God. He didn't need to be the center of attention or always in charge. He always made allowance in the service for the congregation to simply focus on Jesus. Yes, Pastor Harrison was different. He had brought a breath of fresh air to the stale spiritual climate of Deerfield, Ohio. Daniel silently thanked God for sending Pastor Harrison and his family to them and reminded himself to make sure he told the Pastor after the service just how much everyone appreciated him.

Deborah searched the face of Pastor Harrison's wife for the signs of pain or weariness which had been etched into the face of the former pastor's wife, Mrs. Buckley. She was pleasantly surprised to see a face of contentment. Christina Harrison actually had a glow about her. As she watched the Pastor return to his seat, Christina slipped her hand into his. Deborah instantly recognized the simple tender expression of affection that she had never once seen the Buckley's exchange in the twelve years she had attended church at Deerfield First Assembly as a child.

Deborah quickly caught herself and began to refocus her thoughts on the worship. As she did, the music began and the same song that Deborah could not get out of her mind on her trip home began to flow through the sanctuary:

I'm forgiven, because You were forsaken.
I'm accepted, You were condemned.
I'm alive and well, Your spirit is within me.
Because you died and rose again.

She was overwhelmed by the presence of the Lord and the words of the song. As the choir began to sing the chorus, *"Amazing love, how can it be, that You my King would die for me?"* she could no longer contain herself. It didn't matter anymore what anyone thought, she felt compelled to get out of her seat and make her way to the altar. *"Amazing love, I know it's true and it's my joy to honor You, in all I do".* Before the moment could pass, she slipped into the center aisle of the church and walked quickly to the altar.

That was it, nothing else mattered right now but making her way to the front of the church. The deep rich plum color carpet of the stage beckoned her as the singers were singing, *"In all I do, I honor You. You are my King."*

Even though the pastor had made the invitation, she was the first one down front. Today she no longer cared what anyone else thought; it was time for her to make a public commitment to Jesus Christ. Another level of peace and joy filled her heart, *"Amazing love, how can it be…?"*

"How could anything possibly compare to what this feels like?" she thought. Drugs and alcohol were nothing compared to the weight of God's glory surrounding her. From downers to uppers, cocaine to heroin, all of them had only been a momentary high, a momentary relief. "No, I've never experienced anything like this before," she smiled slightly and inhaled deeply.

Daniel, lost in the worship, was a little annoyed when his sister, who was standing next to him, nudged him just a bit. "Not now," he thought, assuming one of the children needed a bathroom break; but, as Daniel opened his eyes, he nearly lost his breath when he saw who was standing nearly right in front of him. There at the altar was Deborah Lynn Noble. He could hardly believe his eyes. Daniel realized he had never been able to call her Debbie like the other kids in church and school; she had always been Deborah to him. His heart began to swell with a love that he knew was not just his own, "Is God really doing something here? Was the dream I had really a message from the Lord? After all, didn't I put out a fleece to the Lord?" his heart was beating more rapidly with every moment that passed.

Although they had seen each other numerous times since she had returned to Deerfield, Daniel really didn't know the woman standing just a few feet in front of him. His sister had told him very little of what Deborah had been through the last twenty years. Anne was always incredibly discreet with any information confided to her from the women she befriended and discipled-she had been no different when it came to Deborah.

Anne was tugging Daniel's sleeve again. "Oh great, now what?" he thought now sure that his son, David, was in need of his morning trip to the rest room. It inevitably seemed to land right in the middle of worship. Anne leaned over and whispered in his ear. It wasn't a trip to the bathroom she was trying to get his attention over, but rather she felt they were supposed to go to the altar with Deborah and make her feel welcome.

Meanwhile, sitting midway in the sanctuary, Elizabeth Noble, was still unable to move or believe her eyes. "Is that really Deborah, my Deborah, who just walked by so quickly?

Can that be her kneeling at the front of the church?" Frozen in her pew and overcome by a feeling of helplessness, Elizabeth had to admit, her own daughter scared her at times. She was never sure what her response might be. Over the years, Deborah's anger and her cruel ability to lash out had paralyzed Elizabeth. Most of the time she found herself doing or saying nothing when it came to her daughter, and once again, she didn't know what to do.

Deborah felt the presence of other's who had also made their way to the altar. She was thankful not to have to be the only one up there.

Suddenly, she felt a familiar arm slip around her shoulders. It was Anne, her friend. In the past, she often found herself still flinching at the warmth and affection Anne would extend to her, but today it was different. The arm around her felt good, warm, strong and secure. She thought, "How will I ever thank her for her prayers and support? I would have never made it without her!" She reached out and hugged her back.

In another church service back in Florida another woman was kneeling in prayer. Soon Lydia was joined at the altar. Both she and Joyce gave each other a "knowing" look. They sensed by the Spirit that something significant was happening with Deborah. It was time to pray.

As the two women interceded for the young woman they had grown to love over the last 5 days the worship team began to sing, *"I'm forgiven, because You were forsaken. I'm accepted, You were condemned."* Once again a knowing glance passed between them-those words had become Deborah's theme song during her stay. The song had been playing in the front room of *His House* the first day she had arrived and Deborah had hummed it to herself throughout the week. The counselors could feel the Holy Spirit alerting them. For some reason, Deborah needed to be covered with prayer right now! Lydia and Joyce interceded earnestly.

Several other people were now gathering around Deborah. "What is that familiar scent?" she thought. How could I forget? It's my mother's dress-up perfume." Her parent's bedroom always smelled of her mother's perfume. In the past, the slightest whiff of it had turned her stomach. Now, she understood why. It had become associated with the secret things Daddy would do to her when her mother was at her prayer meetings or out running errands. In the past, immediate anger and a desire to push her mother away would have risen within her. Today, however, things were different. She felt a new tenderness toward her mother and she remembered how, as a child, she had always loved to see her mother all dressed up. Elizabeth Noble had been a beautiful woman in those days. And as a little girl, Deborah had longed to snuggle up next to her because she smelled so good; always hoping that some of her mother's beauty would rub off on her.

The Holy Spirit had finally nudged Elizabeth and had broken through her immobilized state. She knew her daughter needed her and she finally made her way down to the altar. Elizabeth appeared to be quite uncomfortable, clearly afraid to reach out and touch her daughter. She stood quietly next to Anne with her arms hanging helplessly at her side.

There was an ache in Elizabeth's heart, one she hadn't felt in years. How she longed to take her daughter in her arms and hold her tightly to her breast just as she had done when she was a little girl. Anne sensed Elizabeth's pain as she took Deborah's arm to help her to her feet. Then Anne stepped back as she put Deborah's hand into her mother's. Frozen for a brief minute, mother and daughter stood there looking at each other. Suddenly Deborah was in her mother's arms. Tears flowed freely, not only from both of them, but from the rest of the congregation who had known the family and could appreciate just what was taking place in the front of their church that day.

As Deborah and her mother whispered their regrets and their forgiveness for the many things that had happened over the past years, Daniel began to feel more and more uncomfortable. "What am I doing up here anyway?" he thought. But he too felt helpless to move as he watched the touching drama unfold in front of him. He didn't know what had happened in Florida, but it was obvious it had been more than he and Anne had expected and prayed for all week. Slightly tanned from the Florida sun, Deborah looked radiant and beautiful even with tears streaming down her face; there was a new peace in her countenance and joy in her eyes.

Daniel had forgotten how much sparkle and life there had always been in those unusual green eyes of his childhood friend. He remembered how Deborah's eyes used to dance with mischief and life when they were young. Then one day, they had simply clouded over and became lifeless and cold. He knew someday he would learn what had happened to crush the hope out of Deborah before her life had really begun. "I wonder what could have made such a dramatic change in her." Daniel's thoughts wandered to the summer before they had started junior high.

Both Daniel and Deborah had been twelve or thirteen years old and he remembered wondering if she wasn't just a little scared about transferring from the private Christian school they had attended together to the community's middle school. His family had moved to Deerfield when he was in the fourth grade so he knew the feeling of transferring schools. The small Christian school they attended only offered grades kindergarten through sixth and it had been time to move to the much larger, and somewhat intimidating, public school at the other end of town. It was then that he saw her change. The sparkle had never come back, not until today.

Even Deborah's dark brown, nearly black, hair looked different today. It had been newly styled and it suited her well. It had moved her out of the frozen-in-the-past look into the present. She was beautiful! The Lord's overwhelming love swept through Daniel's heart and he had an intense desire to take her in his arms. He wanted her to know that he would take care of her and protect her; nothing would ever hurt her again if he could help it. Daniel had never experienced anything like this. He had loved and cared for Susan, but it had been gentle and kind, nothing like the intensity of what he was feeling at this moment. He suddenly realized these heart-felt feelings actually sounded like marriage vows. "Is God giving me the heart of a husband or simply sharing with me His heart toward Deborah?" He just wasn't sure. The feelings were so intense.

Before he could answer his own question, Deborah turned toward her right. She had felt the prompting of the Holy Spirit to turn to see who was standing on the other side of her. "Oh my God! It's Daniel," she thought, as she let out a little gasp. She remembered the vision she had seen on her trip back to Deerfield. He immediately saw the look of shock on her face and started kicking himself for being up there and making her feel uncomfortable, "What an awkward situation Anne's gotten me into!" he thought as he shifted his feet awkwardly. Fortunately as quickly as the look came, it left her face.

For the first time in twenty years, Deborah looked Daniel straight in the eyes. His crystal clear, blue eyes, which she had felt contained nothing but disgust and pity for her for so many years, were full of compassion, forgiveness and grace. "They had been the eyes of Jesus all along," she realized. The Holy Spirit showed her at that moment, that when she had run from Daniel's goodness, his steady nature, his unconditional love and the conviction she had always felt whenever she was around him, she had really been running from the Lord inside of him. Now, the same thing that had repelled her and had always been a stumbling block between them became a magnet. She felt her heart drawn to this man who was looking so intently at her.

Actually, it was more than that. She wanted to give Daniel everything: her heart, her life and yes, even her body, completely. Deborah had never felt like this before! She had always begrudged anything she had ever given any man, and always demanded to have something back in return: a place to stay, drugs, a job, something that would even the score. In this moment, standing beside Daniel, she neither needed nor wanted anything but to give herself to him for the rest of her life. She thought of the vision she had seen the day before, of herself standing at the altar of this very church marrying the man who was now standing next to her. She determined at that moment that she did not care how long the journey might take, Daniel was part of her destiny and she was ready to start.

As he reached for her hands, Deborah took a deep breath and took one step closer. They stood there together, their hands locked, eyes searching each other's faces. Had God stopped time just for them?

Lydia and Joyce rose from their knees, their prayer was over and the song was over, too. Whatever God was doing in Deborah's life was settled. They could do no more. They went back to their seats with the peace and knowledge that whatever crossroad Deborah had been at, the right choice had been made. Next week, they would have to call and find out what had happened this Sunday morning. The pastor began to take up the offering and their attention turned toward the church business at hand.

Anne, Elizabeth and the rest of the congregation seemed to be holding their breath as Daniel and Deborah stood before them in front of the church. Pastor Harrison wasn't quite sure what was happening but whatever it was, he could sense God's presence so he motioned to the worship leader to keep singing. *"Amazing love, how can it be…?"*

Deborah quickly said, "Daniel, I'm so sorry, truly, truly sorry for everything." As she said those words, Daniel felt the last bit of fear and apprehension leave his heart. The old invisible wall of hurt and rejection had been melted by God's love. He looked deeply into her eyes. As he did, he was reminded of the parable of the prodigal son returning to his father's house. He could feel the father's joy and excitement in this divine moment.

As he continued looking into her eyes, he felt as if his own eyes were piercing to the bottom of her soul. Genuinely and straight forwardly, he said, "You are forgiven." He knew, as he spoke those three, simple, life-changing words to Deborah that morning that they were not just his words, but the words of their heavenly Father.

The worship team began to sing a modern rendition of *Amazing Grace*. With the exception of Andrea Kline, there wasn't a dry eye in the Deerfield Family Worship Center that morning.

The prodigal daughter had come home.

Freedom Scriptures And Steps

১৯ ৬৯

The New King James Version of the Bible has been used for all scripture references.

Salvation

ॐ ॐ

John 3:16 *For God so loved the world that He gave His only begotten Son, that whoever believes in Him should not perish but have everlasting life.*

Romans 10:9 That if you confess with your mouth the Lord Jesus and believe in your heart that God has raised Him from the dead, you will be saved.

Matthew 10:32 *Whoever confesses Me before men, him I will also confess before My Father who is in heaven.*

- Repent for your sins and receive His forgiveness.
- Believe in your heart that He died and rose again.
- Confess that He is now the Lord of your life.
- Go and tell someone.

Baptism of the Holy Spirit

ॐ ॐ

Luke 11:13 *If you then, being evil, know how to give good gifts to your children, how much more will your heavenly Father give the Holy Spirit to those who ask Him!*

Acts 1:8 *But you shall receive power when the Holy Spirit has come upon you; and you shall be witnesses to Me in Jerusalem, and in all Judea and Samaria, and to the end of the earth.*

1 Corinthians 14:2 *For he who speaks in a tongue does not speak to men but to God, for no one understands him; however, in the spirit he speaks mysteries.*

1 Corinthians 14:4 *He who speaks in a tongue edifies himself, but he who prophesies edifies the chur*ch.

- Ask the Father for the Holy Spirit
- Bind all spirits of fear, unbelief, religion and self-consciousness.
- Receive in faith.

- In an attitude of prayer and worship, begin to share your heart with the Lord by allowing whatever is in your belly to come forth. Don't use your natural language.
- It may start off with stammering lips or just a few syllables or there may be a strong flow of words. Everybody's river is in a different state.
- Remember you cannot make a mistake, the Father said that if you ask, you will receive a good thing.
- It's up to you to open your mouth and cooperate with the Holy Spirit. It is not natural; it is supernatural, so it may feel a little awkward at first. Once you allow the flow to come out, it will feel great. You will wonder where it's been all your life as you receive a sense of greater intimacy with the Lord.
- Continue to use your prayer language daily. Like a natural well can lose it's prime if not accessed enough, sometimes if you do not pray in tongues regularly, it will seem as if you have lost the river. You haven't, it will just need re-priming. It's best to keep a regular flow.

Redemption from Generational Sin

࿎ ࿐

Example of a generational sin and resulting curse:
Deuteronomy 23:2 *One of illegitimate birth shall not enter the congregation of the Lord; even to the tenth generation none of his descendants shall enter the congregation of the Lord.*

Leviticus 26:39-42 *And those of you who are left shall waste away in their iniquity in your enemies' lands; also in their fathers' iniquities, which are with them, they shall waste away. But if they confess their iniquity and the iniquity of their fathers, with their unfaithfulness in which they were unfaithful to Me, and that they also have walked contrary to Me and that I also have walked contrary to them and have brought them into the land of their enemies; if their uncircumcised hearts are humbled, and they accept their guilt–then I will remember my covenant with Jacob, and My covenant with Isaac and My covenant with Abraham I will remember; I will remember the land.*

Nehemiah 9:2 *Then those of Israelite lineage separated themselves from all foreigners; and they stood and confessed their sins and the iniquities of their fathers.*

Acts 3:19 *Repent therefore and be converted, that your sins may be blotted out, so that times of refreshing may come from the presence of the Lord.*

Galatians 3:13 *Christ has redeemed us from the curse of the law, having become a curse for us(for it is written, "Cursed is everyone who hangs on a tree"),*

- Identify a generational sin pattern in your family lines.
- Stand in the gap and repent for your own sin in this area and the sins of your ancestors.
- Forgive them for how their sins affected your life.
- Ask God to forgive you for how you have participated in this sin pattern.
- Forgive yourself.
- Renounce and break agreement with the sins and curses related to the generational sin pattern and rebuke all related demons.

Transformation of Beliefs

ॐ ঔ

Romans 12:2 *And do not be conformed to this world, but be transformed by the renewing of your mind, that you may prove what is that good and acceptable and perfect will of God.*

2 Corinthians 10:4-5 *For the weapons of our warfare are not carnal but mighty in God for pulling down strongholds, casting down arguments and every high thing that exalts itself against the knowledge of God, bringing every thought into captivity to the obedience of Christ,*

Ephesians 4:22-23 *that you put off, concerning your former conduct, the old man which grows corrupt according to the deceitful lusts, and be renewed in the spirit of your mind.*

Exodus 23:32-33 *You shall make no covenant with them, nor with their gods. They shall not dwell in your land, lest they make you sin against Me. For if you serve their gods, it will surely be a snare to you.*

- Identify the ungodly belief.
- Forgive the people who helped establish it in your life.

- Ask God to forgive you for how you have participated in the ungodly belief.
- Renounce and break agreement with it.
- Listen to the Holy Spirit and establish a new godly belief.

Spirit/Soul Healing

⮞ ⮜

Matthew 6:14-15 *For if you forgive men their trespasses, your heavenly Father will also forgive you. But if you do not forgive men their trespasses, neither will your Father forgive your trespasses.*

Isaiah 61:1D He has sent Me to heal the brokenhearted,

Psalm 142:1-2 *I cry out to the Lord with my voice; with my voice to the Lord I make my supplication. I pour out my complaint before Him; I declare before Him my trouble.*

Psalm 23:3 *He restores my soul; He leads me in the paths of righteousness for His name's sake.*

- Ask the Holy Spirit to search your heart and show you any areas of unforgiveness or woundedness.
- Pour out your hurt to the Lord.
- Forgive anyone involved.
- Ask Jesus to reveal Himself in the painful memory.
- Get quiet and listen for His voice, watch what He does, see how He makes you feel. Wait on Him, He is your Healer.

- After Jesus has ministered to you, check the memory, is the pain gone? If yes, you're done.
- If it's not complete, ask the Lord if there's anything standing in the way of your healing. Deal with anything He shows you and once again ask Him to visit the painful situation. Remember it is His Will and Promise to heal you. He loves you and desires to make you whole.

Deliverance

࿔ ࿐

Matthew 12:28 *But if I cast out demons, surely the kingdom of God has come upon you.*

Mark 16:17 *And these signs will follow those who believe: In My name they will cast out demons; they will speak with new tongues; they shall cast out demons,*

1 John 3:8 *He who sins is of the devil, for the devil has sinned from the beginning. For this purpose the Son of God was manifested, that He might destroy the works of the devil.*

Luke 9:1 *Then He called His twelve disciples together and gave them power and authority over all demons, and to cure diseases.*

- Make sure you have removed legal ground of unforgiveness, generational curses, ungodly beliefs and spirit/soul hurts first. This makes the deliverance easier and also shuts any spiritual doors the enemy may try to use for re-entry.
- Ask the Holy Spirit to help you identify areas where you may be battling demonic oppression.

- Renounce and break agreement with the specific stronghold and any related demons.
- Examples: <u>Anger</u>, rage, frustration and destruction. <u>Fear</u>, worry, anxiety. <u>Deception</u>, secrecy, denial and lying.
- Command the demons to go in the Name of Jesus.
- Pray that the Holy Spirit will now fill those places.
- Pray to receive specifically. Examples: If anger has been cast out, pray to receive God's peace. If fear has been cast out, pray to receive faith. If the deception has been cast out, pray to receive truth.
- If you are not comfortable with self-deliverance, find a believer who knows their authority in Christ and ask them to help you.

Hearing the Voice of God

❧ ❦

Proverbs 20:12 *The hearing ear and the seeing eye, the Lord has made both of them.*

John 10:3 *To him the doorkeeper opens, and the sheep hear his voice; and he calls his own sheep by name and leads them out.*

John 15:15 *No longer do I call you servants, for a servant does not know what his master is doing; but I have called you friends, for all things that I heard from My Father I have made known to you.*

- Read the Bible and discover what is personally illuminated to you in the Word.
- In times of worship and prayer, begin to listen for the still small voice within you.
- Write down the things you hear and watch as they come to pass.
- If a dream is particularly vivid or feels somewhat different than your normal dreams, write down the high points and ask the Lord to give you the interpretation.
- Begin to identify; do I normally see mental images, do I hear within my mind or do I feel something in my body.

Seeing, hearing and feeling are all methods through which the Lord speaks to us.

- Check with spiritual authority to see if they have a witness to what you are hearing or sensing.

* Please see Recommended Materials and Ministry Sources on the following page to order "An Integrated Approach to Biblical Healing" or the "Restoring the Foundations Manual." Both of these contain, in more detail, much of the ministry process shared in "The Prodigal Daughter."

Recommended Materials and Ministry Sources

ॐ ⋘

For more information on other products and materials by Kathy Tolleson or for speaking dates and locations, please contact **info@kingdomlife.com**

An Integrated Approach to Biblical Healing Ministry, Chester and Betsy Kylstra, Proclaiming His Word Ministry **www.rtfi.org**

Redeemed, the 2nd novel in the *Prodigal Daughter* series Kathy Tolleson, Kingdom Life Now **www.kingdomlifenow.com**

Birth Assignments, Kathy Tolleson, Kingdom Life Now **www.kingdomlifenow.com**

Bitter Roots Video, John and Paula Sanford, Elijah House **www.elijahhouse.org**

Women's Guide to Freedom
Kathy Tolleson, Kingdom Life Now,
www.kingdomlifenow.com

Prophets and Personal Prophecy,
Dr. Bill Hamon, Christian International
www.christianinternational.org

Restoring Sexuality - Book, DVD or CD Series
Kathy Tolleson, Kingdom Life Now
www.kingdomlifenow.com

Restoring the Foundations Manual,
Chester and Betsy Kylstra, Proclaiming His Word Ministry
www.rtfi.org

Soul Battles,
Kathy Tolleson, Kingdom Life Now
www.kingdomlifenow.com

You are My King; CD Title-*Adoration: The Worship Album* by
Newsboys; Song written by Billy Joe Foote,
www.newsboys.com

In order to locate ministry providers near you, please go to
www.healinghouse.org.

To learn more about Restoring the Foundations training and
equipping contact Proclaiming His Word Ministry at
www.rtfi.org.

For further ministry training contact Christian International at
www.christianinternational.com.

Made in the USA
Charleston, SC
05 December 2014